The Tale of Penelope's Red Hot Pickled Peppered Peanuts

An African American Folk tale

BOOK I TRANSFORMATION

By

Lorie Holloway

DEDICATION

To my beloved aunts—Doris, Gracie, and Shirneata—whose love, wisdom, and spirit have always inspired the magic in my stories. This book is for you.

Table of Contents

THE PEANUT CELEBRATION

In the enchanted riverside village of West Nigeria, dawn broke in hues of rose and amber, gilding palm-thatched roofs and winding dirt lanes. Under the benevolent reign of King Bruno—his laughter as warm as the midday sun—and Queen Utopia—her kindness as gentle as the river's current—the people prepared for their greatest annual festival. It was the long-awaited Day of the Peanut Celebration, a harvest-and-heart holiday born from the culinary passions of their seventh child, Princess Penelope. Her signature stew—a heady, aromatic brew of freshly ground peanuts, sweet okra, vine-ripened tomatoes, and just a hint of fiery pepper—was ladled over steaming fufu dumplings, each pillowy morsel meant to be pinched between fingertips and dipped into the savory broth. From far-flung hamlets and bustling market towns, villagers arrived carrying woven baskets brimming with their finest peanuts—some the size of eggs, others plump as newborn chicks—eager to take part in the ceremonial dance, the vibrant marketplace, and the grand feast where Penelope's stew would flow freely as a reminder that generosity binds a kingdom's soul.

That morning, a lone rooster's clarion cry—"Cock-a-doodle-doooo!"—echoed against the palace's ivory walls and sheer curtain-draped balconies, stirring the princess from her silk-lined bed. She stretched luxuriously, the soft sunlight painting golden patterns on her linen sheets. As she sat up, her dark curls tumbled over her shoulders, and her hazel eyes gleamed with bright anticipation. A gentle breeze carried the mingled scents of blooming bougainvillea, spiced grains of incense burning at the temple gates, and the distant hum of market life. Rising, Penelope padded to the alabaster basin where crystal-clear water, poured earlier by her devoted maidservant, shimmered with flecks of rose petals. Each splash washed away the last threads of sleep, and she let her fingertips graze the surface as she mused on the day's tasks.

Dressed in a gown of pale green silk embroidered with tiny golden peanuts, she slipped past the clatter of tongs and bakers' laughter in the kitchen, her slippers scarcely making a sound on the cool stone floor. Outside, the palace's courtyard garden beckoned rows of tomato vines heavy with ruby globes, fragrant okra blossoms dangling like stars, and clumps of peanut plants with their delicate yellow flowers peeking from the earth. Bending to choose the ripest tomato, Penelope felt the soil tremble momentarily beneath her sandals, a subtle reminder that the world was never entirely still. Determined, she whispered to the morning air, "No time for doubt—so much to prepare." Tucking the plump fruit into a woven basket, she retraced her steps to the hearth, where sunlight streamed through an arched window, illuminating swirling motes of flour and dust.

With deliberate care, she sliced the tomato into perfect cubes on a well-worn wooden board, the bright red juice staining her fingertips. Lost in visions of dancing villagers and jubilant drummers, she murmured, "I cannot wait," just as a slip of the knife nicked her finger. Crimson welled up, and she looked skyward with a soft plea: "Not today,". Snatching a freshly laundered rag from a nearby peg, she pressed it to the wound, the cool cloth soothing the sting. Sunbeams spilled across her face as she hummed the festival tune—its buoyant drums, cheerful flutes, and playful shouts echoing like an invitation to every child in the realm.

In that quiet moment, memories of past celebrations flared in her mind: swirling skirts stitched with Aso-Oke patterns, ribbons of every color twisting in the breeze, and the communal tables groaning beneath platters of honey-glazed plantains, spiced yams, and peanut stew. Gratitude and unity had always been the festival's heart. And yet, amid the joy, her thoughts drifted to a single, absent figure, Aunt Safire. She had never known this aunt, but in whispered tales and faded portraits, Penelope sensed Safire's long-ago spirit: a poignant mixture of sorrow and strength. Closing her eyes, she raised her hands in prayer to the spirits of earth and sky, asking softly for Safire's presence at the Peanut Celebration and, above all, for healing and forgiveness to blossom in every heart. As the last syllable of her prayer faded, a gentle breeze stirred the curtains behind her, a promise that her wish had been heard.

SAFIRE

The very name Safire carried a dark grace, a whisper in the corridors of the palace that lingered like smoke. Before Penelope's birth, she had been Queen Utopia's younger sister—legendary for her fierce beauty, her obsidian hair cascading like a midnight waterfall, and eyes alight with untamed fire. Yet her heart had been claimed long ago by King Bruno's ardor, a secret blaze that flared before he ever pledged himself to Utopia.

Determined to halt the wedding at all costs, Safire stole into the royal chambers under cover of night. She gathered three glittering diamonds from Utopia's crown, tucked a single crimson rose—its petals as velvety as spilled blood—and a silken lock of her sister's hair into a satchel. Then she slipped beyond the kingdom's golden gates and into the ancient forest. There the air hung heavy with damp moss; each breath felt like inhaling centuries. Towering baobab trees arched overhead, their roots gnarled like arthritic fingers clutching at the earth. Deep in that primeval hush, she discovered a warlock's cabin—its shingles bowed beneath years of neglect, walls cloaked in twisted briars, and a lone candle guttering in the dusky gloom.

Within, the warlock emerged from shadow, draped in a robe of midnight feathers. Bone beads clacked softly around his throat, and his eyes burned with otherworldly light. His voice rasped, "Why do you seek me, child of royal blood?" Safire's pulse thundered in her throat, but her resolve never wavered. "I want my sister dead."

He inclined his head. "What binds you to her?" With deliberate calm she produced the lock of Utopia's hair and the blood-red rose. The warlock's thin lips curved into a smile as he beckoned her to set them into a cauldron bubbling atop a roaring fire. The pot's surface shimmered black as tar. She laid in her tokens; he poured in goat's blood that hissed like venom, strips of tiger hide that writhed into curling smoke, and another strand of Utopia's hair—white as moonlight. Pale steam rose, carrying soft voices of malice. "Speak your wish," he intoned. Safire's pulse hammered against her throat as she whispered, "I want her dead." A malicious grin split his face as he poured the bubbling concoction into a slender glass vial. "When this touches her lips, she'll draw her final breath before the next sunset." He pressed a small silver mirror into her trembling palm. "This will show you the moment her soul departs."

The wedding day dawned in a cascade of gold and jade: Utopia in a gown that gleamed like sunlight on a river, her headpiece glittering with diamonds. Unaware of her maid of honor's venomous intent, she smiled and embraced Safire. As Utopia and Bruno danced beneath crystal chandeliers, music swirling like starlight, Safire's green eyes burned with fury. She watched for the perfect moment, heart fluttering with triumph and dread.

At last, Utopia paused mid-twirl and called for her goblet of wine. As she turned to steal a kiss from Bruno, applause rippled through the hall. Safire moved swiftly—only to freeze in horror as the king's gaze snapped to hers. Bruno lunged; the glass shattered on marble. "You would poison your own sister?" he thundered.

Guards seized her on the spot and dragged her before the court. The hush that fell was heavier than any forest gloom. King Bruno's verdict rang like a war horn: "Exile her to the swamps, to live among leeches and jackals." Safire, chest heaving, spat back through clenched teeth, "I shall return—this is not the end." And with that vow echoing behind her, she was cast into the fetid mire.

Years passed. Utopia and Bruno's love endured, blossoming into a family that brought peace to the realm. The old king died, and Bruno ascended to rule both East and West with gentle wisdom. The Peanut Celebration was created and grew into a festival of reconciliation and wonder. Yet on its twelfth anniversary, as laughter and lanterns drifted through the night air, the whisper of a long-buried grudge drifted back on the wind—and Safire's name carried its dark promise once more.

THE ANNUAL PEANUT FESTIVAL

As dawn broke, Penelope leaned against a weathered stone wall, her eyes fixed on the men as they set off in a slow, steady line. Their strong silhouettes moved purposefully along dew-damp trails, carrying hefty bundles of wood that burst with the scent of resin and fresh leaves under the early light. In the distance, she could see the women meandering gracefully through the forest, their baskets slowly filling with plump, ruby fruits and crisp, dew-speckled vegetables. With only ten days remaining until the grand celebration, every heartbeat of the kingdom pulsed with excitement, and Penelope felt its rhythm echo within her chest. Radiating a quiet brilliance, she stood as a living beacon, her anticipation for Olajuwon shimmering in every thoughtful glance and small, hopeful smile.

A new year, ripe with the promise of love, quietly began. This year was special—it would be the day Penelope met Prince Olajuwon for the very first time. He, the dashing son of Ghana's royal couple, had been destined to join their fates since the moment Penelope was born. Their meeting was arranged to take place during the vibrant Peanut Festival. Even though the prince was a stranger to her eyes, Penelope's resolve to leave behind her childhood home was firm and filled with longing. She saw her future in vivid detail: family gatherings where warm voices mingled happily, cross-cultural visits between Nigeria and Ghana, and laughter echoing around steamy bowls of hearty peanut stew. In her daydreams, her future husband stood tall beneath a sapphire sky, his handsome features adorned with a playful, understanding smile.

On the day of the Peanut Celebration, the air shimmered with early golden light as Penelope and her family climbed into their waiting carriage. They merged seamlessly into a bustling crowd where excited faces glowed with anticipation. Proud farmers showcased their prized, oversized peanuts, each more elaborate than the last. Amidst the throng, Penelope's eyes locked onto Prince Olajuwon. He emerged in an exquisite purple robe, his soft, curly hair catching hints of the sun's light, and his smile wide and inviting. As if guided by fate, he ambled toward her, extending his hand in a gesture that whispered promises, "I have been waiting eagerly to meet you, my beautiful bride." With a gentle yet determined grace, Penelope took his hand and led him toward an enchanting garden where the air was scented with blooming jasmine.

After an hour of conversation beneath the dappled light of the garden, Olajuwon glanced at the sun behind a nearby tree. "It's almost time to choose the largest peanut, my love" he suggested, his tone urging a return to the festivities. Rising gracefully, Penelope smiled and, with a soft command, said, "From now on, this will be our day to share. I'll let you have the honor of making the choice because soon we will be united." With her words gently echoing through the crowd, they made their way back among the jubilant onlookers.

Just then, as they reached the heart of the mass of onlookers, a grotesque pillar of black smoke burst forth from the center of the courtyard. Every delighted murmur froze into stunned silence as the dense cloud began to dissipate, unveiling the infamous and much-feared figure of Safire. Her presence was impossible to ignore as she swept into view with a chilling smile. "Penelope, thank you for wishing for my return!" Safire bellowed, her voice slicing through the air, sharp with bitter joy. She advanced menacingly; her eyes locked on Utopia. With a curled, venomous finger, she sneered, "You stole everything I loved; now I will take your precious little peanut girl."

Before the threat could root itself in terror, Utopia's eyes blazed with fierce maternal fire. Her voice rang out, bold and defiant, "How dare you try to harm my child! She has never wronged you, not in the slightest."

Raising her arms high as if summoning an ancient strength, Utopia cried out with unwavering conviction, "Winston, banish Safire —not just from our borders but from this entire continent! I command that she be exiled to a land so distant that we shall never again behold her wicked face!"

From behind the crowd stood a familiar image—the warlock Safire had sought before Utopia's wedding. His ashen skin, once smooth as polished stone, now cracked with age like dried riverbed clay. The midnight feather robe he wore had molted to reveal patches of sallow skin beneath. Where his eyes once gleamed with otherworldly light, they now swam with murky tears. His voice, once crackling like embers, now barely concealed regret as it trembled across the suddenly silent gathering. "Safire," he whispered, "I'm deeply sorry I must do this." With deliberate care, his gnarled fingers—adorned with the three diamonds she had once given him, now set in tarnished rings—pulled out an intricately carved wand of blackened elder wood. His hand shook, causing the wand's tip to trace erratic patterns in the air as he aimed it directly at Safire's heart.

Drawing in a long, measured breath, he declared, "I hereby condemn you to a new land—a place where you can no longer inflict your harm." As his solemn words echoed off the stone walls of the courtyard, a searing bolt of lightning shot forth from the wand. In an unforeseen twist, Safire fumbled for the gleaming magic mirror given to her earlier. The bolt rebounded with fierce determination, racing toward Penelope before Safire herself evaporated into a swirl of mist and darkness.

A collective gasp thundered through the crowd as a ferocious flame suddenly engulfed Penelope. Panic rippled among the villagers, and in a flurry, they scrambled forward with buckets of water, their shouts mingling with the crackle of burning magic. When the acrid smoke eventually thinned, there stood Penelope, trembling. Her hair now towered in wild, defiant spikes, as if each strand had a mind of its own, challenging gravity. Mesmerized by this dramatic transformation, Winston approached her slowly, his eyes softening with concern as he gently ran his fingers through her unruly locks. With each tender stroke, her transformation unfolded into a luxurious curtain of straight, silky hair that framed her face, earning her hairstyle the new and affectionate name, "The Silk Press."

Yet even in this moment of visual wonder, a somber shadow lomed over her future. In a hushed tone weighed by regret, Winston explained that while the wand's heat had wrought a miracle on her hair, the very same curse had signaled her destined exodus—a calling to a distant world where, heartbreakingly, she would be forced to vanish from the sight of those she loved.

In the wake of these climactic events, King Bruno's stern decree resounded throughout the land. A mighty wooden gate was soon erected around the entire kingdom, its robust lock standing as a silent sentinel against any looming threat. Moreover, a relentless twenty-four-hour vigil was established to shadow Penelope's every step, ensuring that she would never have to brave the outside world without the safety of a trusted escort beside her.

DISOBEDIENT

As time moved swiftly, the spell of Safire swirled around the kingdom, waiting for the perfect time to capture the Princess. With moments of bordun and lack of attention, the memory of Olajuwon faded like a dry leaf in the wind, leaving Penelope lonely and wishing for the union to move faster . In the years that came after the meeting, the King's oppressive rules chafed at the free-spirited, headstrong nature of Penelope. The kingdom's restrictions were a cage to her unbridled soul. Though she was ordered to remain within the safe embrace of her home, she often slipped beyond the high stone walls—seeking the wild herbs that imparted a secret magic to her beloved peanut stew. One radiant day, the magic of Safire immersed the Princess's body. Her mind became engulfed, and she began moving toward restricted areas. The guards that were supposed to be watching her suddenly became tired, and before they knew it, they were sound asleep at the gate. As sunlight danced on dew-kissed grass, Penelope's eyes caught sight of the most vibrant, blushing tomatoes clustered just outside the weathered wooden fence. They glowed like rubies in the soft light, beckoning her with the promise of perfection for her stew. Mere steps from the kingdom's secure confines, she knew she could dart over the wooden gate and return before anyone sensed her absence. She crept past the drowsy guards in their crimson uniforms and, with her heart fluttering like a caged songbird, Penelope sprinted across the dew-dampened grass. With an impulsive leap that sent her silk dress billowing around her thighs, she vaulted over the gate and landed with a soft thud before rows of luscious tomatoes.

She plucked one and cradled it in her palm, feeling its weight and warmth against her skin. The fresh, sun-ripened scent filled her nostrils with notes of earth and sweetness, wrapping around her like the memory of her peanut garden. At that moment, a subtle vibration—like the trembling of a spider's web when touched by morning breeze—drew her attention. Turning slowly, the tomato still clutched to her chest, she beheld the most peculiar sight: a man, unlike anyone she had ever seen. Tall and impeccably poised with shoulders broad as an oak beam, his straight chestnut hair fell in a perfect curtain to frame a face of alabaster whiteness unmarked by sun or age. His eyes, framed by thick dark lashes, shimmered in a shade of blue that shifted like the depths of the wild, untamed sea during a gathering storm.

Penelope's pulse quickened as she found herself captivated by this striking, pale stranger, almost as if destiny had scripted their encounter in a single, unforgettable moment. As he strolled out of the village, his presence evoking an aura of mystery and allure, she resolved to follow him—curious where this unexpected spark of love might lead. Leaving behind the familiar comforts of her small village and her beloved Olajuwon, she trailed after him into the open, sunlit expanse. He paused and slowly turned, his gaze locking with hers. His lips, soft and inviting like a succulent, perfectly ripened peach, stirred an irresistible longing within her. When his eyes held hers, a mischievous, devilish grin spread across his face, capturing her very soul.

Stepping closer with a deliberate cadence, he addressed her in tones that mixed tenderness with intrigue, "Who do we have here?" Though the cadence of his words was foreign, her smile spoke the language of her heart. Then, with a gentle, almost reverent touch, he reached out to caress her hand, and to her amazement, he continued speaking in her native tongue. Introducing himself as Pedro, he revealed that he was an explorer from Spain. Though his home was in England, his heart beat for the enigmatic allure of African culture. His eyes twinkled as he confided that his love for Africa was so profound, he dreamed of marrying an African woman and whisking her back to

England. Fate, it seemed, had played its part today, for here they were together, an unlikely meeting borne of destiny.

In a gesture as unexpected as it was tender, Pedro rummaged through his haversack and produced a banana, offering it to Penelope as a symbol of their inaugural encounter. With a lighthearted smile, she then reached into the depths of her pocket and retrieved a small peanut—a cherished token representative of everything she adored—and pressed it into his hand. Slowly, as she began to peel the banana, the sweet fragrance of its ripening flesh mingled with the warm tropical air, sending shivers along her skin. The moment she bit into the soft, yielding fruit, the handsome stranger gazed deep into her eyes; an electric charge passed between them, stirring passions that lay dormant beneath polite restraint.

As if guided by an unspoken rhythm, his lips met hers on the far side of the banana. As they kissed Safire curse surrounded Penelope's body and she became bewitched mind, body and soul. The kiss was a symphony of flavors: the subtle, sweet tang of the fruit intermingled with the warmth of shared desire, creating an experience of succulent delight that overwhelmed all other senses. During this tender abandon, his gentle hands wandered, caressing her soft curves with fingertips that left goosebumps in their wake. The small peanut—golden-brown and still warm from his palm—tumbled from his grasp.

It fell through the narrow space between their bodies, landing in the hollow between her breasts where her heartbeat caused it to tremble slightly. Neither noticed its descent, their attention consumed by the heat rising between them like steam from summer asphalt, their breathing growing ragged as the world beyond their embrace dissolved into insignificance. —an unsung witness to the passion that enveloped them.

Just as their embrace reached a crescendo, Pedro abruptly broke away. With a tone laced with urgent promise, he murmured, "Come with me—I want to show you my ship." Rising with determined grace, he strode away into the dense, whispering jungle, and Penelope, caught in a whirlpool of emotions, followed him blindly. The lush foliage gave way to a rugged shore, where a grand ship loomed against the horizon, its silhouette wreathed in the garish light of a foreign land.

Yet what should catch Penelope's attention on the shore was a sight of profound horror. Chained together like cattle, African people—livid with fear and despair—were being unceremoniously dragged onto the deck. The scene, stark and merciless, shattered the delicate cocoon of her earlier rapture. Overwhelmed by terror and remorse, she turned to flee, but escape proved impossible. Swiftly, a pallid hand clamped down on her wrist, and a voice, rough with authority, demanded, "Where the hell do you think you're going?"

Fighting with every shred of her fiery spirit, Penelope struggled desperately against the man's overpowering strength. Yet he was relentless—his hand struck her face, and before she could gather her scattered thoughts, she was hurled violently upon the unforgiving ground. A coarse rope was pulled from his sack and mercilessly looped around her wrists, binding her delicate hands. Another rope encircled her neck, dragging her unwillingly onto the ship alongside her African counterparts. The charming, enigmatic Pedro had transformed before her eyes into a ruthless captor.

The year was 1845. Though the Atlantic Slave Trade had been outlawed for decades, Captain Pedro Fernando's ship cut through the waves toward Africa, its hold emptied to make room for human cargo. Each person delivered alive to American shores would fill his pockets with gold.

He was a man with eyes like polished obsidian and skin leathered by thirty years at sea—found his way to the Coast of Africa where the air hung thick with humidity and the scent of baobab. His mission was crystal clear as he wiped sweat from his brow with a monogrammed handkerchief: to seek out human cargo. American plantation owners had enlisted his services with gold coins that clinked heavily in his pocket, entrusting him with the grim responsibility of transporting enslaved individuals to cotton fields that stretched endlessly across the rapidly expanding New World. Although his calloused hands would not directly clamp the iron shackles on these unfortunate souls, the enticing prospect of earning five hundred silver dollars per head proved too irresistible for Pedro to ignore. His ship, La Fortuna, a formidable three-masted vessel with canvas sails yellowed by salt and time, stood anchored fifty yards offshore, creaking against its moorings like a predatory beast straining at its leash, ready to embark on its perilous six-week journey across the shark-infested, storm-wracked Atlantic with its tragic human cargo packed below decks in spaces barely eighteen inches high.

Penelope's fingers trembled at the sight of him on deck. This was the same man whose whispers had once set her heart aflame in Africa. Now she saw beyond his Castilian charm to the cold calculation beneath. He had crossed an ocean not for love or honor, but to chase fortune in flesh—a few hundred American dollars that would cost her everything she had ever loved,

Every night, the ship's wooden stairs creaked under Pedro's heavy footsteps as he descended to the hole. The jangle of keys announced his arrival before his shadow fell across Penelope's cell. Her wrists, raw from iron shackles, trembled as he unlocked them. "Come," he would command, his voice flat as he dragged her above deck. There, beneath stars that no longer held beauty, he would splash her with cold seawater that stung her wounds before forcing himself upon her. During these ordeals, Penelope's mind would flee to her village's peanut harvest festival—the earthen bowls steaming with her renowned stew, children's laughter echoing across the square, her mother's gentle hands adjusting her ceremonial headwrap. But these memories, once sweet, now tasted of ash as they collided with the wooden deck pressing against her back and the endless rocking of a ship carrying her far.

After the torment was over, she was dragged back down and chained in the dark, damp belly of the ship—a place reeking of urine and feces. In that oppressive space, Penelope's thoughts wavered between the cold, sobering darkness and the distant, tantalizing visions of the African sun's heat, the scent of mangos, and the sweetness of ripe bananas. Her inner world was a bitter refuge, a place where her vivid imagination became her sole confidant amid a language of isolation, for no one on the ship spoke her tongue or understood her pain.

In those long hours of helplessness, she reached for memories of her siblings, a conflicted mix of gratitude and guilt swirling within her. She silently thanked God they hadn't been taken, even as a part of her wondered—if only she had been less determined, less resilient, perhaps like the others, she might have been spared such misery. The self-reproach mingled with longing, leaving her with an unbearable internal struggle.

One day, several women were dragged above deck for the sailors' entertainment. As the ship pitched forward on a wave, one captive woman broke free from her captor's grip and leapt over the rail into the churning waters below. Penelope watched her disappear beneath the foam, whispering, "She escaped." The words tasted of both honey and bile in her mouth. Pedro's boots thundered across the deck as he shouted, "Five hundred dollars lost! Secure the remaining merchandise properly—I won't have another piece of cargo swimming away!" His words stripped away any lingering illusion that they were still considered human.

Deep in her conflicted heart, Penelope clung to a fragile conviction that all her suffering would someday be redeemed. Whether that salvation would come to her in this life or resonate through the future of her offspring, she believed that someday, in some elusive way, the agony she endured would not be in vain—even if her own escape seemed as distant and conflicted as the visions of home that haunted her every moment.

Mary

Several days later, the ship glided into the bustling port of Antigua, its sails flapping gently in the salty breeze. It was here that the crew unloaded several slaves destined for the auction block. Amidst the chaos and clamor, Pedro's eyes fell upon a strikingly beautiful mulatto woman named Mary. Her presence captivated him, and he decided to purchase her, drawn by an allure he couldn't quite name. Unbeknownst to him, Mary possessed powers of magic, and Pedro was about to face the consequences of his choices. As Mary stepped aboard the ship, Pedro led her to his private cabin, the wooden floor creaking beneath their feet. He unlocked her shackles with a clink and instructed her to bathe and adorn herself in the fine garments he had acquired from the nearby towns. "You will be my mistress, and I will treat you well," he declared, his voice filled with a misguided confidence, before departing the cabin.

Once alone, Mary allowed a knowing smile to play across her lips. "Though you bought me, you will never own me," she murmured softly to herself. As she slipped into elegant attire, each piece of clothing was a testament to her newfound power in this moment. With a deliberate motion, she traced her fingers beneath her breast and retrieved a small, concealed sack of magic powder.

When Pedro returned, the cabin door creaking open, Mary seized her opportunity. She flung the powder into the air, and it swirled around him like an ethereal mist. As he reached for her, his hands suddenly grew weak, and he collapsed to the wooden floor, helpless. "You are my servant now!" Mary pronounced with a voice both commanding and serene. "The devil inside you will emerge and find another host, and you will become my obedient pet for the rest of your days. Now go, release your spirit into one of those wenches below and return when it is done."

Pedro, dazed and compliant, stumbled out of the cramped cabin, his movements sluggish as if moving through a dream. The narrow passageways twisted like a labyrinth before him, dimly lit by flickering lanterns, casting eerie shadows on the walls. He navigated these corridors to the ship's hold; a dark and oppressive space filled with the stench of salt and despair. There, he found Penelope, a woman whose eyes bore the haunting memories of his past cruelty. In a final, brutal act, he violated her, leaving behind an insidious legacy within her womb. As he withdrew, a bizarre sense of liberation washed over him, like a prisoner tasting freedom for the very first time. "I will no longer trouble you," he whispered, his voice tinged with an unsettling mix of relief and remorse. "I am finally free of Satan's curse."

Returning to the cabin, Pedro submitted to Mary's control as she fastened a leash around his neck with a possessive air. She ordered him to sleep on the floor, her voice dripping with condescension. "There, there, my pet, you have done a good job. After your nap, you may fetch my dinner," she purred, asserting her dominance. Pedro was now Mary's slave, a mere shadow of himself.

As the journey ended, under Mary's command, Captain Fernandez instructed the crew to feed the slaves generously, their bodies to be fattened for the impending sale. With a dismissive gesture, he tossed a haversack full of bananas at Penelope, a pitiful compensation for all her suffering. "Here! Take that for all your trouble," he barked, before striding away without a backward glance. Penelope clutched the bag tightly, her fingers trembling as she peeled and devoured three bananas, each bite, a bittersweet reminder of her lost freedom. Memories of her peanut stew flooded her mind, grounding her amidst the chaos. With quiet resolve, she shared the remaining bananas with those around her, a small act of kindness in a world devoid of mercy. Clinging to the bag, she vowed to remember her origins and never again be ensnared by the false promises of love.

MISSING

When Penelope did not return home by the day's end, worry etched deep, furrowed lines into King Bruno's brow. His heart heavy with fear, he immediately dispatched a search party, commanding them to scour every inch of the sprawling kingdom for the young princess. As the sun dipped below the horizon, painting the sky in hues of crimson and gold, shadows stretched long and thin across the land, casting an eerie gloom. For the next several days, the search continued but despite their tireless efforts, nothing yielded but silence. In desperation, they summoned the kingdom's enigmatic sorcerer. With his long, silver beard, twinkling eyes that seemed to hold the secrets of the universe, and a cloak made of lion's skin, Winston exuded an aura of mystique. He sprinkled magic dust into the fire that blazed outside the palace, a sphere glowing with an ethereal, otherworldly light. The orb revealed the fate of the princess, casting a somber shadow over the atmosphere. The news made the royal couple's hearts sink into a chasm of despair, as they saw their daughter lying flat, captured upon a slave ship. They wept tears of sorrow and frustration that seemed to echo through the surrounding jungles of Africa. As they wept, Utopia's cries swelled into a piercing scream that reverberated through the dense jungle. Her anguished wails echoed like thunder, commanding the attention of every creature within the lush, green expanse. The jungle's vibrant symphony fell silent; every bird ceased its song mid-note, and the rhythmic hum of insects abruptly halted as if the earth itself held its breath. From the regal lion resting in the shade to the tiniest ant navigating the forest floor, all life paused in solemn reverence, captivated by the Queen's heart-wrenching lament. Suddenly, she ceased her cries and turned to the warlock, her voice a fierce command that shattered the stillness. Her eyes blazing with a mixture of fury and desperation, blaming him for the ordeal, convinced that his magic mirror had set the tragic events in motion. Her voice, though firm, was tinged with a desperate plea as she commanded him to rectify the situation and ensure Princess Penelope's safe return. "Work your magic and bring my daughter back," she shouted, her words charged with an urgency that brooked no delay. Winston, with a solemn nod, assured them of his commitment. He would attempt a powerful spell, one that required Penelope to mirror an ancient ritual from Africa in the unfamiliar land of America.

As he began his spell work, his voice rose in a powerful, resonant chant that reverberated through the African jungle like an ancient hymn. "When Penelope prays over the peanuts after offering aid to strangers she encounters on her journey, the heavens will part, and the gods will bestow their blessings upon the peanuts, enveloping her in a protective shield as she flees towards freedom. There, she will encounter individuals known as abolitionists. These benevolent souls, driven by compassion, will guide her to board a ship destined for England, where slavery is abolished. In this land, the people will open their arms, extending their help to ensure her safe passage home. She must heed the whispers of the universe, trust in fate, and let the stars be her guide. Should she doubt, she risks the fate of enslavement until her final breath. Let us pray fervently that she trusts her instincts and allows the celestial bodies to lead her back to us."

That night, Utopia was overwhelmed by the unbearable thought of her beloved child being ensnared in the chains of bondage, and she felt a deep mistrust in the warlock's ability to bring Penelope back safely on his own. Determined to connect with her daughter in a way beyond the physical realm, she resolved to take her own life and unite with Penelope through the vast expanse of the universe. Utopia vowed to watch over Penelope's every step until she was returned to safety.

Under the cloak of darkness, she gathered a handful of toxic herbs, their leaves a deep, ominous green, and boiled them until their pungent aroma filled the air. Pouring the bitter concoction into a wooden cup, its surface etched with intricate patterns, she settled herself beside her husband in their tranquil garden, where the moonlight cast gentle shadows on the foliage. Slowly, she sipped the potent brew, then grasped her husband's hand tightly, her eyes glistening with unshed tears. Beneath the canopy of glittering stars, their silver light casting long shadows across the palace gardens, Queen Utopia asked his forgiveness for the drastic choice she was making, leaving him alone in a cruel and cold world. Her ebony skin shimmered with a faint sheen of perspiration, her eyes reflecting the distant constellations as she spoke with a voice that trembled between determination and sorrow. "My darling," she whispered, her slender fingers tracing the weathered lines of his face, "I have a duty to protect Penelope in the new world. This is the only way to guarantee our daughter's safe return back to Africa. I must join her in spirit, guiding her through the unseen paths of destiny." Her words hung in the night air like a solemn vow, carried on the scent of night-blooming jasmine. Upon hearing his wife's intentions, the king, stricken with despair, let go of her hand as if it burned him. His broad shoulders slumped, and his voice cracked like thunder as he urgently cried out for the servants to fetch the Doctor with all possible haste. Yet, despite their frantic efforts, the Doctor arrived too late. Utopia, with a serene look of peace on her face, had already embarked on her journey into the afterlife, leaving behind the earthly bonds to become an ethereal guardian for her child.

Slave

Her fate was sealed, she felt the harsh tug of the chain shackling her body, pulling her toward the auction block. Stripped bare of dignity and possessions, she stood stark naked, clutching the old bag—a poignant symbol of the deception that had led her into bondage.

Soon after Penelope was sold, rough hands hauled her from the auction block and shoved her onto the creaking flatbed of a rickety wagon. The iron chains bit into her wrists and ankles, each link a cold reminder of her new life. Huddled against the splintered boards, tears trailed down her dusty cheeks. Her once-glossy hair lay tangled across her shoulder, dull and matted, and her feet—bare now that her sandals had vanished— pressed into the sunbaked wood of the slave ship.

Around her sat a half dozen other captives, each silent in a different tongue. No one spoke as the wagon jolted onto the red-dirt road, dust swirling in the hot breeze. For hours, they rumbled past fields that stretched to the horizon, the stalks crowned with fluffy white cotton that glimmered in the sun like a snowdrift in midsummer.

At last, the wagon slowed in front of a low-bricked house, its white pillars sun-bleached but still imposing. The enslaved fell from the wagon one by one as wealthy planters strolled out of their doors to inspect them. The air filled with the snap of whips and the click of boots on stone. One man yanked at Penelope's lips, examining her teeth as though she were livestock. Another slapped his palm against her thigh, making her flinch. A third fondled the men's manhood before making his choices. Humiliation washed over the captives like icy water, and each indignity crushed a little more of Penelope's will.

When the last captive had been claimed, the wagon rolled on to the Foster plantation. A pair of sleek horses pawed at the gate as Master Foster's most trusted slaves—tall, sun-browned men and women whose eyes betrayed years of servitude—stepped forward to receive the newcomers. Among them was Ol' Mammy, whose bent back and silver-streaked hair spoke of generations spent in these fields. She approached Penelope, gently brushing the matted curls from her forehead. Her fingers trembled as they moved to Penelope's rounded belly. Looking up into Penelope's wide, frightened eyes, she whispered in the soft tongue of their homeland, "Oh, baby, I think you're with child—and you're only a child yourself."

Mammy straightened and went to Master Foster. She spoke low and urgently, her voice carrying just enough deference. "Massa, may I have this one? She needs care, and I could tend to her." Foster leaned on the rail, his brimmed hat shading a slow smile. "Sure," he said, stroking his graying beard. " looks like she is gonna have a little pickinini, it's like getting two for the price of one." He strode back to the trader and snapped his fingers. A handshake sealed the bargain.

Inside the grand house, polished floors reflected the afternoon light that filtered through gauzy curtains. As Penelope was led in, Mammy murmured over and over, "Don't you worry none. Mammy will take care of you, Your Majesty. By them scars on your face, I know whose you are. Slavery here will be kinder than most." Above them in the high rafters, a little black raven cried out , a sign that Utopia was near, eavesdropping on every promise made in the opulent hall.

Mammy lingered only long enough to see Penelope seated on a wooden chair, trembling but alive. Then she slipped out into the yard, Harry—the small slave child whose quick feet and quieter manner had earned Master Foster's favor—following close behind. Mammy crossed the sunlit expanse to where Foster stood beneath a magnolia, its heavy blossoms dripping pink petals.

"Massa," she began again, as though it were the first time they'd spoken, "we've no use for a pregnant wench in the fields, and she don't know our tongue. Miss Darcy needs a nurse for her newborn. I reckon this one would suit her fine." Foster tipped his head, considering the angle of the sun. "You're a sharp one, Mammy. You're right. Send her to Darcy once she's washed and fed." He patted her weathered hand and added, "And you can go with her, if you like. Show her the ropes—teach her English, proper manners. Keep her out of trouble."

Mammy's eyes glistened, and she bowed her head in gratitude. Then Foster retired inside, returning moments later with a folded note addressed in elegant script.

"Hello, Darlin',

I'm sending you someone to care for your newborn—and for you, too.

Love, Pappa."

The young slave boy sprinted off toward Darcy's house, paper clutched tight in his fist. Penelope, carried forward by hands she already half-trusted, felt as if she'd been plucked from one world and set trembling at the threshold of another. One where hope and despair rode side by side on the wind.

As Utopia heard the words of the Master of the plantation, her eyes filled with tears, not knowing the fate of her child in this distant world. As her tears began to fall, clouds filled the air, and buckets of rain fell on the boy as he ran through the fields to give the message to the Master's Daughter.

As Penelope stepped out of the imposing mansion to embark on her new life as a slave, a heavy dress was thrust upon her. The garment felt oppressive, its weight pressing down on her shoulders. The fabric was coarse and abrasive against her skin, a stark contrast to the soft, simple cotton garments she had worn back home in her village. The dress, a uniform marking her new status, hung on her as a constant reminder of her captivity.

Once inside the grand entry hall, Mammy gently peeled the heavy cotton dress from Penelope's trembling arms. "It's all right, child," she murmured in her soft, rolling dialect. "Ise gone take care of you. Let's get you cleaned up and dressed so you can meet your new mistress, Miss Darcy." She guided Penelope toward a low basin of warm water scented with sweet grass. As Penelope wept, Mammy leaned close and spoke in their secret tongue, weaving the tale of how she'd been captured. Long before Penelope's birth, Mammy had stood at her mother Utopia's side when bride and groom—The King and Penelope's mother— joined hands beneath a canopy of blossoms. It was the finest celebration the village had ever known, until Safire, consumed by jealousy, unleashed a terrible spell across the countryside. The following year, soldiers swept through the hamlets, snatching dozens of villagers and sending them to this foreign land.

With gentle hands, Mammy wiped Penelope's face until the tears and dust vanished. Then she dipped a brush into the warm water and drew it slowly through Penelope's ebony curls. Next came a small jar of rendered animal fat infused with crushed petals— jasmine and marigold—whose heady perfume filled the room. Mammy warmed the grease between her fingertips and smoothed it along each strand, coaxing the hair back into a neat bun at the nape of Penelope's neck. Finally, she tamed the tiny curls along Penelope's forehead, pressing them flat against her skin. "There, there, Princess—you look beautiful," she whispered. Over her head, she slipped the hard, coarse dress so that Penelope stood poised, heart pounding, before the towering doors of the big house.

Inside, Darcy greeted them with bright curiosity. "Hello, Mammy—who do we have here?" Mammy inclined her head, "This here is Penelope, Miss." Darcy's lips curled into a dismissive smile. "Penelope? What sort of name is that for a slave? I think we'll call her Nelly. Papa says she's expecting—like getting two slaves for the price of one!" Mammy returned the smile, though concern flickered in her eyes. Darcy folded her arms. "And why are you here, Mammy?" "I is here to teach the child the King's language," Mammy replied, voice steady. "She's just a poor, ignorant child from Africa, and your papa sent me to train her as your house servant." Darcy tapped her chin. "How long will that take?" "Perhaps a month or two, Miss," Mammy answered. "It won't be long." Darcy's gaze drifted to Penelope's sleek bun. Her eyes widened. "Good gracious! A Negra with such straight hair—if she can work this magic on mine…" She clapped her hands. "Take her to the quarters. Feed her, then begin lessons at once. I need a lady's maid who can brush and style my hair."

With a respectful bow, Mammy led Penelope to the slave quarters. Inside her small cabin, she laid a pallet of straw and an old potato sack on the rough planks. "You rest, child," she said, brushing a stray lock from Penelope's temple. "Mammy will be back soon with your supper." Then she closed the door, leaving Penelope alone in the flickering lamplight.

Sobbing softly, Penelope's tears fell onto her dress. Between her sobs, she felt something hard against her chest. With shaking fingers, she drew out a single peanut, the very one she had offered the captain before her capture. Its smooth shell brought a rush of bittersweet memories. Under the watchful moon streaming through the small window, she dug a tiny grave in the cool earth just outside and buried her token from home. Falling to her knees, she lifted her voice in a desperate prayer to the gods. Overhead, her mother Utopia's spirit leaning close, whispering, "Prepare the peanut stew, share it with those around you, and it will open a path to lead you home." But distance from

Utopia shut Penelope's ears; she only wept, lamenting her own trust and longing for the life she had lost.

When dawn painted the sky in rose and gold, Mammy returned and ushered Penelope back to Darcy's house. There, inside the bustling kitchen, Penelope met the kindly kitchen maid—an elderly woman whose smile crinkled the corners of her eyes. "Hello, darlin'," she greeted, her voice warm as fresh biscuits. Penelope's lips curved into a shy smile, the first spark of hope returning to her heart. The woman beckoned Penelope to come closer with a gentle gesture, and Penelope instinctively mirrored her movements. The woman turned to Penelope with a tender expression, placed a weathered hand on her own chest, and said, "Me, Patsy." Penelope nodded, absorbing the lesson, and echoed, "Patsy." Her earnest attempt elicited a hearty laugh from Patsy, who replied with delight, "Yes, I'm Patsy. You're a fast learner."

Over the following weeks, Patsy would pick up various utensils and objects scattered across the bustling kitchen, pointing them out and articulating their names with patient precision. The fragrant aroma of freshly baked bread and simmering stew filled the air as Penelope learned the names of pots, pans, and spices. After several months of dedicated learning, Penelope could speak and understand English fluently.

While Mammy taught her the latest hairstyles and all of the techniques it took to be an excellent lady's maid. She also taught Penelope how to care for Darcy's infant with lessons on diaper changing and feeding, tasks she would take on between taking care of Darcy.

With her newfound language skills, Penelope was then promoted to the upstairs quarters, where she took on the role of Darcy's lady's maid and wet nurse to her infant child. The nursery was a serene space filled with the soft glow of morning light filtering through silk curtains, and Penelope embraced her responsibilities with a sense of purpose and newfound confidence.

Although Darcy conversed with Penelope in a gentle and considerate manner, her husband was as mean as a rattlesnake, a fact that Patsy had warned Penelope about, highlighting his selfish tendencies. Whenever he strutted into the house, he would cast a disdainful sneer at the house servants, demanding his meal accompanied by a glass of whiskey, and dutifully, they complied. Mr. Brown was notorious for his greediness, hoarding the finest parts of the crop and meat for himself, selling what remained, and leaving the slaves with only the meager rations that were left. Behind his back, the slaves mockingly referred to him as "Cheap Brown," a nickname that spread quiet chuckles across the miles of fields. In contrast, Darcy found joy in the company of the other slaves, fostering a vision of union among them for two practical reasons: married slaves were generally happier, reducing the likelihood of escape, and more slaves meant increased wealth for the plantation, an additional bringing forth a child could be an asset to sell if financial times became tough.

Three months of patient training had slipped by beneath the relentless Southern sun, and at last the day arrived when Mammy was to return to her own plantation—yet nothing prepared her for what was to come. Mammy had always believed she held a special place in Mayor Foster's heart. He'd grown up under her watchful care, and in his youth, he vowed to keep her by his side forever. But a prosperous family from upriver near Louisiana, having heard of the miraculous way Mammy taught a newly arrived African girl to speak flawless English and behave like a refined lady's maid, offered three thousand dollars on the spot— an irresistible sum. Within hours, Mayor Foster had signed the papers. In two days, Mammy would be handed over to the local slave trader.

That evening, a slender note found its way to Darcy:

Dear Darcy,

Send Mammy back home.

Her work with the new slave is done.

Thanks, Darlin'.

Your Pappa

Darcy summoned Penelope. "Bring Mammy at once," she said, voice trembling. Penelope found Mammy sitting in the garden mending a frayed hem. When Darcy read the note, Mammy's weathered face crumpled, and a single tear slipped free. Gathering Penelope into her arms, she whispered, "Don't you fret, child. I'll only be a hop, skip, and jump away—we'll be neighbors still." Then she looked to Darcy. "Miss Darcy, could Nellie and you walk me to the property line? I'd like one last goodbye."

Under the glowing embers of sunset, the three crossed the dew-wet lawn. Cicadas droned from the magnolias overhead. At the worn fence that marked the Foster estate's edge, Mammy embraced first Penelope, then Darcy, her rough hands trembling against their soft dresses. Her chest ached with each faint heartbeat.

The next morning, Mammy stepped onto the broad white porch of the big house. Mayor Foster lounged beneath a column, a fat cigar glowing between his stained fingers. She straightened her skirt, smoothed her faded headscarf, and offered a deep bow. "Good morning, Massa," she said, voice steady though her heart quaked.

He peered down at her over tarnished spectacles. "Well, Mammy, how did you find your time away?"

"It was mighty nice, Massa," she replied softly. "Wish I could've stayed longer."

He grinned thinly. "Glad to hear it—because I've decided on a permanent change."

For a brief moment, Mammy dared to hope she might remain with Darcy. But his next words shattered her world. "No, Mammy. You won't be returning here. You're too old to work the fields, and there are no little ones to tend, so, I sold you."

A strangled sob escaped her lips. "You promised you'd never sell me!"

"That was my father's promise, not mine," he snapped, rising. "He's dead and buried. Now pack your things. The trader arrives at dawn."

Mammy bowed her head. Summoning the last of her courage, she whispered, "Massa—may I at least say goodbye to Nellie?"

He turned, eyes cold as river stone. "No." Then he strode inside, slamming the door behind him.

At first light, iron shackles bit into Mammy's ankles as she trudged down the dusty lane toward the river. Under draping Spanish moss, her old life slipped from her like water through cupped hands. Yet within days, she found a new calling: the Louisiana family employed her as a teacher. In a small cabin beside their sugarcane fields, she opened a humble schoolhouse, hanging lace curtains in the windows and filling its rooms with worn furnishings—an oval mirror, a chipped teacup, a velvet chair salvaged from the Master's parlor. There she taught newly arrived Africans to speak English, to cook rice and sugar cakes, to braid hair in neat rows, and to polish silver.

A year later, Mammy approached the mistress under an oak's spreading limbs. "Ma'am," she began, voice trembling like the bayou at dusk, "Could I ask you to purchase Penelope for me?" The family begged Mayor Foster for permission, but his daughter Darcy refused. That final refusal sealed their fates: Mammy never saw or heard another word from the Fosters again .

The Red Hot Pickled Peppered Peanuts

The days passed, and Penelope would nurture this tiny promise of a peanut, watering the earth with hope and dedication. As time passed, the peanut sprouted, stretching towards the sun, eventually flourishing into a modest crop. When the time was ripe, Penelope harvested the peanuts, planting more seeds until a small oasis of verdant peanut plants encircled her cabin in the slave quarters.

Each night, as the shadows lengthened, instead of consuming the offered pork and grits, Penelope would roast the peanuts over the glowing embers of the fireplace, savoring their warm, nutty aroma. Her dinners transformed into a simple yet satisfying feast of roasted peanuts and grits. One day, when the Master distributed rations, she received peppers, vinegar, and a few other sparse ingredients. With nimble fingers, she extracted the seeds from the peppers and sowed them alongside the thriving peanuts in her secret garden.

Ingeniously, she poured the vinegar into a mason jar, nestling in a handful of roasted peanuts, then topped them with the fiery, seedless peppers before sealing the jar tight. The following day, her meal was a revelation; she relished the fiery crunch of red-hot pickled peppered peanuts. The flavors danced on her palate, an unexpected symphony of heat and tang, while the peanuts snapped and crackled delightfully in her mouth. Keeping this culinary treasure, a well-guarded secret, Penelope understood the scarcity of food during the harsh winter months and knew that if Master Brown discovered her bounty, he would surely claim it for himself.

With this knowledge, Penelope buried the jars deep in the earth, knowing the cool, dark soil would shield them from the relentless sun, preserving their contents through the harsh winter months. Each night, under the cloak of darkness, she filled the jars with plump, golden peanuts and gently laid them in the garden beside the small slave cabin. There, nestled in their earthy beds, the peanuts remained fresh and savory, a hidden treasure to sustain them through the cold season.

BUCK

Time passed, and Penelope gave birth to a child as pale as newly fallen snow. In Penelope's eyes, his hair was straight and his eyes a striking shade of lavender, eerily reminiscent of the man who had torn her from her homeland. She named him Buck, for every glance at his innocent face summoned a silent scream of anger within her. For the rest of her days, Penelope would face the constant struggle of looking upon the features of the man she despised yet finding the strength to love her son. When the baby arrived, Darcy descended to the slave quarters to visit. Her heart twinged with an indescribable ache as she gazed upon him. Despite her words praising the baby's beauty, in her eyes, he was the most unsettling sight she had ever encountered. His skin was as pale as a ghostly apparition, and his eyes blazed like a fiery inferno, tinged with a sinister yellow hue. His cries pierced the air, a wail that seemed to claw at her very soul.

Each day, Penelope brought the child to the big house, leaving him in the bustling kitchen with the servants. The staff eyed him with a mix of fear and unease, as if he were some otherworldly being. And whenever Darcy entered the kitchen to converse with the maid, an irrational urge would grip her—a fleeting, dark impulse to seize an iron skillet and dash his little brains out.

A few months passed, and Darcy's cousin Leona visited. Though married, Leona had never been able to bear a son. Seated in Darcy's parlor while sipping tea, she recounted her own struggles, then said, "Bring me the child you've been writing to me about." Darcy got up and went into the nursery where her son and Buck were playing. She instructed Penelope to gather flowers for the dinner party later on that evening, while the children played in the parlor with her and her cousin.

Penelope rose, picked up Buck, and led the young master into the parlor with Leona, while Darcy followed behind. As Penelope wandered the grounds selecting blooms for the dinner party, Darcy began negotiating for young Buck. While seated in the parlor with Buck between them, Darcy's cousin burst out, "Good gracious alive, what in the lord's tarnation— this is the little white Negra child you've been writing to me about? Look at those gorgeous lavender eyes; they have a slightly mischievous gleam, but that's the fashion in Paris. All I need to do is put a little wig on him, dust him with talcum powder, and he'll look just like Louis the 15th. How much do you want for him?"

Darcy leaned back in her chair and smiled, "I want a thousand dollars."

Her cousin blushed deeply, "A thousand dollars? Are you crazy? That is a baby—I suppose you're going to throw in his mammy too?"

Darcy's expression tightened, "I don't think so; I need his mammy to brush my hair. Have you ever seen a Negro wench with straight hair? Nelly is worth her weight in gold, and I'm not about to give her up. So, do you want this white pickaninny or what?"

After a moment of thoughtful silence, Darcy's cousin replied, "My husband does need an heir, and since he's away on business—a venture that can take years—I'll take him. You've got yourself a deal. I'll write to him and say I am with child; he'll never suspect the child isn't his."

That evening, while Penelope was getting Darcy ready for bed, a gentle glow of the setting sun filtered through the bedroom window, casting warm amber tones on the walls. As Penelope neatly folded Darcy's nightgown and placed it on the bed's edge, where the last light of the day touched it. Darcy moved to the dressing table and handed the brush to Penelope to brush her hair. As she brushed, the soft rustling of hair was the only sound in the room. Casually, Darcy mentioned to Penelope that a Harvest Dance was approaching. "Perhaps you'll meet a beau," she remarked with a warm smile. "Don't worry about your little boy; he can stay here with my child, and the old woman from the quarters will watch over them both. Just drop him off at the old woman's place before you head to the dance." Penelope's heart filled with excitement at the idea of dancing and mingling with others like her, sharing moments of joy and camaraderie. As Penelope imagined being at the dance, Darcy arose, as she disappeared into the closet and returned with a simple white dress and matching sandals. "You can wear this," she said, her voice filled with anticipation. "I can't wait for you to enjoy the dance with the other Negras. You're going to look so beautiful." Penelope nodded, her face glowing with happiness as she finished dressing her mistress.

After her duties were done for the day, she gathered Buck in her arms and waved goodbye. That night, Penelope ground peanuts into a fine paste, mixed it with creamy milk that she got from the mistress's house, and fed Buck the nourishing mixture. As she watched him eat, her thoughts wandered to the dance. Even if she met a man there, she wondered with a sigh, how could any man accept a woman with a child whose pale skin set him apart from the others?

As the week flew by, Penelope found herself in her cabin preparing for the Harvest Dance. Holding Buck in her arms, she carried him to the elderly woman who would be looking after him for the evening. A chill of fear ran through her, as if this might be the last time, she would see her little boy. She quickly dismissed the thought. "Who would want to take my baby? This thinking is ridiculous," she reassured herself as she headed for the door to drop him off.

The old woman came to the door, "Are you here to drop off the young'un?" she said in a sweet little voice. "Yes, and I'll be back to pick him up as soon as I get home". The old woman scoffed, "Come back in the morning, I go to bed early, plus I don't like yungons to break sleep, and lose their pattern." Then she waved Penelope goodbye. As soon as she saw Penelope walking down the road with the other slaves, the little woman picked up the child and walked through the back door, down the road to the big house. "Do you need me to tend to the child for the night?" She said to her mistress. Darcy smiled, "No, just go back home, and I'll send someone for you if I need you". With that, the old woman left and went back to her cabin.

Penelope arrived at the harvest dance around six o'clock. It was set to be a grand celebration, with the rhythmic beats of drums and lively tunes of fiddles filling the crisp autumn air. Slaves from nearby plantations were invited, their laughter and footsteps blending under the vast, starry sky, creating an evening of joyful respite and community amidst their daily toil. At the event, she met a man named Sam, who was from a neighboring plantation. Sam was about six feet tall, muscular, with noticeable dimples on his strong, dark face. As he approached her, he asked, "Hey, pretty lady, would you like to dance?" Penelope smiled, nodded, and they spent the night dancing together. By the evening's end, Sam proposed to Penelope, as was customary at the time. There was no time for lengthy courtships; slaves who cared for one another simply jumped the broom to marry. Overjoyed, Penelope spun around in delight as she returned to her cabin, collapsing onto the cool, damp grass in a dizzy spell. Finally, her son Buck would have a father figure. She then reflected on Prince Olajuwon and wondered how life might have been different had she not defied her father, and tears began to fall.

Second Sold

The next day, Penelope went by the old woman's home to pick up her child, and the old woman said that the mistress had picked him up already. Shocked, Penelope ran to the big house where Master Brown was standing at the door. "My wife is sleeping. How can I help you?" Penelope, terrified, whispered, "I came to pick up my boy". He yelled, "What, say it louder, I can't hear you." Penelope yelled, "I came to pick up my boy" He looked down at her and said, "come back in an hour she should be woke by then." Penelope turned around and went back to her cabin, confused about what could have happened to little buck.

Within the next hour, time passed swiftly. Penelope walked over to the mistress's quarters, picked up the prepared breakfast, and delivered it to her room. The mistress greeted her with a bright, "Good morning,

Nelly!" Confused, Penelope replied, "Good morning—I'm looking for my boy Buck. Have you seen him?" With a secretive smile, Darcy remarked, "Now, Nelly, you know that boy is as white as I am. It would be far too confusing to have a white child living among the slaves. Someone might even assume he's Master Brown's, which I simply cannot allow—so I got rid of him." Shocked, Penelope recoiled, causing the tray to fall. Rising from the bed, Darcy continued, "That white child belongs with his own kind. I want you to have a proper life, and you won't if you keep carrying around a white Negra baby." Gasping and choking on her words, Penelope realized that the woman she trusted had just stolen and sold her baby.

Darcy then called a servant from the hall, instructing, "Please take Nelly down to the kitchen. Tell them to prepare something warm to calm her nerves, then come back and clean up this mess." The servant complied. While she began tidying the fallen tray, Darcy inquired about the harvest dance. The servant explained that Penelope had met a man named Sam from a neighboring plantation who had proposed that they jump the broom together. Smiling, Darcy added, "That should distract her from thinking about the child. When you go downstairs, tell Nelly to come back up—I need her to brush my hair." Meanwhile, as the servants tried to comfort Penelope, Patsey dabbed away her tears and said, "Nelly, that's just the way it is. White folks want your baby—they snatch it away and sell it like a loaf of bread. You've got to put up with it, or you'll find yourself in the cotton fields for the rest of your life. Just smile and say it's alright, Missus—there's nothing you can do about them selling your child. If anger begins to rise, the best remedy is to laugh or hum a hymn. White people love that; they don't like it when a slave gets mad. An angry slave might even seek revenge and cause trouble. It's better to keep smiling, laughing, and acting happy no matter what they do. You see, slaves often joke about things they can't control—because a slave is denied everything, even his own feelings."

Penelope nodded and slowly picked up a corncake to nibble on. Then a large, robust woman with rich, dark skin said, "Now Nelly, make sure you wash your hands—the Missus is allergic to corn. She'll break out in a rash and have difficulty breathing." With that, Penelope went to the sink, washed her hands, and climbed the stairs to the mistress's room. Before entering, she offered a small smile. "Are you okay, Nelly?" the mistress asked. With a gentle smile, Penelope replied, "I'm fine, Missus. You're not sore about me selling your little ugly pickaninny, are you?" Still smiling, Penelope added, "It's alright, Missus. You're right—I don't need that baby. I'm okay," and then she began humming a hymn. Darcy's face lit up as she exclaimed, "I just love those Negra hymns!" She sprang out of bed and walked over to her dressing mirror.

At the dressing table, while Penelope assisted, Darcy handed her a brush and commented, "I heard you met a man at the party last night. Looks like we're heading toward a wedding." Smiling through her sorrow, Penelope replied, "Yes, Missus." "So, tell me, what's his name?" the mistress inquired. With a bittersweet smile, Penelope answered, "Sam Peterson—he's from the Peterson plantation." "Oh, good, now you can have some all-Negra children—that's exactly what you need, all Negra children." Penelope managed a soft smile as she agreed, "Yes, Missus."

Lynch

The following morning, Darcy informed Penelope that she wished for her to join her on a ride into town. As the horses trotted along the dusty road, Darcy began to speak about the grim fate that awaited any slave who dared to escape. Her voice was laced with a chilling amusement as she chuckled, "Oh, Nelly, this is your life now. You've been sold into a life of servitude, and should you ever attempt to flee, oh my, you'd be lynched." Penelope, with a childlike curiosity, asked, "What is lynched?" Darcy laughed again, the sound as cold as the winter wind, "Oh Nelly, that's when they loop a rope around your neck and tie you up to a tree. The rope grips so tightly that it cuts off your breathing, and you slowly choke to death. I'm taking you to a lynching right now, so you can see what I mean." Penelope smiled innocently and replied, "Okay, missum," her voice carrying a naivety that was stark against the grim reality Darcy described.

In the sweltering afternoon heat, Darcy's eyes shone with a frigid, unwavering intensity as she held tightly onto Penelope's hand. "You ain't never seen a lynching, have you, girl? You'll see one today. I'm takin' you to watch one right now, so you can see what I mean." Penelope, her heart pounding like a trapped bird, managed a tremulous smile and whispered, "Yes, mis sum."

As they stepped out of the carriage into the dusty street, the town square sprawled before them, a grotesque spectacle already unfolding. A Black man, his dark skin glistening with sweat and fear, stood in the eye of a human storm, a crowd of jeering, sneering faces. Chains clanked around his wrists, and two white men, their faces contorted with hate and triumph, flanked him, gripping his arms like vices.

Darcy, her eyes wide with a feverish glee, began to jump and clap, her voice piercing the air like a shrill, discordant note. "Hang that nigger!" she screeched; her face flushed with a perverse joy. Penelope watched, her stomach churning with a mix of fear and incomprehension. What was this spectacle that could evoke such joy in her mistress?

Two men, their faces set in grim determination, dragged the man towards a towering tree, its thick branches stretching out like gnarled, accusing fingers. A rope, a sinister serpent, swung gently from one of the branches, its noose a gaping maw waiting to be fed. The man struggled, his body writhing in a desperate dance of defiance. But the crowd, a monstrous beast with a thousand arms, descended upon him, sticks and fists raining down blows until his body went limp, his spirit beaten into submission.

One of the men grabbed the noose, pulling it over the poor, defenseless soul's head like a grotesque crown. The other man tightened it, the rope creaking like a grim symphony as the crowd grabbed hold, their hands eager to deal death. They pulled, their faces contorted with effort and hate, the rope taut as an executioner's bowstring. The man's body jerked, his feet dancing a macabre jig as life was choked out of him. His body spasmed, a marionette controlled by the strings of death, until it hung limp, a grim pendulum swaying gently in the breeze. The crowd erupted in cheers, their faces a chorus of gleeful, triumphant masks. But Penelope, her soul weeping, could only stand in silent horror.

On the journey back to the plantation, Darcy's hand, cold and unyielding like a shackle, gripped Penelope's. "If you ever try to run away from me," she hissed, her voice a poisoned arrow, "I will catch you and lynch you. My father bought you and gave you to me as a gift, and I own you for life. If you ever think about leaving, you just remember that Negra jerking in the middle of the town square and get it out of your head."

Prayer

As Penelope lay on a rough pallet on the earthen floor, her tears mingling with the dust as she mourned the loss of her child, a persistent knock at the door shattered the stillness. A small, timid voice, trembling with hope, asked, "Is somebody in there?" Rising slowly, her tear-stained face set with a determined resolve, Penelope opened the creaking door to reveal an elderly couple cloaked in threadbare rags. The man's hair, a soft curtain of gray that receded with time, revealed a subtle, raised bump on his forehead—a silent testament to his life of hardship— while his wife, a diminutive light-skinned woman dappled with freckles, wore a faded red and white checkered bandana. Despite the fear evident in their eyes, her smile radiated warmth, a beacon of light in the darkness.

"Come in," Penelope said gently, gesturing for them to enter the modest shack. As they stepped inside, their voices lowered to a hushed, desperate murmur, "We is runaways, and we is powerfully hungry. We been traveling for days, and we are so very tired—can you spare some food for the children of God?" Her heart aching in sympathy, Penelope welcomed them to sit at her worn wooden table. With careful tenderness, she produced strips of salted pork from her meager rations and then moved to a creaking cupboard to retrieve remnants of grits, which she heated slowly over a small, sputtering fire.

As the couple recounted their dangerous escape from the bonds of oppression, their voices filled with a mix of exhaustion and hope, as Penelope divided the modest meal equally between them. Her eyes, full of compassion, then met theirs as she inquired, "What's your name and where are you headed?" A soft chuckle escaped the old man as he introduced himself with pride, "I am Reverend Petunia, this is my wife, Sweet Pea, and we are journeying towards Freedom Land—a place they call Canada. It lies far ahead, but with the help of the Lord, we will reach it. Why don't you come with us?"

For a moment, Penelope's face fell, her memories darkening as she recalled the chilling words of Darcy and the ghastly image of a poor soul dangling from a rope—a fate that loomed over anyone who dared run. The sharp recollection of Buck's fate, sold off to

Darcy's cousin, stung bitterly; the fear of never seeing him again held her back. With strained resolve, she confessed, "I would love to go, but my mistress warned that if I ever ran, I would be caught, and I would be lynched. She even sold my baby to her cousin. I must stay, hoping that he might return someday. And there's more—I met a man, and our marriage is set in a few weeks."

The elderly couple shared a knowing chuckle. "Who is he? Perhaps we know him," they inquired. With a tender smile, Penelope replied, "His name is Sam Peterson, from the Peterson plantation. He is well known to many because he is often rented out to work on other plantations. Yes, he's a big, beautiful man— strong and handsome." At that moment, Sweet Pea stepped closer, draping her arms around Penelope's shoulder in a comforting embrace. "We know Sam Peterson well," she murmured gravely. "Master Peterson often leases him out to sire children with slave women, so that his slaves can be bred to labor harder and longer. Perhaps you should come with us and leave all that torment behind."

As Sweet Pea's words washed over her, a conflicted longing stirred within Penelope—a desire to escape mingled with the paralyzing fear instilled by Darcy. Clutching her emotions tight, she replied softly, "You must go without me. I have suffered unspeakable wrongs— I was raped and my future husband was raped too. I must hold together what remains of my little family." With a resigned sigh, she continued, "I will pray to my ancestors to guide you every step of the way. It is getting late; you should set forth before daylight reveals you too easily."

Gathering what little supplies she had, Penelope carefully bundled the remaining pork and grits in a faded cloth and handed them a small jar filled with her fiery, red-hot pickled peppered peanuts. "Now off with you," she whispered earnestly, "And one more thing: As I pray over these peanuts they will connect to the gods. Never lose them, for they will hold the power to protect you and keep you together. The moment they leave your possession, their magic will seal, and the jar will become unbreakable, leaving you defenseless if they fall into the wrong hands. Cherish them, just as I cherish my memories of Africa. Our fate, our hope, rests in your hands. Now go, and may my ancestors on the other side watch over you on your journey to Freedom Land."

With that, the tender farewell was sealed in an embrace filled with both love and sorrow, and the old couple melted into the embracing night. Left standing in the dim glow of her little cabin, Penelope stepped out into the side yard. The cool, damp grass pressed against her knees as she knelt, her voice echoing into the sprawling darkness as she called out to the spirits of her ancestors.

"Hear me, Mother Africa, hear my prayer,

Cover the two who just left here.

Protect the sweet couple from all that wish to hurt
and scar,

Protect them near, protect them far.

Take them safely to Freedom Land.

Far away from where they ran."

As Penelope began to speak, the spirit of Utopia descended from the heavens, cloaked in a swirling, majestic purple cloud that shimmered like an otherworldly curtain. Her countenance burned with anger as she denounced Penelope's refusal to accept the gift of freedom; in her fury, Utopia smeared the sky with thick, oppressive clouds. Meanwhile, tears flowed relentlessly from her mother's eyes, glistening and falling like silver raindrops through the heavy clouds onto the earth, drenched in sorrow yet carrying a strange, sacred blessing for her little peanut girl.

Penelope craned her neck upward, her eyes filled with a mixture of hope, fear, and confusion, as Utopia's resonant voice echoed down from the stormy heights: "Penelope, how could you let fear keep you from your dreams of freedom?" In a soft, trembling whisper, Penelope replied, "Momma, is that you?" The voice responded, laden with both reproach and lament: "I have watched you from afar, listened as you placed the blame on your siblings for your confinement, when in truth it was your own disobedience that brought this upon you. Had you obeyed the words spoken to you, you would not be ensnared in this predicament. You defied your father's command not to stray beyond the gate, and you ignored the pleas of the kindly couple urging you to depart with them. Disobedience is a grievous sin, and now all must suffer the price of your folly. You prayed for the gods to guide you home, and when they granted your earnest request, you relinquished what was given without understanding its true value. It is the harshest slap in the face to divine grace. Consider how many souls beseech God for the means to secure land or build a home, only to squander the blessings bestowed upon them. God must wonder why He opened a path to you when, the moment your desire was fulfilled, you abandoned the essential needs that sustain you. Penelope, like so many women, you traded the precious freedom of your spirit for the fleeting promise of a man and a child. Trust me, had they been the true gifts they appeared to be, they would not have demanded the price you paid. That child, half white, may never fully grasp his heritage nor feel the unconditional love of his mother. Instead, he might grow to mirror the contempt of his father—a man who has known little but survival and the harsh lessons of a loveless existence. You made a dangerous bargain, and now my very being must bear the anguish of your choice. Penelope, you cannot fully understand the depths of what you have wrought! The Peanuts, though mighty and powerful with their ability to connect souls, also harbor the capacity to divide us. I must depart now, compelled to follow the unpredictable power of these sacred peanuts. My spirit must leave you and seek them out wherever they may lead, for they are destined to bring all our scattered souls together and reunite the spirits of our people, young and old alike, in some distant corner of the universe. Farewell, my child, though my prayers remain with you—be warned, you are fated to endure a life of bondage."

At that moment, as if in response to her words, a blinding flash of lightning struck a nearby tree, setting it ablaze in a fierce burst of fire. As the relentless rain quickly subdued the flames, Utopia pronounced a curse upon the very ground and all that held her daughter captive, and with that final, searing condemnation, she vanished into the roiling sky.

Soon after, as a dense, swirling cloud enveloped the small couple, a palpable fear took hold of them. Utopia, draped in a radiant gold coat that caught the fleeting light amidst the darkness, pulled it closely around them. Her voice, gentle yet commanding, filled the air: "Do not be afraid. I am Utopia; I was called forth by my child's desperate plea to safeguard you. I will guide you safely towards freedom. Place your hand in mine, and know that no harm shall touch you." With trepidation and reverence, the couple tentatively reached out and touched her delicate fingertip. A subtle electric tingle raced through them, a small shock of divine energy threading their hearts together, and then she faded away like a whispered secret.

"Momma, did you see that?" Sweet Pea's voice quavered in wonder as she smiled, nodding in quiet amazement. As they pressed on through a vast, whispering field under a dimming sky, the sound of galloping horses shattered the silence. When they turned, they could see torches blazing like scattered stars in the encroaching darkness. Reverend Petunia, his voice hushed and filled with urgent dread, murmured, "That's the Patrollers. Oh, Momma, we have no place to hide; it seems we must return to the chains of slavery." Frozen in alarm, they clutched each other, standing in the field as if time itself had stopped, awaiting the inevitable. Yet, in a most unexpected turn, the patrollers rode past as if the couple were nothing more than an illusion, unseen in the eyes of their pursuers.

Once the threat had receded into the distance, Utopia reappeared, her form ethereal against the backdrop of the field. In a voice that soothed their burdened souls, she reassured them, "Fear not, I will guide your weary feet to abundant berry bushes and flowing streams, ensuring you never suffer from hunger again. My spirit will remain your constant companion on this journey, leading you to the refuge called Freedom Land, where you will always find your way." As she hovered above them, her gentle light shielding them from curious eyes, she gave one last promise: no one would detect their presence until they reached safety. Then, as quietly as she had arrived, Utopia disappeared into the welcoming twilight.

Since Penelope did not accept the gift of freedom, Utopia would exist between two realms, compelled to follow the peanuts and observe her child from afar. However, thanks to the peanuts, there was communication through the spirit world, for which Utopia was truly thankful.

FREEDOM

After a grueling journey of thirty days with the unwavering support of Utopia, Theodore Petunia and his wife, Sweet Pea, found themselves standing in Buffalo, New York. The air was crisp, and the promise of freedom lingered just a few hours north, across the Canadian border. As they paused to rest, a gust of wind delivered a crumpled page from a newspaper, Reverend Petunia could read because the old' Master taught him from the good book to prepare him for his preaching days. As the page from the newspaper fluttered to their feet, bearing the life-altering headline: "The Fugitive Slave Law Abolished." Reverend Petunia's heart soared, and he erupted into joyous leaps, his voice ringing out in pure elation. He turned to embrace his wife, Sweet Pea, whose fragile frame bore the marks of their arduous trek, sustained only by the wild berries they had foraged along the way. Despite her hunger pains, she joined him in exuberant celebration, her voice breaking through with triumphant cries, "This means we can't be captured and taken back into slavery; the Lord has answered our prayers!"

Reverend Petunia placed his foot firmly on a large, weathered stone that stood resolutely before him. "On Christ the solid rock I stand," he proclaimed with fervor, "all other ground is Cheektowaga, Lackawanna, or Niagara Falls." Their laughter rang out, a harmonious blend of relief and happiness. With renewed determination, Reverand Petunia declared, "Today, we shall call Buffalo our home. I will purchase this land and erect a sanctuary in the name of our Lord Jesus, who has delivered us from the chains of slavery."

Sweet Pea, her eyes bright with hope, reminded him, "What about Utopia?" The Reverend nodded, his expression softening with gratitude. "Utopia was an angel sent by the Lord, and yes, we thank her for coming." He lifted his gaze to the heavens, his voice carried by the breeze, "Utopia, we..." His words trailed off into the sky, a silent prayer of thanks for the divine intervention that had guided them to freedom. Immediately after Reverand Petunia concluded his solemn prayer, he glanced over his wife's shoulder and caught sight of a bright "Help Wanted" sign glimmering in the window of the local mercantile. With an eager nod and a hint of divine excitement in his eyes, he pointed at the sign and declared, "Look, God knows just what I need. The Lord done gone and got me a job!" Striding purposefully toward the store, his jubilant proclamation echoed through the quiet street.

Moments later, he burst out of the mercantile, his voice ringing with exuberance as he bellowed, "Praise God Almighty—I got me a job! C'mon, let's get set up in a nice, quiet spot deep in the woods on some government property, far out of the way. We don't want no trouble!" Without hesitation, he and his delicate, frail wife gathered their few treasured belongings and set off toward the secluded, whispering woodlands.

Deep amidst the towering trees, the couple unfurled a large sheet that served as a makeshift tent beneath the dappled sunlight. Not long after, Sweet Pea revealed a cherished jar filled with fiery red hot pickled, peppered peanuts—a gift from Penelope— and with a burst of hunger and delight she exclaimed, "I forgot about these, praise the Lord—I'm starving!"

Reverend Petunia swiftly snatched the jar from her grasp, his tone both firm and reverential as he chided, "Sweet Pea Petunia! You can't eat those peanuts—they were made by the angel who sent the spirit to protect us on our perilous journey. We must preserve them as a constant reminder of Penelope and of where we came from." With gentle care, he returned the sacred jar to the bag holding their few possessions, then stepped away to gather twigs and kindling for a comforting fire, while Sweet Pea meandered towards a nearby sparkling stream to fetch fresh water.

Upon her return, Sweet Pea unveiled a modest repast: salted pork accompanied by a small bag of grits, another precious gift from Penelope, and began preparing their humble dinner. As the savory aroma of cooking meat mingled with the cool forest air, the Reverend unrolled soft blankets on the forest floor in preparation for the night. The couple spent that evening tossing and turning with restless excitement, their hearts brimming with the thrill of being truly free—free from the fear of capture and abuse. Together, they envisioned a new life: one in which nightly camp meetings would transform into earnest church gatherings until winter's bite forced them to seek shelter in a nearby barn until spring's gentle revival. Their dreams, while grand, were tempered by the understanding that hard work lay ahead if they were to see these aspirations materialize.

The following day, as Pastor Petunia diligently managed his work in the store, an unexpected visitor approached—a wizened old woman whose weathered face told tales of hardship. A jagged scar marred the delicate skin above her left eye, and she was missing two front teeth, giving her a particularly rugged look. Her head was swathed in a lustrous black silk scarf, contrasting starkly with the threadbare, grimy fabric of a dress fashioned from an old potato sack. On her feet, she wore a pair of sturdy men's boots, which she claimed had been taken from a dead prisoner found along a lonely roadside.

Without delay, the old woman made a beeline for Reverend Petunia and, with a voice both weary and resolute, declared, "I have walked hundreds of miles to claim my freedom. I am powerfully hungry, and my back aches from the long journey—will you help me?" The moment the storekeeper noticed this interaction, his face twisted in disdain as he barked, "Get that unsightly woman out of my establishment before she distracts my paying customers!"

Calmly raising his hand to interpose himself, Reverend Petunia replied, "Perhaps the Lord has sent her here to bestow a blessing upon your store. The ways of the Lord are indeed mysterious." Extending his hands toward the downtrodden woman, he instructed, "Please, venture into the woods; there you will find my wife. She will feed you and take care of you." With that, he offered gentle directions, and the old woman departed, slowly vanishing into the quiet embrace of the forest.

When he returned home, the old woman met his gaze with a serene, knowing smile, then she softly uttered, "Thank you for sending me here and saving my life. I am forever in your debt. I am, in truth, an enchanted angel, shunned by many because of my outward appearance—but you saw beyond the surface and recognized the woman within who was in dire need. Because you helped me, I shall remain in your service for as long as you desire. And for your kindness, I grant you three wishes—be careful of what you wish for, for you only have three."

At that moment, Reverend Petunia's heart sank as if a heavy stone had taken root within it. Though his mind was awash with gratitude for the help rendered, he could not dispel the profound repulsion he felt at the sight, overwhelmed by the woman's ghastly appearance—a visage he simply could not embrace, a face that resembled hers, and being a man of God, he had to tread lightly to avoid hurting her feelings. So, he declared, "I love Sweet Pea so deeply that I've even attached her first name to the church we're founding. We shall call it The Church of God and Sweet Jesus—placing her name right between God and Jesus. You are kind, but I long to have Sweet Pea back." In that instant, the old woman's face shifted back to that of his wife, and in Sweet Pea's voice the woman announced, "You have two more wishes—choose wisely."

The same night, the Reverend savored a sumptuous meal of leg of lamb and freshly dug vegetables—arguably the most delicious feast he'd ever had. Yet, he missed his wife terribly and understood that he must complete his remaining wishes swiftly, so the imposter would vanish and his true love would return.

Later that evening, when the woman tried to embrace him, he pushed her away, saying, "Even though you look and sound like my wife, you are not her, and I have no desire to be intimate with anyone else. I am a man of virtue, and I must honor our union—even if that means sleeping outdoors." The woman nodded in understanding, and the Reverend stepped outside, soon finding another equally lovely tent where he spent the night.

Throughout the restless hours, he tossed and turned, contemplating his next wish. It was the first night in ten years that he went without the comfort of Sweet Pea's presence, and despite their decade-long marriage, she had never borne him a child—the one thing he yearned for most. By morning, he resolved to ask the mysterious woman for a boy who could carry on the Petunia name.

That morning, the old woman busied herself reheating leftover lamb while an egg fried in another pan. Sitting by the fire, he watched as she placed the breakfast onto a large stone that served as their table. With a warm smile, she remarked, "I just love being your wife." That comment infuriated Reverend Petunia, and he quickly responded, "I wish for my wife to bear a boy, one to carry on the Petunia name." Nodding, the enigmatic woman replied, "The child will come to you in about a year. Do you desire anything more?" With no further request, Reverend Petunia shook his head, finished his meal, and set off on the long walk to work.

Upon arrival, he found the store owner in a foul mood—angry about poor sales and taking it out on him by forcing him to unload bags of wheat and corn all day, then sending him on lengthy errands with impossible deadlines. By the time he was ready to leave, his feet were blistered. Frustrated, he declared, "I wish I had a horse and buggy so I wouldn't have to walk home." In an instant, a horse and buggy materialized before him, and he climbed aboard, heading home with relief. When he reached his destination, everything was as it had been before the old woman's interference—the tents, clothes, and food were all gone. Sweet Pea galloped up to him, asking, "Where did you get the horse and buggy, husband?" With a smile, he replied, "The Lord granted it to me." Then he inquired, "What's for dinner?" Sweet Pea produced a metal pan filled with cornmeal mush, promising, "I'll heat it up in no time." As he enjoyed the moment, he thought to himself, "Why didn't I ask for money? With cash, I could have bought a horse and buggy, maybe even my own store, or better yet, managed the church until it could self-sustain. I was foolish; I wish I had one more wish." he murmured. At that moment, the old woman reappeared and said, "I can grant you that wish, but it comes at a cost. You must pay with the jar of peanuts and your very name. Should you ever give me the peanuts, your name will vanish, taking with it The Church of God and Sweet Jesus, and I shall live forever. However, if the peanuts are opened, your church and all you've built will remain intact, and my life will end."

The Reverend nodded in agreement and handed her the jar of peanuts, after which she disappeared into thin air.

Reverend Petunia had been unaware that he had unwittingly traded the peanuts to Safire, Utopia, and Penelope's adversary, a cunning foe who would employ the peanuts to drive a wedge between Mother and Daughter, pushing them even further apart. As he reached into his pocket, his fingers brushed against something unexpected. With a jolt of surprise, he pulled out a crisp five-dollar bill, its edges sharp and clean, the paper smooth and new against his skin. "Five dollars? What am I meant to do with five dollars?" he grumbled as he placed the bill on the stone table, then moved behind Sweet Pea to embrace her.

"Oh, baby, I missed you!" he exclaimed. Sweet Pea laughed and replied, "Honey, you've only been gone for ten hours. Remember the days when we were slaves? You toiled in the big house while I picked cotton, and only after nightfall did, we see each other. I'd be so exhausted I could barely move, and you'd comfort me with a salve made from peppermint leaves and pig fat from leftover chitterlings. Those were dreadful days indeed. Reach into your pocket—I always keep a small jar of that salve there in case we need relief from those old pains."

To his amazement, when Reverend Petunia reached into his pocket again, another crisp five-dollar bill emerged. Realization dawned on him: this was the fulfillment of the wish granted by the old woman. Every time he reached into his pocket, there would be a five-dollar bill, ensuring he would never run out of money. Overjoyed, he looked at his wife and said, "Things are about to change—let's go out to dinner." As they rode the horse and buggy to the town's restaurant, he added, "God has smiled upon us; let's give thanks for our newfound fortune."

Years passed, and the small tent in the woods blossomed into a grand tabernacle. The son that Reverend Petunia and Sweet Pea had grew up to have children of his own, and those children, in time, had their own offspring. As the Reverend looked down at his grandchildren, he recognized that everything would eventually end—the church he and his wife had built, and even his own name, would vanish. Though this thought brought a measure of relief, for he had always resented carrying the name Petunia—a name linked to his days of servitude—it also filled him with sorrow. The sorrow lay in knowing that all the hard work he and Sweet Pea had so diligently labored over might one day disappear into nothingness.

Meanwhile, Safire raced through the dense forest toward Niagara Falls with a sense of urgency pounding in her chest. She had to intercept the tiny ship meant for Penelope, the vessel that would carry her closer to her distant home in Africa. The voyage was an exhausting seven-day ordeal, and with the ship set to leave in 7 hours, she had no alternative but to sprint through the underbrush if she hoped to make it. As she neared the ship, the peanuts she carried blazed with a brilliant light, signaling her origin from Utopia.

Upon boarding the ship, she thrust the glowing peanuts toward the crew, who instantly recognized their significance. "We've been anxiously awaiting you, Penelope," they exclaimed, their voices tinged with excitement as they clasped Safire's hand, guiding her to a cabin. The small quarters, though modest, offered a sanctuary with a bed draped in a sumptuous goose quilt and satin pillowcases cradling plush cotton pillows. In this haven, she prepared for the journey ahead.

On the nightstand stood a crystal-clear vase cradling a solitary, long-stemmed rose, its petals a deep crimson, with a note delicately attached: "Welcome, Penelope." Safire let out a sharp, incredulous laugh before collapsing onto the bed, slipping into an abyss of deep, dreamless sleep. Hours later, a thunderous knock echoed through the room. It was Mary, her presence electric and demanding. Safire jolted awake, eyes wide with shock as she stammered, "Who are you?!"

Mary's response was a fierce, righteous roar. "Who am I? I was on the slave ship with Penelope, and I missed saving her by mere seconds! I've returned to claim Utopia's daughter, and instead, I find you? Where is Penelope, and how did you come by the peanuts?" As Mary's voice thundered through the room, her gaze fell upon the jar of peanuts, glowing with an unearthly light. She lunged for them, but Safire reacted with equal ferocity, grabbing Mary with a desperate grip.

They clashed brutally, bodies slamming against the floor, rolling and tumbling in a violent dance of desperation until Safire wrenched herself free from Mary's iron hold. She bolted toward the glowing jar, snatching it with frantic hands, and raced up to the boat's deck. Mary pursued her relentlessly, her footsteps pounding like war drums. As they reached the edge of the boat, the sky erupted with the apparition of Utopia, her voice a thunderous command, "Give me those peanuts! They are all that remains of my daughter!"

With a heart-pounding finality, Utopia reached down, her spectral fingers grazing the air. But Safire, driven by a wild, reckless courage, leapt from the ship, plunging into the frigid embrace of Lake Erie. The icy water engulfed her as she cried out her final curse: "By the power of the peanuts, I condemn the earth that cradles Penelope and her descendants! I curse all women born of Penelope's line!" As she descended into the depths, her words rose like bubbles to the surface, drifting through the air until the malevolent spirit of Safire encircled the small cottage where Penelope dwelled.

Meanwhile, her body transformed into solid ice, sinking into the lake's murky depths. For a hundred years she remained there, her frozen form gradually moving toward the distant shores of New York, with Utopia's spirit tethered to her like an anchor, drawing her ever farther from Penelope—a spectral guardian throughout the passing decades.

LOVE

Penelope and Sam leaped gracefully over the ceremonial broom at the Brown plantation amid the relentless, sweltering heat of mid-July. The blazing sun hung high in a cloudless sky, its rays blazing down and casting long, dramatic shadows on the dusty ground—a small slave congregation witnessing their union. Penelope appeared as a radiant vision in her pristine white dress, a simple yet elegantly flowing garment that Darcy had once gifted her for the harvest dance. Her feet were encased in delicate, finely crafted sandals, and upon her head, she wore a repurposed lace curtain—once discarded by the household after the mistress had acquired lavish new drapes from France— imbuing her with a look that was both resourceful and graceful.

Beside her, Sam stood proudly in modest attire: a pair of well-worn trousers and an old shirt handed down by his Master. Though the garments were humble and edged with the wear of labor, he wore them with unwavering dignity, his quiet strength and rugged handsomeness lighting up his stern features despite the hardships of his life.

After the heartfelt ceremony, the newly united couple celebrated with a modest feast centered on Penelope's rich, aromatic peanut stew. The savory scent of simmering spices and roasted peanuts mingled with the warm summer breeze, each inhalation deepening the anticipation of their first night together as husband and wife. Yet every precious moment was shadowed by the inexorable march of time—Sam was bound to another plantation and held only a temporary pass for the evening. As the sky hinted at the coming dawn, duty called him back to the fields, forcing him to depart before the first light of day.

At the tender hour of four in the morning, Penelope woke with a fervent eagerness born of both love and devotion. With gentle care, she prepared a basin of hot, steaming water for his morning wash and reheated the remnants of their celebratory meal—a humble yet deeply nourishing combination of rich peanut stew and hearty grits—to serve as his breakfast. This quiet ritual was the life Penelope had long yearned for: a daily opportunity to nurture the one she loved with every fiber of her being. In the soft pre-dawn light, while Sam remained in a deep, peaceful slumber, she stepped forward with graceful determination. With warm, tender hands, she wrung a cloth in the steaming water and softly wiped the perspiration from his brow—a silent act of care to soothe the weariness etched by the relentless sun.

Slowly, his eyelids fluttered open, revealing eyes that gleamed with both recognition and deep-seated affection. A gentle smile curved his lips, and as Penelope leaned in to press a tender kiss upon his forehead, she whispered, "Good morning, my love. I hope you slept well," her voice a soothing whisper that melted into the calm of the early hour. With a soft nod, Sam sat up in bed to ready himself for the day, while Penelope gathered his simple breakfast upon a timeworn wooden tray, each gesture imbued with unspoken love.

Once the breakfast was savored, the inevitable moment of separation arrived. The bittersweet gravity of their parting clung to the air as Penelope gripped Sam's calloused hands, her voice trembling with raw emotion. "Why must we be torn apart? We are husband and wife, bound by vows exchanged before God's watchful eyes. How can we be made into mere possessions, subject to the whims of others, when our hearts are filled with love, joy, and hope?" she cried, the anguish in her tone echoing the injustice of their reality.

Sam, his eyes shadowed with resignation, gently pushed her hands away. "Now, woman, I know you once tasted freedom, but those days are long past. It's fine to love and find joy in fleeting moments, but be cautious of hope, for hope will only leave your heart filled with disappointment. Now come here and give your old man some sugar." In that moment, Penelope leaned in and kissed him tenderly, a bittersweet farewell that hinted at the long wait before their next embrace.

This, however, was the cruel and unyielding reality of a slave's existence: lives controlled and manipulated by the capricious whims of a slave master, stripped of any genuine personal freedom.

Each weekend, Sam would miraculously secure a brief pass to visit his family, and slowly, their family expanded. Yet even as new faces joined the fold, many were eventually sold away, leaving Penelope to cling to the cherished, fleeting memories of those irreplaceable moments they once shared.

First Middle Last

Penelope had once borne ten children, yet only one remained in her care—a tiny girl named Melanie, affectionately known as Lil-bit because of her small stature. As the other children grew and became deemed capable of pulling cotton, they were callously sold along the river to distant plantations. Darcy justified these heart-wrenching separations by insisting that the enslavers simply could not afford to feed another mouth, or perhaps they were struggling to pay the mortgage. In a soft, sorrowful tone, Darcy would gather all the slaves together and explain, "The sale of the child is for the good of all. Because of this sacrifice, we will live and thrive." Almost immediately after, the enslaved community would break into a mournful hymn of "Precious Lord," clinging to the fragile semblance of normalcy that life on the plantation demanded.

Penelope never forgot the children that Darcy had sold away, and within her heart, a quiet, burning resentment for Darcy grew over the years. The first lost child was delivered into the care of Darcy's own first cousin and came to be whispered of as "Nelly's bad seed." In letter after letter, Darcy's cousin recounted the grim details of her so-called investment: an account filled with bleak, disheartening updates. In one harrowing missive, she described how she and her husband had bought the child a small, endearing puppy. Only three weeks later, a horrifying discovery was made in the forest—an image of the puppy hanging by its neck. The child had insisted that the puppy had run away, but a neighbor's eyewitness account told another grim story: he had seen the child tie up the poor animal and hang it, laughing as the puppy's life ebbed away. After the puppy died, the child had set the motion for an even darker act, piling wood to burn the creature's remains and then setting ablaze a nearby shed—a fire that spread to a barn filled with terrified horses. The neighbor recalled, in even grimmer detail, how the child would capture insects in jars and leave them helplessly under the scorching sun to dry out and die. Darcy had never encountered such cruelty in youth and inwardly wished that this child had been sold off to a stranger, never allowed to commit further atrocities.

Despite Darcy's attempts to shield Penelope from the truth of the child's actions, fate forced painful encounters. On one early occasion, when the child was about eight years old, he was running in the yard when he fell in front of the big house. When Penelope rushed to help him, her gentle touch was met with a venomous retort: "Get your hands off me, you filthy nigger." Shock and disbelief paralyzed her—these harsh, wicked words issued by her own flesh and blood stung like a lash. The boy scrambled to his feet and fled in disgust, leaving Penelope standing in aching silence. The bitter memory was compounded several years later when, at fifteen, he attended a birthday party for the Misses' son. As Penelope offered him a simple scoop of ice cream, he erupted with a hateful cry: "I don't want no niggers near me, get away from me and let me eat my ice cream in peace!" The cruelty escalated to its darkest form when, at twenty-one, mirroring the monstrous behavior of his father, he raped her—an act that shattered the delicate bond of life itself and left Penelope numb and broken.

In a further act of unspeakable depravity, during one of his visits to the Browns' home, the degenerate boy remarked casually to his cousin that he had yet to experience intimacy with a woman. The young master, in a disturbingly callous tone, suggested that he consider violating Penelope. Oblivious to the horrific irony that Penelope was Buck's mother, the boy retorted, "No one cares if you rape a slave, everyone does it." Thus, they conspired to commit an act of violence against Penelope while she innocently gathered wildflowers for her mistress's bath. Concealed behind a nearby bush, the duplicitous pair awaited the moment; as soon as she bent down, they lunged forward, seizing her and casting her harshly to the ground. With a cold, calculated cruelty, they restrained her until her son—embodying every betrayal and horror in that moment—pulled down her pant legs and forced his manhood inside her until he exploded in a final act of defilement. Weeks later, Penelope discovered she was pregnant. Sam, who had long assumed fatherhood of her children, believed the child was his. However, when the baby was born with a delicate, light mulatto complexion, Penelope was reminded of the brutal rape she had suffered at the hands of her own son—a secret she knew she could never allow Sam to discover.

In a bid to safeguard the child from the stain of its origins, Penelope confided the painful truth to her mistress. With a heavy heart, she presented the baby, recounting in subdued tones what had transpired. Upon laying eyes on the beautiful, mixed-race infant, Darcy instantly fell under a spell of calculated affection. "What are you going to do, Nelly? We cannot sell this beautiful child," she declared. "I have a distant relative who can care for her—a woman named Lisa Hartford. She is a wealthy, single woman in her forties who lives in New York, and she leads the women's movement against slavery in Yonkers. I will contact her immediately and ask that she take this child under her wing." Convinced that it was the best fate for the child, Penelope agreed and relinquished the baby into the custody of her mistress. When Sam next visited, Penelope coldly informed him that the baby was lost, and no further discussion ensued.

A week later, an imposing, well-dressed woman with tall stature and thin, refined features arrived at the plantation in a modest black carriage. Penelope watched as the dignified stranger accepted a neatly folded paper from Darcy. "Nellie, bring me the child," Darcy ordered. With trembling resolve, Penelope entered the quiet room where the baby napped. She carefully dressed the infant in a delicate yellow dress and matching booties—an ensemble chosen from cherished relics the mistress had once brought from the mercantile store. Exiting the room, Penelope handed the little one over to the waiting woman. Darcy then motioned for her to leave, allowing the elegant lady to cradle the baby. In a hushed, tentative inquiry, Darcy asked, "What would you like to call her?" The woman's eyes softened as she smiled gently and murmured, "Sasha; she has the look of a Sasha." Cradling Sasha tenderly, the woman continued, "She is a beautiful little bundle of joy. I promise you that she will receive the finest schooling. And tell me, are the freedom papers in order? I can't abide the thought of those foolish rednecks snatching her back into bondage." With a reassuring smile, Darcy explained, "It's all taken care of. You have a bill of sale along with the freedom papers, so on the train to New York, you can secure her freedom without any trouble." The woman's eyes widened at the casual mention of a "bill of sale," as if the life of a human child could be reduced to a transaction fit for a puppy. Yet, resolved in her mission to rescue this beautiful soul, she accepted the terms.

Sasha flourished far from the oppressive life of a slave, nurtured under the tender care of her adopted mother, who provided her with a home where love and respect reigned supreme. She received an education of the highest order, with scholars and tutors carefully chosen to refine her mind and spirit. Madame Hartford went so far as to hire a kind, resilient black woman named Sissy—a former runaway slave—to serve as Sasha's devoted caretaker. When Madame Hartford first found Sissy, the woman had been huddled beneath a dilapidated shed, her body emaciated and her spirit nearly broken from the long, arduous journey to freedom. Over time, Sasha grew to love Sissy dearly, secretly hoping that her gentle caretaker might be her true mother. However, as the years passed and Sasha began to inquire more deeply about her identity, she was confronted with the painful truth: Sissy was not her biological mother, and she had never even met the woman who had given her life—Penelope. This revelation left Sasha with a lingering emptiness and a cascade of unanswered questions about her origins. In an effort to soothe her aching heart, those close to her insisted that her mother had died in childbirth, and that the unwavering, loving embrace of her adoptive family was a comfort all its own.

Despite the bittersweet mystery surrounding her past, Sasha thrived academically and socially. Embraced by the warmth of the Negro community, she became known for her melodious singing and spirited dancing. Often, she would sit at the piano during family dinners, filling the room with the soulful strains of "Give me Love," a song that had come to represent both hope and longing in her heart. In quiet moments, she dreamed of one day gracing the stage in a Negro musical, much like those celebrated performances on the bustling streets of Paris.

Determined to nurture Sasha's burgeoning talent and promise, Madame Hartford spared no expense. She arranged for rigorous ballet lessons and ensured that Sasha received every opportunity to master her craft. Once her schooling was complete and her skill undeniable, Sasha was sent off to France—to the free, vibrant stages of Paris, where she could pursue her dreams unencumbered by the cruel chains of slavery that had so long haunted her past.

FRANCE

On June 12, 1862, Sasha and her close companion Sissy embarked on an unforgettable journey aboard The Lie de France, their hearts filled with dreams of experience and education in the enchanting city of Paris. Arriving in the City of Light, Sasha would soon take up residence at the elegant home of Madame Hartford's cousin, Lily, situated in one of the refined 16th arrondissements. The posh villa nestled just a short distance from the illustrious 19th-century Auteuil Villas—once the playground of high society—boasted sprawling gardens and intricate architectural details that whispered tales of old-world charm.

Sasha's voice lessons would come from Rochelle DuBarry herself—niece of the infamous Madame who had once enchanted a king of France before Marie Antoinette banished her from court after his death.

That scandal had helped ignite the march on Versailles. Madame DuBarry emerged with a title, modest wealth, and a bestselling memoir called "The King and I," which funded Rochelle's dance education and eventual stardom on Parisian stages. Now Rochelle sought Sasha Hartford as her protégée—this talented Black woman from New York might help her escape her family's notorious shadow.

Sasha waited in the mansion's parlor, surrounded by ornate moldings and velvet drapes, her fingers brushing the gleaming piano as her heart raced. Would Rochelle, like her aunt, look down on a woman of color? Her thoughts scattered like windblown leaves until the door opened, and a slender figure appeared, smiling warmly.

"Bonjour!" Rochelle's voice lilted with charm. "I am Rochelle DuBarry—please, just Rochelle. My aunt is the Madame. You're American, yes? I've always wanted to visit, but Paris keeps me dancing, n'est-ce pas?

A relieved smile spread across Sasha's face as she nodded. With a gleam in her eye, Rochelle continued, "I won't burden you with more of my whimsical fantasies. I know you aspire to shine as a great dancer, and I am here to help you achieve that dream. Are you prepared to work hard and show the world—and the Americans—what you are truly capable of here in Paris?" Sasha's nod was resolute. "Then let's begin!" Rochelle declared enthusiastically. With graceful poise, she led Sasha toward the antique piano and began to play soft, intricate melodies that danced through the luxurious room. "Now, Sasha, show me what you've got," she coaxed. "We shall practice diligently for a month or two before you begin auditioning."

Sasha hesitated, her voice timid as she asked, "Auditions?" Rochelle's smile widened in reassurance as she explained, "Yes, my dear. You must build your career here, for America's ingrained prejudices may not allow you to shine as the beautiful entertainer you are. There is a peril in those lands—where a fleeting performance could result in your talents being dismissed, or worse, your freedom compromised under the weight of oppressive laws. Even if your mother were to fight to reclaim you, who knows how long you might be lost to an unjust system? I am deeply sorry, but you must remain here for now—to learn French, to remain safe. Do you understand?"

Sasha, with a determined glimmer, replied, "I only dance." Rochelle laughed softly; her voice as melodic as the notes that filled the room. "In Paris, my dear, we do it all! Oui?" With a mischievous twinkle in her eye, Rochelle added, "Now, let's not waste another precious moment. The day will come when you can speak and sing in French, when you can earn your keep and savor the sweet taste of independence, freedom, and liberty!"

Months of rigorous practice passed, and soon Rochelle DuBarry arranged for Sasha to secure a modest role in a musical production at the illustrious

Theatre Comedies Francoise. There, she was to perform "Donne Moi Amour," a soulful song that she had sung countless times within the intimacy of family gatherings and among cherished friends. Her debut arrived on a rainy April day; the streets of Paris were washed in a shimmering cascade of reflections. As Sasha watched the diverse crowd streaming into the theater, she searched for a face that mirrored her own. Instead, she saw only unfamiliar features and noted, with a pang of loneliness, that none of the faces belonged to someone like her. Her eyes then drifted upward to the balcony, now occupied by new aristocrats, where Marie Antoinette and Louis XVI once secured seats. Overwhelmed by a terror that they might disapprove of her very presence on stage, Sasha broke down, collapsing into Sissy's supportive embrace, tears streaming down her cheeks as she sobbed, "They won't accept me, I am a nigger, I don't belong!"

Gently, the elderly woman cradled Sasha's hair and whispered tenderly, "Of course, you belong. If you did not, you would not be here. Dry your eyes, my child, and go forth onto that stage to fulfill your destiny. Remember, God walks with you, and so does your mother, watching over you from heaven." Encouraged by those comforting words, Sasha lifted her head, took a deep breath, and straightened her dress with careful precision before returning to the stage, ready to seize her moment.

As Sasha stepped forward to perform her solo, she paused to quietly observe the expectant audience. Closing her eyes, she began to sing, letting her voice flow with the soulful cadence of her heart. When her song came to an end, she opened her eyes to the sight of teary-eyed applause and a standing ovation that filled the grand hall with resounding support. With a graceful bow, she retreated to the back of the stage to continue with the rest of the performance.

Later that evening, amidst the glittering opulence of a soirée attended by all of France's high society, Sasha found herself mingling amid the refined elite. It was there that she encountered a striking young aristocrat named Christian Sinclair. Approaching him with cautious hope, she was greeted by his amiable smile and the playful remark, "What's a pretty little package like you doing in a place like this? You have the loveliest voice, my dear." Those words, filled with both humor and genuine admiration, resonated with Sasha deeply—coming from a stranger and suggesting that someone might truly appreciate her art and bring laughter to her heart. She had long questioned whether the praise from friends and family had been given out of love or mere duty, but here, Christian's sincere compliments seemed to be born from pure appreciation.

As they conversed, Christian signaled a waiter and had a chilled glass of champagne presented to Sasha. With the first sip, the effervescent bubbles danced on her tongue, lifting her spirits even as they coaxed a pleasant dizziness. The sensation grew gradually until Sasha suggested that they move to the garden, where the cool night air could offer gentle relief. Amid the twinkling lights and soft murmurs of the party, the garden provided a serene haven—a perfect setting for a night that promised whispers of new beginnings and daring dreams under the Parisian sky.

Monstrosity

Penelope's firstborn, Buck, had at last found a bride—a captivating Southern belle from the historic streets of Charleston, South Carolina. In the very first year of their union, the couple jubilantly announced to the world that they were expecting a child. In honor of this momentous occasion, Buck's mother organized an extravagant party, attended by family and friends, including Darcy, her husband, and their only child. The night was alive with the sound of jubilant music, spirited dancing, and lavish feasting—a celebration of the new life soon to brighten their world in less than a year.

However, the months to come were paved with both hope and hardship. Buck's wife endured a long and agonizing pregnancy as the child within her kicked with wild, relentless fury. Each night, as exhaustion set in, her feet swelled painfully, and her body ached under the strain. Finally, in the throes of her ninth month, she delivered an 8-pound, 2-ounce baby whose skin was as dark and profound as midnight. The moment Buck laid eyes on the infant, he erupted in a scream of disbelief— "Whose baby is that?"—and, in a fit of rage, struck his poor wife, forcibly knocking her from the bed.

Blinded by shock and unable to comprehend the truth, Buck lashed out with a vicious accusation, claiming that his wife had been unfaithful with a slave. The small town's gossip added fuel to the fire, as neighbors whispered derisively behind his back, jeering, "Buck's baby is a darkie." The venom of their ridicule stirred an uncontrollable anger within him; when he overheard a man chuckling at the child's appearance in broad daylight, Buck's fury reached a climax. He pulled a pistol from his pocket and, without hesitation, fired a shot that silenced the mocking laughter with tragic finality. Realizing that his act would not go unpunished, he retreated home, stepped into the nursery where the innocent child lay, and extinguished its life with a cold, deliberate shot.

The nightmare escalated further when his wife, hearing the echo of gunshots, raced to the nursery. As she confronted him, pleading for an explanation to the unfolding horror, he turned the chaos back upon her. Without a word of remorse, he fired her in the face. In one final act of despair and cruelty, Buck then directed the pistol upon himself, ending his own life in a grim, irrevocable storm of violence.

At his funeral, Darcy was overwhelmed by a cavernous guilt—haunted by the thought that she had once had the chance to prevent this monstrous chain of events. In a tearful moment of reflection, she silently thanked God that the darkness within Buck had been buried forever, and that it had not tainted the beautiful child destined for a fresh start in Paris. Each week, her cousin's letters arrived, filled with vivid descriptions of Sasha thriving amid Negro high society, her graceful talent taking center stage in Parisian dance halls and theaters. These letters were read aloud to Penelope, in hopes that the recounting of Sasha's successes might soothe the deep-seated pain that lingered relentlessly in her soul.

As the years passed and Darcy grew older, she bore no more children. In a gesture of calculated affection, she ordered that all the precious diamonds be removed from her jewelry and carefully placed into a velvet sack intended as a keepsake for the beautiful child when she reached adulthood. It was clear to all that Darcy wished the "golden child" would remember her, and not the sorrows wrought by her own mother—a fact that stirred a profound, simmering hatred in Penelope's heart towards Darcy. Over time, Penelope's weariness of Darcy's selfish ways deepened. Darcy had divested herself of all her children, keeping only Melanie, and had bestowed a lavish gift upon the one child she secretly coveted in her final will and testament. Penelope knew in her heart that Sasha was the child Darcy had long desired—a little girl whom

Darcy would have claimed as her own if she had not been marked by dark skin. And so, in the quiet recesses of her soul, Penelope vowed that one day, retribution against Darcy would be exacted, and that the day of reckoning was drawing ever nearer.

FORGIVENESS

Melanie was the sole confidante—aside from Darcy and Penelope—who secretly knew of Sasha's existence, and in hushed confidences beneath a starlit sky, she vowed that one day she would return Sasha to the family that had been forever denied to her. Though Melanie and Sasha had never met, the two shared a radiant artistic soul. Sasha had once expressed herself through melodious song and graceful dance, while Melanie, bound by the heavy chains of slavery and deprived of formal training or proper supplies, turned to nature itself as her medium of expression. Resourceful and determined, Melanie transformed the discarded scraps left scattered about the vast plantation into a form of art. It was one October, at the dawning of the harvest season, when the enslaved workers were busy tearing down the tall, golden corn crops and clearing the fertile ground to plant anew. As they gathered the corn remnants, bundling them tightly to be burned away, Melanie's voice rang out above the clamor: "Let me have 'em!" The other workers erupted in mocking laughter. "What are you going to do with this garbage?" they jeered. With fierce indignation, Melanie cried, "Garbage? I will make a sculpture out of it!"

Slowly and deliberately, she began collecting every stray stalk and husk, carefully piling the fragments to the side of Penelope's modest cabin. Her quiet labor soon drew the attention of Penelope herself, who descended from the looming big house to lend a helping hand. Together, they gathered every scrap, creating a modest heap that shimmered with the promise of transformation under the waning light of day. When twilight had fallen and their work came to a pause, Penelope gently asked what marvel Melanie planned to create from these remnants. Melanie, with a soft, resolute smile and eyes alight with quiet faith, replied, "I don't know, but the Lord will guide my hands as I work."

From that day forward, as the crimson hues of sunset ushered in the end of a grueling day in the fields, Melanie retreated to that secret nook beside the cabin. There, under the whisper of the cooling air, she dedicated herself each evening to crafting her divine work. Though many fellow slaves passed by whispering criticisms and laughter, dismissing her endeavor as a foolish dream, Melanie never raised her eyes in despair. Instead, she poured her heart into what she called a "work of God." Using the long, supple leaves of corn stalks, she wove a grand basket so large that two people could comfortably fit inside. Carefully, she braided additional stalks through the top rim to secure its form, leaving an opening at the side, designed for ease of entry. She then climbed inside and meticulously wove a bench spanning from one side of the basket to the other—a place where two souls might sit in repose. To complete her creation, she attached two weathered wagon wheels salvaged from a broken pull-cart, and as a final flourish, she brushed the entire structure with shellac discovered in a forgotten barn near the slave quarters. Not content with just this, Melanie also created a charming rocking chair from leftover corn husks: she wove, sun-dried, and then artfully brushed it with shellac, decorating its arms and legs with carefully dried corn kernels that glittered like tiny gems. And so, it sat, hidden beneath a well-worn blanket, until the day Darcy's fever set in.

As time ambled onward, Melanie embraced the old tradition of "jumping the broom," ensuring that the long-forgotten customs were passed down from generation to generation—a rite that included a promise of one day reuniting with her elusive sister somewhere in Yonkers. In the quiet evenings, once the fields lay silent and Penelope had finished caring for Darcy, the air around the modest cabin would fill with the soft crackle of a fire. In that tender glow, Penelope spun vivid tales of Africa: stories of hearty peanut stews simmering for villagers, lively contests celebrating the humble peanut, and festive gatherings in sunlit village. She spoke of her grandparents, who had once ruled a small but splendid kingdom, and demonstrated the intricate, ceremonial dances passed down through generations. Enraptured, Penelope mimicked every graceful movement, her spirit dancing alongside those distant memories. Yet, as laughter mingled with tears, Penelope also recounted the dark tale of how she fell in love with a man whose beguiling promises led her aboard a slave ship, sealing her fate and tearing her from her family. Amid the rapture of her recollections, she would pause, collapse to her knees in silent sorrow, and then, with trembling resolve, clutch a jar of red-hot pickled peppered peanuts. "One day," she would whisper, "this jar of peanuts will free us all from bondage and guide us back to our ancestors."

Years passed, and Darcy, having outlived her husband and the son lost in the ravages of the Civil War, slowly withered under the weight of time. One bone-chilling winter morning, Darcy was struck with a fever so terrible that even the doctor, with a heavy heart, predicted that her end was near. On her deathbed, as the room lay cloaked in sorrowful silence, a spectral figure emerged—the ghost of Penelope's formidable mother, Utopia. Radiant and ominous, Utopia's voice filled the space as she declared, "Darcy, I am Utopia, mother to Penelope. I have silently borne witness to your torment, year after year, as you stripped away my grandchildren from their rightful dignity. I have seen you drag her to witness hangings, and utter cruel threats should she ever attempt escape." With an air of dread and divine retribution, Utopia drew three gleaming chains from the folds of her long, golden gown. Reaching over with a ghostly hand, she chained Darcy's trembling arms and legs, declaring, "To free yourself, you must reach for me." But as Darcy stretched, a monstrous ball and chain materialized, anchoring her limbs to a transparent, glistening floor—its crushing weight pushing salvation just out of reach. "This," Utopia intoned, "is punishment for confining my child to endless bondage. When the day comes that my beloved reenters the heavens, you shall be condemned to labor in a field—a field of stars." When Darcy timidly asked, "What is the field of stars?" Utopia's tone grew icily poetic as she explained, "Imagine the cotton fields where slaves once toiled, only here, instead of cotton, you will harvest stars, not on the soft earth, but in a universe two miles from the scorching sun. Beneath a relentless blaze, you will tend these stars until six o'clock, when the overseer will collect them before they ascend to the heavens. And then you will rest until dawn, condemned to repeat this futile labor for eternity." Darcy, stunned into silence, managed a whispered query, "We pick stars?" To which Utopia replied with chilling finality, "Yes—you pick them. Without your heavy hand, how else would the stars rise? And do not expect to see your family there, for they shall labor on another star plantation." With a final cruel taunt, Utopia continued, "Will you find Satan there, you wonder? Know that his name is Lucifer, a despicable overseer who takes perverse pleasure in ravaging tender souls like yours. Should you dare defy him, prepare for even harsher punishment. At least you need not fear death, for you are already condemned to the afterlife." With these damning words, Utopia led a trembling Darcy towards the fate that awaited her.

Entering a dilapidated shack designated as her living quarters, Darcy was met with a cold, hard dirt floor and the grim presence of others—fellow plantation souls trapped in perpetual misery. In the pale morning light, she noticed a man named Buck sleeping on the ground. Bewildered, she turned to Utopia and implored, "I thought you said none of my family would be here?" With a sad, wry smile, Utopia replied, "I said your family would not be here. Buck is not of your blood—he is my grandson. It is a tragedy he ended up in such a place, along with his father. I made an exception for them because, in many ways, they are alike. Perhaps it is like getting two for the price of one—an echo of what your own father once claimed when he purchased my pregnant daughter." With those haunting words, Utopia vanished, leaving Darcy to spend a restless, fear-filled night, her heart pounding with terror of Buck and his father.

At the break of dawn, the other condemned souls stirred, and Buck remarked gruffly, "Girl, you better get yourself together because we've got a whole lot of stars to pick." Desperation coloring her voice, Darcy asked softly, "Are we in hell?" Buck's coarse reply came laced with cynical humor: "Hell? No, Sister. They say niggers go to hell 'cause they got no soul. You're better off here with us—don't you want to be away from that place full of evil, like those abolitionists who claim slavery is wrong, when everyone knows it's ordained by God? You're on a star plantation now, among your own kind, and you ought to be thankful." As they spoke, Darcy's eyes caught sight of other planters shuffling toward a long trough filled with a thick mush of grits and peanuts. Bent low to scoop up the mush, she thought she saw her husband and son. Dashing forward in a desperate embrace, they dissolved like mist into nothingness, leaving an aching emptiness inside her soul. A weathered planter approached with a tone equal parts pity and cruelty, whispering, "You can't be here with your family. We are your family now. The moment you acknowledge one of them, they'll be sold away—such is the unforgiving law of the plantation." Overcome with agony and defiance, Darcy cried, "How can you separate us so heartlessly? How can you treat us as animals, feeding us without honor? I am a human, not an animal!" His eyes filled with sorrow as he replied, "This is how we have always treated black people—sold off like cattle on auction blocks, without even a thought for their suffering. It is an abomination, and now we must atone for our sins. Now hurry and eat—there are stars waiting to be picked."

Throughout that grueling day, as Darcy stooped to pluck the glittering, imperfect stars—each one with jagged edges that pricked her tender fingers until they bled—a fellow planter would pass her makeshift bandages and order her on with a merciless tone. When the pain and sorrow became too much, Darcy's cries broke through the oppressive silence. Whispered admonitions swept around her, "Shut up and stop crying. Lucifer hates tears, and you don't want to be whipped or sold again. Just smile and say, 'Everything's all right, Massa." With trembling resignation, she complied.

At last, as the day waned, Lucifer himself, a sinister overseer with a devilish grin, approached her. "Is there a problem, missy?" he asked, his tone mocking yet predatory. Forcing a smile, Darcy replied, "Everything's fine, Massa." His eyes glinted with perverse delight as he murmured, "That's good, for I wouldn't want you to be unhappy. You're quite pretty, and I think I'll come see you tonight." Casting a calculating glance toward the other planters, he commanded, "Make sure she is alone in a shack—we will need some privacy."

An entire day of toil and torment eventually gave way to restless anxiety as Darcy contemplated what horrors might await her once she was alone with Lucifer. To distract herself from the scorching pain of the fields and the cruel rhythms of her labor, she clung desperately to memories of her life on earth—of calmer moments, particularly the soothing care of Penelope when she tenderly brushed her hair. But as night fell, it was time to measure the stars that she had gathered.

The harsh rules decreed that failing to meet a quota of three hundred pounds would exact punishment. That day, her labor yielded only two hundred and ninety-five pounds. When Lucifer noticed the missing five pounds, his anger erupted. With brutal efficiency, he bound her trembling hands, ripped away her dress, and forcibly shoved her against the cold, rough wall of the shed. With each resounding crack of his horse whip, her back split open, blood staining the plain floor. When his vicious beating finally subsided, he sneered, "Now! Get yourself cleaned up—I'll see you tonight," as he opened her battered bag and let the gathered stars fly upward, as if released from a broken promise.

Later that night, within the cramped interior of a battered shack, several caring women gathered around Darcy, tenderly washing and dressing the deep wounds that marred her skin. Their voices, soft and measured, pleaded with her, "Remember, you must tell Lucifer you are enjoying what he's doing to you, or he'll whip you again. And don't forget to say, 'Thank you.'" Once they had finished tending to her, Darcy wandered into the empty shack where Lucifer had consigned all the new, broken women. There, a brilliant light suddenly burst through the darkness, and behind it stood Utopia once more. With a voice that dripped both disdain and somber relief, she asked, "How was your day of terror?" Darcy, voice ragged with pain, confessed, "It was excruciating." Utopia's tone turned chillingly final, "That is what you have inflicted upon black people for hundreds of years—each day a mere fragment of a lifetime of suffering, and still, you complain of injustice. Now, do you wish to leave the star plantation?" In a desperate, quavering cry, Darcy pleaded, "Yes! Please!" Utopia smiled grimly. "Although you once promised to care for my child upon your death, I find your promises unfulfilled. I will allow you to return to the living world for three days. But if you cannot mend the wrongs you have done to Penelope and her family in that time, and if Penelope does not grant you forgiveness, then you shall be condemned to the star plantation for all eternity." In a heartbeat, Darcy found herself lying in bed with Penelope's watchful presence hovering over her.

In the quiet murmur of the night, faint voices of other slaves drifted through the room, "Is that old heifer dead yet?" To which a soft reply came, "No, I don't think so—not yet." With a weak voice, Darcy whispered, "Nelly, is that you?" Penelope responded warmly, "Yes, ma'am, it's me—right here, taking care of you." Slowly, Darcy sat up and commanded, "Now, Nelly, bring me some paper and a pen." Obediently, Penelope did as she was told. Soon after, Darcy sent one of the other slaves to fetch the town's lawyer. As Penelope escorted him up to the room, he burst out in incredulous exasperation, "Are you crazy? You want to leave all your assets to a slave?!" Then, in a quieter tone, he added, "There is no law against a slave receiving property, so I suppose you can do as you please." He took the documents, mounted his horse-drawn carriage, and departed.

After he left, Darcy composed a letter to her cousin, Madame Hartford, enclosing a copy of her will. In her careful, trembling script, she instructed that Penelope and Sasha Hartford were to inherit all that she possessed. She promised that, by righting even the smallest wrongs, she might someday bring back the beautiful golden child to her family—a portion of the cherished land reserved as a legacy. As Penelope held Darcy's frail hand, the old woman wept bitterly, and her final words, heavy with regret and sorrow, tumbled out: "Nelly, I always knew that boy was a demon. Something warned me to sell him, but I sold him to the wrong person. I felt that upon his birth, fate beckoned me to end his evil life; yet, blinded by greed, I let him live in exchange for money. That man, who lured you into bondage with his rotten soul, has cursed us all with his sins. You have suffered rape and unendurable trauma, and my cousin, too, has borne the scars—her suffering even scarred her husband. One dreadful night, after returning from a tavern, her husband found the boy awake; the boy, with a cold knife, said, 'I had that black wench now—I want a white buck.' Shocked, her husband stumbled and fell. The boy pounced, ripping his trousers and overpowering him until his manhood bled. In horror, my cousin discovered the terrible betrayal, and though the boy retreated and locked himself away, her husband vowed vengeance. One night, as he crept in with a loaded pistol to strike, a sudden fire erupted. Rushing to his room, she found him dead on the floor—the boy, waiting in darkness with a rifle, had silenced him before any justice could be served. Fearing exposure of his vile acts, my cousin claimed an intruder had killed her husband. Over time, he eventually married, only to later take his own life. Penelope, all of us have suffered under that cursed man who lured you onto that slave ship—your parents, who were forced to live apart; your husband, torn from his family; your children, forced into unspeakable circumstances; and even those who enslaved you. Therefore, I leave all my possessions to you and your descendants, in hopes that it might mend the eternal scars of our past."

As Penelope listened to Darcy unload her soul, riddled with guilt and regret, she could not conceal the simmering resentment inside her. "Everyone has suffered—except you. I do not forgive you. You will know true suffering before you leave this world." With that, she retrieved the intricately wrought rocking chair—crafted long ago by Melanie from corn husks— and placed it beside Darcy's bed. "Miss Darcy, you must get out of bed. Trust me, you will feel better," she insisted gently, lifting Darcy and easing her into the creaking chair. But as Darcy began to rock back and forth, a fit of violent coughing and desperate gasps seized her. "What is wrong with this chair?!" she screamed as her body began to swell with burning hives. "Nelly, help me!" Darcy shrieked, clawing at the arms of the chair. Penelope's footsteps faded down the hall as the door clicked shut. Alone with her panic, Darcy's throat constricted from the corn allergy, each gasp more desperate than the last. Her fingers found Penelope's jar of Red Hot Pickled Peppered Peanuts, and she gulped the vinegar, seeking relief from the fire in her windpipe. The liquid burned a path down her throat until a single peanut broke free, wedging in her narrowing airway. Her struggles weakened as oxygen abandoned her cells. Moments later, death claimed her completely—her final silence an echo of countless souls torn from their families across generations.

"Once all was quiet, Penelope entered Darcy's dim room one final time. Gazing into her lifeless eyes, she whispered with cruel finality, "Now you know how it feels to be lynched."

In that moment, as Darcy's spirit seemed to hover in a broken limbo, she saw Utopia looming ominously at her shoulder. A single tear tracked down her cheek as Utopia pronounced, "It appears Penelope is not pleased and has not forgiven you. Since you have not atoned for all your wrongs, you are condemned once again to the Star Plantation for eternity." In a blinding flash, Darcy was thrust back into the squalid little shack, naked and resigned to a fate entwined with Lucifer.

Later that day, Penelope sent a small slave boy to fetch the doctor. When the doctor arrived, he discovered the peanut lodged in Darcy's throat and casually labeled her death accidental, adding that he would notify her cousin in Yonkers. As soon as he departed, the newly freed slaves, their rage barely contained, tore away all of Darcy's remaining clothes, dug a shallow grave beside a fetid swamp, and callously dropped her lifeless body within. They interred her in cold, unforgiving earth, mingled with writhing worms and hissing snakes, and prayed that her tormented soul would decay for eternity. Once the makeshift funeral was over, a grim celebration began—a feast of roasted herb chicken and wine marking the end of their oppressive days of slavery.

When the lawyer received the news, he promptly sent a copy of the will along with the sack of diamonds to Madame Hartford. Upon its arrival, she carefully taped the will to the underside of a drawer in a desk, an heirloom from her father. Nestled with the will was a note that read: "Dear Sasha, this is the will of the property left to you by your mother's ward, Darcy. Upon my death, please inform your descendants of their inheritance. Furthermore, there is a special gift at the back of this drawer from your mother, Nelly Brown, a woman carried from the distant shores of Africa, who loved you dearly and trusted me, Madame Lisa Hartford, with her most precious possessions." With deliberate care, she slid the drawer back into the desk, gently pushing the sack of diamonds to the rear and concealing it with a neat stack of papers to obscure its valuable contents.

As the years drifted by, nature began its quiet reclamation of the neglected burial ground. Tall, unruly grass swayed in the breeze, and gnarled weeds entwined themselves over the grave, until Darcy's memory—

alongside her very name—faded quietly into oblivion, like a solitary leaf carried away on a whispering breeze.

The war's bitter end brought freedom's proclamation, yet Penelope chose to remain on the plantation while her husband Sam fled northward. Upon the mistress's death, the estate fell to their stewardship, with Madame Hartford overseeing their management of the land and its tax obligations.

Meanwhile, Melanie found love with Marcus, a man newly freed from bondage. Her belly soon swelled with child, and one spring afternoon, as she walked among wild bluebells, her waters broke without warning. Her cries scattered birds from treetops, but no help came as she fell to the earth and delivered her daughter alone. When they discovered them, Melanie had already slipped away, leaving behind her newborn girl. They called her Maybelle—for May's bluebells that had witnessed her birth.

The child grew strong, inheriting more than just her mother's features. She absorbed the culinary wisdom of generations: how to coax flavor from the humble peanut into rich stews and fiery pickled delicacies. These recipes became her birthright—a testament to ancestors who had created sustenance and joy even when denied their humanity.

Turn of Luck

As the days turned into weeks and the weeks turned into months, the bond between Sasha and Christian blossomed like the first hints of spring, their connection deepening until whispers began to circulate that they were utterly inseparable. Every night, Christian would claim his seat in the audience, his eyes alight with wonder as he watched Sasha perform as though he were seeing her for the very first time. Together, they strolled hand in hand through the romantic streets of Paris, savoring the rich aromas and bold flavors of local coffee houses and dining in restaurants that oozed elegance and quiet sophistication. With time gently passing, Sasha found herself falling ever deeper into the arms of love with Christian, blissfully unaware of the cruel twist fate was about to reveal. It wasn't the color of her skin that barred their union—it was her heritage. Without a noble father to bestow upon her a title that would open society's hallowed doors, marriage became an unreachable dream.

Under the serene glow of a starlit night, with the heavens silently witnessing her hopes, Sasha laid bare her heart to Christian. Amid soft whispers and trembling confessions, she recounted the passionate nights they had shared and revealed the most exquisite secret of all: the promise of a beautiful child cradled tenderly in her womb. Her words, rich with love and longing, were met not with the warmth she had anticipated but with a bitter dose of reality.

"Sasha, I love you, and I will love this child," he began, his voice heavy with sorrow, "but it is unfortunate that France does not acknowledge love as a right to matrimony. Society's rigid walls dictate that I can only marry a woman of equal rank, and since you do not have a name of nobility, I cannot wed you."

In that heart-wrenching moment, tears cascaded down Sasha's face as she cried out in despair, "What is to become of me? How will I support myself? I am a performer gracing the stage—how can I possibly perform, visibly pregnant and without a husband? How can I face the public when I cannot even return to America with a baby and no man by my side? My mother will never tolerate such disgrace!"

With a serious demeanor, Christian stood up and gently pulled Sasha into an embrace, as if to comfort her. "Sasha, I promise to look after you and the baby," he whispered gently. "we'll tell everyone that you were hit by a severe fever, which requires you to stay in the mild warmth of the South of France. Your caring nursemaid Sissy will be with you, and I'll visit every weekend to provide you with love and attention until the baby is born. Meanwhile, my parents will take care of the baby, and we'll say the child is a distant relative whose mother passed away during childbirth. "But Sasha's spirit flared with fierce defiance as she broke free from his embrace, her voice resonating with the intensity of a mother's love, "I want this child—I will not give away my baby. I have already lost my mother; how can you ask me to surrender my flesh and blood?"

With a heavy heart and eyes glistening with sorrow, Christian revealed the devastating truth: their child would be taken from her, entrusted to his family, and adopted by his parents. "Sasha," he said in a pained tone, "your child will never know you. This baby, bone of my bone, flesh of my flesh, must be kept within the bounds of society—a society that forbids the stigma of our unconventional beginnings. You must learn to let go, the sooner the better."

Overwhelmed by grief and betrayal, Sasha fled from his grasp, racing through the labyrinthine streets of Paris toward her only confidante—the wise, weathered Sissy who had always offered solace in times of turmoil. Breathless and anguished, she cried, "Oh, Sissy, I believed he truly loved me. Now he demands that I relinquish my baby to him, so that our child may be raised properly, blessed with a noble name and title."

The elderly woman held her quivering body, her gaze gentle yet filled with a lifetime of hard-earned wisdom. With a tired sigh, she murmured, "Just as your mother once gave up everything to offer you a better future, can't you consider giving up your own child for a better life?" Sasha, you shine on the stages of Paris, a dream few Black people can achieve. You've been given a rare opportunity; seize it or you might regret your decision forever. Sasha's voice resonated with defiance, "No!" In response, the old woman sat down on a nearby bench, her worn hands resting in her lap, and suggested a cautious scheme, "I believe he has a well-thought-out plan. We should follow it for now. But when the moment is right, we will escape with the baby and return to America. Ms. Hartford will then guide us on how to best handle this difficult situation. What was meant to be a celebration of new life and love had instead unraveled into a tapestry of nightmares. The joyous anticipation gave way to frantic scheming and whispered plans of escape, as the enchanting city of Paris transformed from a cradle of romance to a backdrop for heartbreak and loss.

As Sasha departed for the sultry south of France, her only trusted companion gripping her hand as though it were her lifeline, the sumptuous velvet interior of the coach cradled her tired body. Inside her, the secret of her beloved infant, safely nestled in her womb, was a bittersweet reminder of both hope and despair. Every bump along the journey, every fleeting moment in the sumptuous carriage, deepened the ache in her aching soul, as memories of leaving her baby behind and abandoning the man she loved on the sun-kissed beaches of France tormented her relentlessly.

When Sasha and Sissy arrived at the grand and imposing Chateau de Beauregard, where she was confined, the housekeeper, whose every step echoed the authority of her role, escorted them to their room. As they walked down the seemingly endless corridor, Sasha couldn't help but gaze at the walls adorned with portraits of the many dignified people who once graced the mansion with their presence. The house was eerily quiet, the only sound being the soft jingling of keys that danced against the housekeeper's thigh, a gentle reminder of her dominion over the household.

Sasha was gripped by a fear of the unknown, the kind that twists the stomach into knots, yet found solace in the warm, reassuring touch of her confidante, Sissy. Once they settled into their room, a maid entered, carrying a tray laden with a sumptuous feast: slices of savory beef drenched in rich gravy, herbed root vegetables, a crisp, fresh salad, and buttery, golden croissants. The aroma was intoxicating, filling the room with a sense of comfort and luxury.

As the maid placed the tray on the table in the dimly lit far corner of the room, she spoke of the possibility of visiting the enchanting Island of Hyères and experiencing the breathtaking Côte d'Azur. Sasha's eyes lit up with excitement at the thought, having often listened to Christian's tales of the stunning beaches that graced the southern coast of France. "I will have the cook pack you a delightful lunch and wake you at nine," the maid promised with a smile, "So you can savor a full day on the beautiful beaches that await you." With that, she quietly exited the room, leaving behind an air of anticipation.

As Sasha began to savor her meal, each bite a harmony of flavors, Sissy gently reminded her of the need to write to Madame Hartford, to convey the unfortunate turn their trip to France had taken. Later that evening, Sasha sat at the ornate desk, her heart heavy as she penned her thoughts through a veil of tears. She recounted the ordeal they had endured, her words a plea for understanding and a hope for a response from the distant shores of America.

The following morning, Sissy rose at the crack of dawn to assist Sasha in preparing for their excursion to the charming beachside town, a mere forty-five-minute carriage ride from their cozy residence. True to their arrangement, as they descended the staircase, they were greeted by the maid who had thoughtfully prepared a delectable picnic lunch, and the coach stood ready for their departure. Before leaving, she handed the maid the letter to Madame Hartford, asking her to deliver it to the post. As the carriage swiftly traversed the lush meadows leading to the glistening shore,

Sasha lost herself in daydreams of Christian sitting across from her instead of Sissy, envisioning the day he would accompany her to this serene retreat.

Upon their arrival, they ventured into a quaint boutique, its exterior adorned with colorful awnings, to purchase swimsuits suitable for the refreshing embrace of the sea. With eager anticipation, they hurried to the inviting, sun-kissed sands of the shore. Sissy meticulously spread out a vibrant blanket, positioning it perfectly on the soft sand, and placed the picnic basket brimming with treats on top. Meanwhile, Sasha dashed toward the quaint bathing machine, a relic designed for modesty, to change into her specially crafted suit, eager to plunge into the cold, rejuvenating sea that promised to wash away her sorrows.

Sissy lingered on the shore, her watchful gaze never leaving her delicate companion. She derived immense joy from observing her innocent charge frolic in the sea, her laughter mingling with the rhythmic sound of the waves. While Sasha leaped and splashed, sending sprays of salty water high into the air, she temporarily forgot the troubles swirling in her mind like the waves that relentlessly crashed upon the sea.

Over the next few hours, the two soaked up the sun of the French Riviera, enjoying the breathtaking beauty of the Mediterranean Sea before reluctantly returning to the coach that transported them to the house. Dinner awaited them in their room, and Sasha noticed with discomfort that they were not invited to dine in the dining area or any other part of the house. The maid, with a pained expression, delivered the dreadful news that Sasha would be kept hidden out of sight, confined due to the family's fear of anyone discovering her situation. She explained that Christian's family would visit in a couple of days, but after that, they wouldn't return until the child was born, only to take the baby away, never to be seen by Sasha again. She would remain there for several weeks and then return to her Aunt's apartment under Madame DuBarry's watchful eye.

Sasha was torn apart, having hoped Christian would visit every weekend. Now, it seemed all he wanted was the baby she carried. As the days dragged on, Christian's mother finally arrived, accompanied by a frail-looking woman. She introduced herself and the woman as Christian's sister, explaining that his sister couldn't have children and was eager to raise the baby as her own. Sasha sat in shock, struggling to process the woman's gratitude for making her dreams of motherhood come true.

Later that day, Sasha and Sissy watched the two women leave the mansion, their hearts heavy with uncertainty, wondering what fate awaited them in the days to come.

As time relentlessly marched on, the life within Sasha burgeoned, and with each tick of the clock, her heart became a leaden weight of dread. The mere thought of her child being torn from her arms gnawed mercilessly at her soul. Then, like the crack of thunder, a letter arrived from the cunning Madame Hartford. With a mind sharp as a razor, Madame Hartford devised an audacious plan to whisk the baby away to the States. She enlisted the aid of a doctor she had encountered during her sojourn in France. This Doctor, a key player in the daring scheme, would rush to Sasha's side as labor gripped her, swiftly claiming the newborn under the guise of illness, insisting the infant required hospital care. The following day, Sasha would flee to the nearby town, her destination a coach bound for Paris. There, the Doctor would await her and Sissy, ready to execute the next phase. Once they reclaimed the child, they would make a hasty retreat, boarding the SS City of Paris, their passage booked for New York, a voyage fraught with the thrill of the clandestine.

REUNITED

As the years slipped by like river currents, Penelope and little Maybelle grew inseparable, bound by blood and shared history. The shackles of slavery lay broken behind them, and Penelope felt a quiet joy that neither she nor her grandchild would ever again be sold away. Still, deep in her heart, she knew the day would come when Maybelle must walk the world alone. Determined to arm her with every tool for survival, Penelope set about teaching Maybelle the art of tending the red Mississippi soil.

By dawn's first light, Penelope led Maybelle among neat rows of peanut plants, their silken roots twisting through the earth. She showed her how to coax fiery pepper vines up trellises, pluck the glossy red pods at peak heat, then swirl them in briny vinegar until they blistered with flavor. In the dusty shade of an old oak, she taught Maybelle the secret family recipe—a precise balance of smoke, spice, and a hint of cane sugar—that gave their pickled peanuts their signature tongue-tingle. "Promise me you'll keep this close," Penelope whispered, pressing her weathered hand to Maybelle's, "for it is our legacy."

When harvest rolled around, Maybelle would help load the jars into the cornhusk-woven wagon that once belonged to her mother. The wagon's faded gold husks rustled in the breeze as they trundled down the sunbaked road, pausing for wayfaring travelers with dusty boots and empty bellies. At the roadside stand, the peanuts gleamed—glassy crimson pods nestled against twisted kernels—and eager customers lined up to taste the zing that set tongues dancing. Penelope taught Maybelle to count coins with nimble fingers, then roll each crisp dollar bill and tuck it into one of the pickle jars hidden among the stacks—an artful camouflage against prying hands.

At evening's close, Penelope brought out a pot of steaming peanut stew: tender peanuts simmered until soft, ladled over fluffy rice they had bought from the nearby mercantile. Under a canopy of fireflies and the watchful presence of Utopia—Penelope's mother's spirit, she believed, drifted among the flames—Penelope spun tales of distant Africa. She painted vivid scents of ripe mango and sun-warmed banana leaves, of red-dirt roads beyond the seas, until Maybelle's eyelids drooped with wonder and longing.

Over the years, Maybelle's small hands grew sure and strong. She mastered every step: from blanching peanuts in boiling brine to threading pepper pods on drying strings. She took up the reins of the cornhusk wagon, rolled the coins with practiced ease, and even shouldered her grandmother up the incline when it was time to pay the land taxes. Each evening, she prepared the stew exactly as Penelope had taught her, watching Penelope rest with a smile of pride.

In Penelope's final days, her breath frail as autumn leaves, she walked Maybelle once more through the fields at sunrise. She pressed her secrets into Maybelle's heart—the recipe, the hidden coins, the stories of their ancestors. That night, the fire died down to embers, and Maybelle kept vigil until dawn, ready at last to carry their legacy forward on her own.

With each passing day, Penelope's strength waned, leaving her increasingly frail. Her decline compelled Maybelle to hire a nearby neighbor, a kind soul who would regularly check in, heat up the aromatic peanut stew, and keep the home in order. Each evening, after returning from a long day at work, Maybelle would wash up and lovingly prepare a fresh batch of the nutty, comforting stew. With gentle care, she would feed Penelope, ensuring she was nourished, before tenderly washing her and tucking her into bed.

That night, while Maybelle slept, Penelope's spirit ascended with a swift grace into the ethereal realms. Before she could fully reach the heavens, a warm, radiant presence enveloped her—Utopia, who had been longing for this reunion. "My child, I've waited for so long to hold you in my arms," Utopia cried, embracing her tightly. Weary from the burdens and toil of her earthly life, Penelope rested her head against Utopia's comforting bosom.

Utopia declared with a serene assurance, "Now we can both watch over Sasha and Maybelle, keeping a close watch on the peanuts that have the power to unite us all." From afar, Penelope could hear a familiar voice, sweet and melodic—Melanie's voice. "Here I am, Momma," Melanie called out, her words resonating with warmth and welcome. "I have been waiting for you."

When dawn's pale light filtered through the curtains, Maybelle rose and crossed the creaking floorboards to the basin. She splashed cool water onto her face, the sharp scent of soap mingling with the lingering hush of morning. But across the room, Grandma Penelope lay motionless. Maybelle's heart fluttered; she knelt beside the bed, brushing back wisps of silver hair. "Grandma must have slept soundly last night," she murmured, gently shaking her shoulder. When there was no response, she drew back the threadbare quilt—and spotted the dark stain on the linen. Grandmother had slipped away in her sleep.

A raw cry ripped from Maybelle's throat. "Grandma—no!" She sank into Penelope's old rocking chair; its slow, mournful sway mirrored the tears coursing down her cheeks. Yet even through her grief, she understood what had to be done. Wiping her face on her apron, she steadied herself and rolled up her sleeves. With shaking hands, she lifted Penelope's frail form, laying her on fresh white sheets. Maybelle ran warm water over her grandmother's hands and temples, tenderly washing away the night's final breaths. She smoothed the linen, eased Penelope into a clean cotton nightgown embroidered with tiny blossoms, and straightened the pillow beneath her head.

In the pale morning light, Maybelle unhooked jars of coins from the kitchen shelf—each copper penny and silver dime saved over the years. She counted out enough to hire a carpenter to fashion a coffin of polished pine, a gravedigger to carve a resting place in the clay soil, and a preacher to speak words of comfort. She loaded the coins into her mother's old two-wheeled wagon and set out down the narrow dirt road, dust rising in small clouds behind her.

At the roadside stand, a kindly woman sold wildflowers—blue cornflowers, a spray of white Queen Anne's lace, and sun-bright marigolds. Maybelle selected a tight bouquet, its heady fragrance promising a burst of life atop the fresh grave. Further along, she entered the town's dressmaker's shop, where bolts of fabric lined every wall. She chose a gown of cream silk patterned with tiny peanuts: a garment fit for a princess in the spirit world. "My grandmother deserves nothing less," she whispered as the seamstress slipped the billowed skirt from its hanger.

That evening, by lantern light, the carpenter arrived with polished boards and brass handles. He worked by the window while Maybelle, tear-streaked but resolute, dressed Penelope in the silk gown. Beneath gentle hammer taps and the saw's rasp, the coffin took shape. Outside, the gravedigger staked out a small plot in the red Mississippi clay, his shovel carving a simple rectangle in the earth.

At dawn the next day, two silent men lifted Penelope's still form and laid her upon a bed of silk pillows. Maybelle stood alone on the sun-warmed clay, dressed in a simple black gown, clutching her grandmother's favorite scarf. Even with just one mourner present, the ceremony felt grand: the preacher's soft words, the hushed rustle of dry leaves in the breeze, the ribbon-tied bouquet laid lovingly at the casket's foot. When the final blessing faded, the gravedigger closed the lid, and the men lowered Penelope into the earth. They shoveled warm clay over the coffin, packing it down gently, and smoothed the soil—collected from the peanut patch—into a new mound.

Maybelle lingered until the last spadefuls fell silent, then knelt at the fresh grave. Against the pale blue sky, she pressed her forehead to the cool earth and whispered, "Rest now, Grandma. You are forever my queen." After the funeral, Maybelle stepped into the small cabin, its once-warm atmosphere now cold and empty, void of the love and support her grandmother had always provided. Her voice echoed through the quiet space as she screamed, "I can't do this, I need you, Momma Lil bit, I need you, Grandma Penelope! How can God allow this to happen to me, leaving me without anyone to console or love?"

Above in a place of peace, Utopia, Penelope, and Melanie sensed the deep hurt of their beloved child, her loneliness cutting through their ethereal existence. Utopia, with a voice filled with wisdom and comfort, called out, "The peanuts will be your protector; they will guide your future. Do not worry or fret, my child. Throw yourself into the peanuts."

As these words of assurance floated down to her, Maybelle walked over to the counter, her eyes falling upon the familiar sight of jars filled with peanuts. She picked one up, feeling its cool, smooth surface beneath her fingers, and whispered to herself, "I will bury myself in my work until the pain of losing my grandmother fades. I will protect the legacy and the land, this precious gift, and cherish the name of 'Penelope's Red Hot Pickled Peppered Peanuts' for the rest of my life.

Farewell Paris

At the break of dawn, the housemaid rapped sharply on the door, only to discover the room that had sheltered Sasha and Sissy was now ominously empty. Heart pounding, she tore through the house in a frantic frenzy. At that very moment, Christian galloped up to the estate. Bursting through the entrance, he halted, eyes locking onto the maid, demanding to know the cause of the chaos. Her words tumbled out in a rush— Sasha and Sissy had vanished, leaving the baby with the doctor who delivered her. Panic surged through Christian like wildfire. He bolted back to his horse, spurring it into a wild gallop straight to the doctor's office, desperate to find them. But upon his breathless arrival, the nurse delivered a gut-wrenching blow: the doctor had departed with the baby hours before. When hearing this Christian turned, mounted his horse, and moved in the direction of Paris.

When Sasha and Sissy entered Paris, their thoughts were consumed with the urgency of finding the doctor and embracing the baby. Finally, from a distance, Sissy spotted the tall man holding the infant and shouted, "There he is!" while tapping the coach roof to signal the driver to stop. Sissy extended her arm out the window, pointing toward the doctor. Suddenly, the coach moved toward Sasha's precious treasure. Upon reaching the doctor, they leaped out of the stagecoach and dashed eagerly toward the bundle Sasha longed to hold once more. As they approached, he gave the two women the tickets to board the ship, then he handed over the baby with delicate care and instructed them to board the SS City of Paris, which was set to leave in less than an hour.

As they hurried aboard the ship in a flurry of urgency, Sasha pressed the newborn to her breast; arms curved around her as if she could shield her from every danger. Her head bowed beneath the brim of her straw hat, she felt her pulse thunder in her temples, eyes flicking through the busy deck where travelers jostled and laughed under brilliant sunlight. Below the chatter and the slap of waves against the hull, she feared each voice might carry the secret to the child's father. Sissy—her loyal companion—scanned the throng until she caught sight of Christian weaving like a dark ribbon through the crowd. He reached the stern where a tall, austere doctor stood flapping his arms as though to part the sea itself. The gap to the dock widened with every deliberate pull of the ship's line, the wood creaking and groaning in farewell. Together, Sasha and Sissy lifted trembling hands in a silent adieu to Christian, the salt-tanged breeze carrying away their grief and hope alike.

Once inside the snug cabin, Sasha let out a breath she scarcely realized she'd been holding. The polished mahogany walls seemed to cradle her resignation. Gone were the vivid daydreams she'd once spun amid Parisian boulevards; in their place bloomed tender aspirations for the tiny life at her side. She unwrapped the infant with deliberate reverence, laying her on the narrow berth beneath the flicker of a lantern. The dancing shadows painted constellations on the ceiling, and Sasha curled around her daughter like a guardian spirit, rocking until sleep's gentle tide washed over her weary mind.

Late that afternoon, a plaintive wail stirred Sasha from rest. Golden light slanted through the porthole, warming the room in honeyed pools. She rose, limbs slow and careful, to cradle the child to her breast. Outside her door, Sissy knocked softly before gliding in, cheeks rosy with kindness. "vv?" she offered. Sasha nodded, gratitude shining in her eyes.

Sissy's footsteps carried her toward the dining saloon, where strains of a string quartet drifted through open doors. Candlelight flickered across linen-draped tables set with gleaming silverware and porcelain plates, each place a vignette of genteel promise. In the galley, she approached a waiter in a crisp white jacket whose smooth drawl held the sweetness of magnolia blossoms. "A tray for my mistress, please," she said. He smiled, voice warm as sunlit amber, and struck up a light conversation until she discovered his home was Hardeeville, South Carolina, the very town she had fled. Stunned delight crystallized in her chest. He introduced himself as Harold, and with a final tender handshake arranged to meet again that evening. Sissy walked back to Sasha with a fluttering heart and the scent of possibility in her mind.

Meanwhile, Sasha pondered the future Madame Hartford had designed for her—a marriage arranged before she'd even set sail. Would her husband be severe, with furrowed brow and graying temples? Or gentle, yielding as a summer breeze? Just then, a warm hand settled on her shoulder. She looked up into the bright eyes of a tall mulatto gentleman whose dark curls framed a smile both curious and kind. "A penny for your thoughts?" he asked, voice rich with humor. He introduced himself as Theophilus Augustine of Long Beach, New York. Intrigued, Sasha listened as he conjured images of rolling sand dunes, newly erected white-columned estates in the Hamptons, and his own snug home in Glen Cove. He pressed an earnest invitation for her and Sissy—and her infant— to visit once they disembarked. Sasha's lips curved in both sorrow and warmth as she confessed her solitary state and the child's father, whom she'd left behind in southern France. He only chuckled and promised that Long Island could soothe a restless heart.

The weeks slipped by as the great vessel cleaved the sea, its wake glittering like stardust in the setting sun. Sasha and Theophilus often walked the deck hand in hand with the babe swaddled at Sasha's hip. Fellow passengers assumed they were husband and wife and showered them with admiring nods. One evening, while the lantern light shimmered on the polished rail, Theophilus turned to her. "Since everyone believes I'm the father, I'll embrace that joy—for this child and for you. When we reach shore, let us court in earnest: I will claim her as mine and ask your guardian for your hand." The promise in his eyes warmed Sasha deeply.

Ten days later, the skyline of Manhattan emerged from the morning haze. On the pier, Madame Hartford awaited with an air of stern delight, flanked by Theophilus and Harold. As they descended the gangplank, Harold and Theophilus fell into animated conversation about plans and prospects, their laughter echoing through the salt-soft air.

That evening, back at Madame Hartford's brownstone, the three women recounted their voyages and the trustworthy souls they'd met. Madame Hartford, never one to delay opportunity, promptly sent invitations to Theophilus and Harold for dinner that coming weekend.

Saturday found Sasha attired in olive-green silk that curved around her like moonlight, her hair swept into an elegant chignon. Sissy chose a modest cream gown that rippled like milky satin, her own tresses pinned high with pearls. Their pulses thrummed in time as they awaited their gentlemen guests in the parlor. When the doorbell rang, Theophilus entered with his dignified parents, and Harold followed, hat in hand, cheeks flushed with eager anticipation.

In the candlelit dining room, platters of herb-crusted prime rib, buttered spring vegetables, and duchess potatoes released their savory perfumes. Theophilus rose, voice resonant with emotion, and lifted his glass. "Sasha," he declared, "You are the light that guides my every day. Will you honor me by becoming my wife?" He knelt, unveiling a diamond that caught the lamplight in a thousand sparks. Overcome, Sasha's tears glimmered as she whispered, "Yes."

Theophilus smiled broadly, then turned to Harold. "And you, my friend—any announcement?" Harold took a breath; eyes fixed on Sissy. "I'm no orator, but I know that life without you would be emptiness. I lack a ring worthy of you, but my love is boundless. Sissy, will you marry me?" Sissy rose, heart soaring, and took his hands. "Yes," she replied, voice steady with joy.

In the weeks that followed, both couples prepared for weddings—Sasha's at the grand Augustine estate, gowns chosen from Manhattan's finest bridal shops, and Sissy's to follow nearby. Nine months hence, Sasha bore a daughter, Camille, before slipping into her bridal gown one bright morning. Their ceremony was intimate, the air alive with laughter and lace. For their honeymoon, they traveled to Niagara Falls, awe-struck beneath the roaring cataract while Camille stayed in Sissy's gentle care. Upon their return, Sissy and Harold wed on Jones Beach at sunset, then danced into the night at a Westbury soul-food hall.

With both brides happily wed and the infant cradled in loving arms, our story turned to Camille's future. Determined to spare her daughter the hardships of her own youth, Sasha arranged for Camille's marriage into a distinguished Brookville family and devoted herself to guiding her education, ensuring the next generation would flourish without the shadows of bias or fear. Camile was a shining star, excelling in dance, singing, and academics with a natural grace that captivated those around her. She was adored by her peers, and her popularity soared throughout the school. When she turned sixteen, a grand coming-out party was organized, marking the occasion where she would meet the man destined to be her future husband. The evening was a whirl of elegant gowns and lively music, filled with anticipation and promise.

Over the next two years, Camile and her suitor courted, their relationship blossoming with each passing day. By the time she turned eighteen, the excitement of planning a wedding filled the air. The ceremony unfolded in one of the most opulent mansions in the Hamptons, a place where chandeliers sparkled like stars and the gardens bloomed with vibrant colors. This lavish setting was a testament to the grandeur of their union.

Camile's new home was conveniently located near her beloved Sissy, providing support and assistance for the children that would eventually come, ensuring a nurturing environment for her growing family.

Buffalo

One hundred and seventy years rolled by as if swept along by the relentless tides of time, and Buffalo blossomed into a bustling, chaotic city; its wild heartbeat fervently with the sounds of commerce and vice, infamous for its flourishing brothels and legions of prostitutes. A sprawling fifteen-mile radius of red-light district enveloped the city's core, a lustful magnet for the thriving businesses that sprang up on every corner. Amidst this sea of sin, a stalwart beacon stood firm: Pastor Petunia's Church of God and Sweet Jesus, which had burgeoned into a resplendent sanctuary. Its congregation was known far and wide for its tireless efforts to shepherd the wayward souls of pimps and prostitutes into the fold of Christianity. Against all odds, the prophecy foretelling the church's demise seemed as distant as a fading echo, especially under the leadership of the indomitable Bishop Theodore IV. As the most influential minister in Western New York, he commanded the spiritual helm of countless churches across the state with an unshakeable resolve. His steadfast wife, Ella Mae, came from a neighboring congregation, and with the death of her father, the two congregations merged. They became a formidable force, the union making The Church of God and Sweet Jesus one of the most prominent houses of worship in the entire country. The church's unyielding growth and influence made it seem as though no challenges could dim its luminous presence, as if it were shielded by divine providence. Yet, as unstoppable as their rise appeared to be, destiny had a different path in store.

Every summer, Bishop and First Lady Petunia launched a spiritual offensive to redeem the lost souls that thronged the backstreets of Buffalo, holding fervent tent revivals that were renowned throughout the city. Each year, the season would commence with the Deacon Board erecting a massive canvas tent on the blacktop beside the sanctuary. Eager women and children would line the asphalt with rows of folding chairs, spreading sawdust beneath them to cushion the hard ground. As the clock struck seven, the tent would teem with the restless bodies of those who wandered the streets, drawn by the promise of salvation and the vigor of the evening's gathering. A vibrant choir would lift its collective voice to the heavens, and Bishop Petunia would invite distinguished guests from the numerous churches that bore the name of The Church of God and

Sweet Jesus. This summer, however, would break from tradition and forever alter the congregation's fortunes. The summer of 1958 began just like any other. Then, during a packed revival one sultry night, disaster struck with the fury of an Old Testament scourge—a storm surged, and lightning ignited the tent in a sudden, roaring blaze. Amid the pandemonium, as frantic souls fled for their lives, First Lady Ella Mae fell, and despite Bishop Petunia's frantic efforts, he could not pry her free. As torrents of rain quenched the raging fire, there he remained, cradling his wife beneath the drenched fabric of the collapsed tent.

The next day, Buffalo's painted women returned to the strip and found the Bishop and his wife in an appalling state. With unexpected compassion, they removed the heavy canvas, lifted the injured couple, and carried them to the hospital. As Ella Mae lay in a sterile room, one of the prostitutes tenderly held her hand until she stirred. When the first lady regained consciousness, her eyes fixed on the unfamiliar woman, and she demanded, "Who are you?" The young woman recoiled, her face a mix of hurt and **indignation**. "My friends and I found you under the church tent, it must have fallen on you and the Bishop during revival. Ella Mae's voice rang with hostility, "Get this harlot out of my room, in Jesus' name!" A nurse hurried in at the commotion and questioned, "What seems to be the problem?" Ella Mae's accusing finger pointed at the woman. "She's a hooker who struts where we do our revival meeting. I want her gone." The nurse's voice was firm yet tinged with reproach, "This woman saved your life; you should be thankful." Turning to the young woman, she added, "Thank you so much for bringing her in." With a defiant nod, the woman's eyes bored into Ella Mae as she declared, "You are very ungrateful and judgmental. Just because you're married to a preacher, you think you're better than me. When I pulled you out from under that heavy canvas, people shouted. 'Leave that self-righteous holier-than-thou gremlin right there.' But my compassionate soul wouldn't let me. I'd rather have the mercy of normal everyday people than the title of First Lady any day. The pain you cause with your piety will come back to you. One day, you will bow down to my kind." And with that, she left. After she was gone, Ella Mae's bravado crumbled. "Okay, Nurse, give it to me straight. Am I messed up in the wound or what?" The nurse replied with soft-spoken seriousness, "Yes, I'm sorry to say you will not be able to have children, and to be intimate with your husband will be totally impossible because of the damage that was done to your uterus during the accident." These words pierced Ella Mae like arrows, and she buried her head in her hands, sobbing bitterly—the woman's prophecy haunting her. Perhaps, she thought, if I wasn't so mean, this wouldn't have happened. The following Sunday, when she appeared at church, scandalized whispers spread like wildfire through the sanctuary. *"Ella Mae done fell out in the spirit and knocked her hind parts out of place. Now she can't perform her wifely duties. Lord Jesus, the Bishop is going to have to be strong in the lord until she can heal up*". Although that was a good thought, all knew that he would find comfort in the arms of another woman.

Twins

In exactly one year, Camile and Cecil's simple life shifted forever with the birth of twins—yet what should have been unbridled joy soon curdled into despair. Williamina and her sister Williston—so named by Cecil's mother, whose own maiden name was Williston—were affectionately called Willie and Willow, two halves of a broken mirror. In their elaborate Glen Cove home, pale morning light sifted through the lace curtains, pooling on the shiny hardwood floor covered with plush rugs imported from India. The closets, overflowing with table linens, polished silver, and yellowed photographs inherited from Madame Hartford—Camile's grandmother, who had died of pneumonia when Camile was a child—gave off the sharp, musty tang of mothballs.

Camile—once brimming with her own dreams—felt suffocated by the endless demands of motherhood. While her college friends danced beneath strobe lights and laughed through late-night study sessions, Camile was trapped in a loop of midnight feedings, lullabies hummed to two wide-eyed infants, and the constant ache of isolation. Cecil worked long hours to support the family, returning home each dawn to find his wife exhausted and the children crying.

Over time, Camile's resentment crystallized around Willie, the child whose delicate cheekbones and bright, curious eyes so unmistakably mirrored Cecil's. mother, a woman she detested. Strangers stopped on the street to marvel at "the most beautiful baby they'd ever seen," and as Willie grew, she taught herself to sew exquisite outfits for her dolls, weaving together scraps of lace and ribbon with focused devotion. Camile's envy burned hotter with each marvel until it at last flared into cruelty. She poured her affection onto Willow—the quiet, plain-faced twin who preferred folding laundry to designing dresses—showering her with trinkets and praise. Willie, by contrast, heard only biting words and felt the sting of her mother's hand. Day after day, Camile dragged her eldest daughter into the corner of their cramped living room and struck her until bruises bloomed like dark flowers along her arms.

One afternoon, Sissy—Camile's devoted caretaker—burst through the doorway just as Camile raised her hand for another blow. Dust motes danced in the slanted light as Sissy flung herself over the trembling girl, arms coiled tight around Willie's shoulders. Tears streamed down the teenager's cheeks, and Sissy's voice, fierce and broken, rang out: "If you won't cherish her, give her to me." Shamed into silence, Camile stood back as Sissy pulled Willie into her arms and carried her away.

That very night, Cecil strode into Sissy's small parlor, lantern in hand, determined to bring his daughter home. He pressed soft apologies into Willie's ear, tracing the outline of her bruised arm with trembling fingers. "I swear, by all I hold dear, no harm will ever touch you again." But Willie had learned better than to trust well-meaning promises. Curling beneath a quilt that was two sizes too small—its fabric threadbare from years of washings—she wept herself to sleep, whispering prayers for a dawn when she might slip away from this house of sorrow into a place where peace and real love waited.

Just then, Utopia gazed down at Penelope's great-great-grandchild, the girl who bore the same sorrow in her eyes. She recognized the dark heritage passed down from Buck, Sasha's father, flowing through generations until it surfaced in the child's mother. With a solemn gesture, Utopia waved her hand, and a soft, silvery light coalesced around the girl. "I will carve for you a path out of this wretched existence," she vowed, her voice like wind through willows, "but you must never return. Should you turn back, your future will be shrouded in uncertainty." And with that promise, a doorway of light shimmered open before the child, offering her the chance at a new life—and at last, the love she had always longed for.

A GOOD TIME

Maybelle's heart had room for only one man: a tall, broad-shouldered sharecropper whose skin bore the deep bronze glaze of sun and toil. He worked the Palmer Plantation, twelve dusty miles from her clapboard house, and every inch of his presence spoke of strength tempered by hardship. One afternoon, as Maybelle rode her basket home along the cracked red road with jars of roasted peanuts under her feet, she spotted him leaning on a fencepost. His eyes—smeared faintly with sweat and smudges of river mud—brightened the moment he saw her. He tipped his battered straw hat and grinned, the deep lines at his temples softening into warmth. "That's a mighty fine wagon you got there, little lady," he drawled, his voice low and steady, filled with gentle admiration.

Maybelle paused beneath the broad maples lining the road and turned, her laughter like tinkling bells. Wisps of her dark curls framed her face, dancing in the light breeze. "You wanna ride?" she teased, her eyes gleaming. He chuckled in reply, voice rumbling like distant thunder. "I'd love a ride. What time do you want me to come over tonight?" Their laughter mingled with the hush of cotton leaves rustling overhead. Yet when his gaze grew more earnest, Maybelle squared her shoulders, the conviction in her tone unshakable as an old oak's roots. "First, you rest your weary bones at my house," she said firmly. "Tomorrow, I'll drive you back—no funny business, no shacking up." With that resolve, she led him down a narrow path to her modest cabin, where she drew steaming water for his bath and laid out a simple supper: green beans fresh from her garden, corn pone warm from the skillet, and tea sweetened with honeysuckle honey.

After dinner, under a ragged patchwork quilt of stars, Maybelle guided him across the fields that had shaped her family's history. She showed him the old Brown Plantation house, its white paint peeling like sunburnt skin, and the long rows of peanut plants still heavy with yellow blooms. They paused at a narrow creek, its water dark and slow, where the mistress Darcy lay buried beneath a fury of wild, stray weeds. Maybelle then recounted how her grandmother Penelope —born beyond the sea—had inherited this stretch of land through the spirit of transformation from the Mistress Darcy. On the path back to the cabin, she knelt at her grandmother's grave; a single tear rolled down her cheek, and her lips quivered in reverent memory.

Gently, he wiped the tear from her cheek and spoke in a low drawl, "Honey, you can't always keep to yourself. Have you ever thought about having a good time?" He paused, eyes alight with inspiration. "Your 'ol plantation's got bones that could dance again. What if we turned it into a juke joint? You'd have folks coming from miles around—black folk hungry for food, music, and laughter." He painted the scene for her: long wooden tables set with platters of fried catfish, collard greens simmered in ham hocks, buttery macaroni, candied yams, and cornbread still warm in its skillet. Sweet tea, lemonade, a bit of corn liquor to loosen tongues and loosen hips. A guitar player strumming dusty Delta blues in the corner, voices calling out, clapping in time. "I'll man the door— penny a head—and you run the bar. We hire someone to cook and serve; pay 'em off with a share when the night's done."

With the harvest a month away, the plan felt as real as the heavy summer air. They discussed painting the old house a deep moss green to match the pines, hauling in picnic tables so men could sit and play cards—Maybelle suggested a small cut of the pot for the house. His eyes shone. "Yes, ma'am. Now you talking!" And in that moment, Maybelle smiled, her heart fluttering at the promise of laughter and music filling the fields where cotton once reigned.

Every evening that followed, he appeared with brushes and cans of paint, turning the battered clapboards into a welcoming façade. Maybelle bent over tender new blooms—petunias, marigolds, and purple salvia—to dot the porch with color. Yet always, she made him leave at least two hours before darkness swallowed the sky, for in those perilous times, no Negro dared linger after nightfall without risking the patrols of cruel ghostly men.

One dusky evening, Maybelle set a cast-iron pot of her grandmother's famous peanut stew on the stove. The rich, nutty aroma curled through the cabin, mingling with the fragrant steam of creamy grits. The sharecropper inhaled deeply, his eyes soft with gratitude. Together, they sat at the rough-hewn table and tasted the flavors of memory and hope—two souls forging a tender, unconventional love and a dream that might just bring joy back to those weary fields.

One late-summer evening, as golden light pooled on the cracked boards of her porch, the sharecropper ambled up the steps in his worn boots and broad straw hat. He brushed sweat from his brow and said, "Maybelle, since you're the owner now of this here juke joint, I need you to shine on opening night—and every night after. No more selling peanuts roadside. I want you in a new dress, hair pressed and curled, looking mighty fine."

Maybelle's heart fluttered at his words. She smiled and agreed. Before dawn the next morning, she climbed astride Clover, her gray donkey, and trotted down the red-dust lane toward the mercantile. Once entering, sunlight slanted through the tall windows, illuminating rows of bolts: silks that shimmered like oil on water, cotton prints alive with daisies and gingham checks. She fingered a bolt of emerald-green silk, felt its cool smoothness, then chose deep purple and ruby-red as well—perfect for the dim glow of her juke joint's lanterns. For her peanut cart, she selected sunny yellows and sky-blue calicoes, hoping to lure customers as they drifted down the dirt road.

As she turned, her eyes settled on a glass display at the counter: delicate powders, rouge cakes, lipsticks in crimson and rose. Above them hung an advertisement of a pale-skinned woman with long curled lashes and lips like fresh-picked cherries. Maybelle beckoned the counter girl. The woman sauntered over, nose tilted, and asked coldly, "What can I do for you?"

"I'd like to buy a few things from that case," Maybelle said, smiling.

The girl's lips curled in contempt. "That's for white women. We don't make makeup for coloreds."

Maybelle kept her voice gentle. "Oh, no, ma'am— I'm buying it for my neighbor next door. She used to visit my grandmother before she passed. I want to give her something lovely."

The girl's surprise bloomed into grudging respect. "Well, ain't that kind. A darkie buying gifts for a white lady. She must've been good to your grandma."

"She was," Maybelle replied softly. Then she added, "May I have one of everything in the case?"

Smiling, she also picked out a few yards of cotton with tiny wildflowers, a Sears catalog bound in thin cardboard, and a jar of brown food coloring. When the clerk rang up the total, her jaw dropped. As Maybelle strode out, the girl hovered by the register and whispered to the store owner, "How'd she come up with all that money?"

The owner leaned in. "That's Maybelle—the granddaughter of Nelly, who sold fiery red-hot, pickled pepper peanuts by the roadside. Folks came miles for that secret African recipe. I even keep 'em in stock now—hard to keep them on the shelf."

Envy curdled in the clerk's eyes. She watched Maybelle ride off and began plotting how to smother Penelope's peppered-peanut trade once and for all.

A mile down the road, Maybelle pulled Clover to a halt before the dressmaker's small clapboard shop, its lace curtains backlit by the afternoon sun. Inside, the dressmaker greeted her with a broad smile. "Maybelle, I have just the thing for you. A client ordered this gown months ago—silk with hand-stitched beading—but she never came back to pay. She said she couldn't afford it and left it here." She held up a gown of dusty rose silk that caught the light like a mellow sunset.

Maybelle slipped into it, and the moment the fabric brushed her skin, her breath caught. The skirt swirled around her ankles; the bodice hugged her waist like it was made for her alone. She stood before the tall mirror, and for the first time, she saw herself as the businesswoman she longed to be. The reflection seemed to whisper, "This is the new you." Tears sprang in her eyes—tears of joy.

When she emerged, the dressmaker hushed her. "For the balance she owes, you can have it." Maybelle paid the modest sum, then spread out her catalog and sketched designs for several more dresses—one in indigo silk for opening night.

At the mention of her juke joint, the dressmaker clasped Maybelle's hands. "Oh, honey, it's high time our people had a place to dance and laugh together again. I'll spread the word by moonlight—no paper trail, just word of mouth. You won't regret it."

When Maybelle arrived home from town, the late afternoon sun slanted gold through her kitchen window. She set down her tins and sacks on the scuffed wooden table and lifted her mortar and pestle—worn smooth by years of grinding peanuts for her grandmother's beloved stew. The cool, heavy stone pressed against her palm as she remembered the rich aroma of simmering peanuts and spices that had filled Grandma Penelope's kitchen.

Next, she unpacked the small boxes and bottles of makeup she had purchased at the mercantile. She could still see the clerk's skeptical glance, as if Maybelle, a dark-skinned woman, could never hope to look as lovely as those pale white ladies. A quiet determination settled over her. "I am beautiful," she whispered, "just a different shade of beauty."

She carefully retrieved the wooden pestle and placed the square block of face powder in the mortar. With gentle, circular motions, the block ground into a fine, pale dust. Maybelle pinched open the vial of brown food dye, dropping tiny beads of color into the powder. The once-ashen dust deepened to a warm, cocoa hue, perfect to match her skin. A few drops of cool spring water turned it into a soft paste. She then spread the paste back into its compact with a small butter knife, pressing it smooth and even. Then she set it in a sunlit corner by the window, letting the light bake it dry to a solid cake once more.

While that dried, she opened the blush container. The rosy cake crumbled under her blade, scattering pink specks across the table. She shook in a little red dye until the pinch of pigment glowed bright and alive against her cocoa-brown cheeks. She reassembled it in its compact, careful to keep the blush separate from the powder, and placed it beside the drying face cake.

Last came the liquid foundation. She poured its creamy base into a porcelain bowl, patiently stirring in more brown food color until the mixture was a perfect match for her complexion. When it gleamed just right, she funneled it back into its tiny glass bottle, sealed the cap, and tucked it onto her grandmother's old dresser alongside her newly filled compacts.

Maybelle moved to the kitchen, humming as she washed last night's beans under a rush of cold water. Each bean slipped through her fingers like a promise, and she pictured opening night at the juke joint she and her sharecropper dreamed of owning. She imagined herself in a shimmering new dress, her hair fresh from the colored beautician's curling iron, silk stockings hugging her legs. But her shoes—her battered, sunbaked shoes—wouldn't do. She couldn't bear to ask the mercantile clerk for another pair; she'd already bristled at the clerk's condescension. Instead, she'd have to find her size in the rag box—unless she ordered a pair by mail. All she needed was her foot measurement.

At the thought of this, she set the pot of beans to simmer and stepped into the yard, bending to pull sweet potatoes from the cool earth. A strange flutter caught her eye: a scrap of newspaper drifting across the cotton field. She chased it, caught its corner, and brought it inside. On the page, she traced both feet with a stub of pencil, carefully noting every curve and arch. Then she leafed through the mail-order catalog, her heart fluttering at each stylish shoe.

That evening, back under the fading sky, Maybelle sat on her porch in her new rose-silk gown. She ran her fingers over the smooth fabric, smiled into the twilight, and felt her grandmother's pride warming her from the inside out.

The next morning, dressed in her plainest frock, Maybelle visited the dressmaker to check on her gown. While the seamstress pinned delicate lace, Maybelle asked if she could also order the shoes she'd circled and a fine cloth for her sharecropper's opening-night suit. The dressmaker's eyes lit up. "I have just the thing," she said, digging beneath her fabric bolts. She pulled out a pair of dainty leather shoes—someone's debt payment, she explained—left by a white customer who'd outgrown them. "Try them on," she urged. Maybelle slipped her feet inside. They fit like a dream.

"I'll take them," Maybelle breathed. "How much?"

The dressmaker chuckled. "You're a smart businesswoman. Never accept the first price." She coached Maybelle through a gentle negotiation: express appreciation, express reservation, suggest a fifty-percent discount, and offer barter—free juke-joint admission and refreshments. Maybelle repeated the lines, her confidence blossoming. When the deal was sealed, the shoes were hers for a dollar fifty and a few nights of festive merriment, the dressmaker rattled off the expected two-week wait for the mail order. "Just remember to bring your man in for measuring before the suit arrives," she winked.

That night, Maybelle served rice and beans, roasted sweet potatoes, and warm cornbread to her hardworking sharecropper. After supper, she fetched a bucket of well water and drew roses from the yard; their petals drifted across the water like tiny boats.

A scoop of baking soda turned it clear and soft. She bathed under the stars, fragrant with flower-scented steam.

Once fresh, she donned the new dress—soft linen in a pale cream—and slipped into the leather shoes that felt as light as feathers. At last, she approached Grandma's dresser, where her handiwork awaited. She washed her cheeks and brow, then dabbed liquid foundation on her forehead, nose, and chin, blending with gentle taps. She dusted on the pressed powder until her skin looked porcelain smooth. With a small brush, she stirred the rosy blush onto her cheeks in warm swirls. She lined her eyes with ebony kohl, then coated each lash with coal-black mascara. Finally, she pressed ruby lipstick to her lips, watching her reflection shift from country girl to glowing belle.

She gathered her hair into a high bun, softening stray curls with a spritz of warm water before twisting them into place. A single braid framed her face, and she secured everything with a ribbon borrowed from her grandmother's sewing box.

Just then, her sharecropper pushed open the door. His eyes widened, then lit in a smile as he crossed the room. He swept her into his arms. "Belle," he whispered, "you look more beautiful than any dream I've ever had."

Maybelle laughed softly, the name sparkling on her tongue. "Transformation," she said, "that's what it's all about. If we want more, we must become more." She rested her hand against his chest, feeling the steady beat of his heart. "In a few weeks, you won't just be a sharecropper—you'll part-own a juke joint. And I won't be a peanut-seller by the roadside—I'll be its madame, your partner in this new life."

He pulled back, his eyes shining. "From now on," he said, "I will call you 'Belle'. 'Belle is the perfect name for you. Then Maybelle questioned the sharecropper," What will you call yourself? "The sharecropper tilted his head and smiled. I think I'll call myself "Cotton". He decided, remembering the fields he'd worked in, the stubborn fibers of his past. "It reminds me of where I started—and why I will work hard so I never have to return. How I will cherish you, because without Belle, there will always be cotton."

He kissed her gently. "Without Belle, there is no beauty. Without cotton, there is no foundation." Together, they stepped into the warm lamplight, two partners ready to claim their shared dream.

OBSESSION

When Maybelle stepped out of the little general store clutching her newly purchased trinkets, the shopkeeper's eyes followed her like a hawk in flight. Each day that passed, the pale-faced woman's fascination with Maybelle grew more feverish: How dared a colored woman—once a slave's daughter, now saving firmer than most white ladies—afford makeup, fancy fabrics, even a crisp dress that gleamed in the sun? The shopkeeper's admiration curdled into bitter envy. She fumed at Maybelle's inherited success, at the steady clink of coins in her pocket that came without a single day's labor for a white employer. Finally, unable to bear it, she resolved to pay her rival for a personal call.

Late that afternoon, beneath a sky bruised purple with coming dusk, the shopkeeper pressed her knuckles to Maybelle's weathered front door. When Maybelle opened it, her face blossomed in warm greeting—her deep brown eyes alight with gentle curiosity, her clean yellow dress patterned with sunflowers soft against the fading light. A pair of plush, catalog-ordered slippers peeked from beneath the hem. For a moment, the visitor hesitated, repelled by the unexpected freshness of it all. But she forced a polite smile. "Hello," she murmured, voice slick with feigned concern. "I thought I'd see how you're holding up, with your grandmother gone and all."

Loneliness still clung to Maybelle like a thin shawl. Since her grandmother's passing, the only companionship was the sharecropper who called at dusk. She welcomed the visitor inside, motioning her into the parlor warmed by the dying glow of lamplight. Maybelle moved to the kitchen window, busying herself with fragrant tea leaves—strange, glossy leaves she'd bought months ago, yet never used. The kettle's whistle sliced the quiet; steam curled upward in pale tendrils. The shopkeeper watched, her envy tightening like cold iron around her ribs.

"Why aren't you out selling peanuts today?" she ventured, masking her resentment with casual interest.

Maybelle turned, offering a serene smile. "I've got a fine friend now. He says I ought to ease up. So I only work Mondays, Thursdays, and Fridays—those are our busy days. Weekends, we set the table for Sunday dinner, and he tends the yard. We're making a home."

The shopkeeper's gaze flicked to a thick catalog lying on the table. Maybelle picked it up and flipped it open to pages of delicate lace curtains. "I'm going to repaint Grandma's old dresser," she said softly, tracing a finger over a swirled pattern. "And hang these in the windows. I reckon I'll take to decorating." She laughed.

As Maybelle spoke, the shopkeeper envisioned herself in that rosy scene: afternoons sipping tea from a porcelain set, resting in a softly furnished parlor, leaving behind the drudgery of shop work. This was the proud life of white gentility, she seethed inwardly—never that of an ex-slave. "Those Blacks are taking everything," she thought, lips tight. "I must claim it for myself."

At sunset, they parted with polite farewells. As the shopkeeper walked home, a plan grew in her mind like a seed in dark soil. Once inside her modest kitchen, she laid her hand on her husband's shoulder. In a hushed tone, she outlined her scheme: one evening in a few weeks, he would ride through the woods, rifle slung across his back, and rob Maybelle as she sold peanuts by the roadside. He would scare her so badly she'd never return—and then they'd start their own peanut business, for good. Her husband's eyes glinted. "When shall I do it?" he asked. She smiled, a cold, triumphant curl of her lips. "In a few weeks," she said. "She trusts me now. I'll find out what else she's hiding that's worth taking."

WARNING

As the weeks passed, the shopkeeper—Anna—began stopping by to see Maybelle after work. When Maybelle was at her roadside peanut stand, Anna would stop by to lend a hand, thinking all the while that this was perfect training for running the business for herself someday.

One evening, Anna lingered too long in the kitchen while Maybelle prepared dinner. The sharecropper came in the front door, spotted the white woman, and asked sharply, "Hey, baby, who is this?" Maybelle smiled and said, "She's my new friend," then realized with a jolt that she didn't even know Anna's name. Excusing herself, she asked, "What's your name? There's so much going on, I just forgot." Anna laughed lightly. "I'm Anna. We've been so busy talking, I never got around to telling you." Maybelle hurried to plate her dinner: "Let me make you something so you won't have to cook later." Anna accepted the plate, waved goodbye, and stepped out into the dusk.

The sharecropper followed her to the porch, watching until Anna disappeared down the road. Turning back to Maybelle, he hissed, "What are you doing, inviting a white woman into our home? She could get us robbed—or worse." Maybelle placed a gentle hand on his arm. "No, she's a friend. She works at the mercantile where I sell Grandma's peanuts. She's been checking on me since Grandma passed." He shot back, "And you don't even know her name. How long has she been coming by?" "About two weeks," Maybelle replied. "Has she helped you at the stand?" he asked. "Yes," she said softly. Sinking into Grandma Penelope's old rocking chair, he muttered, "I don't want her here anymore. If she comes, you shut the door. I mean it." With a heavy heart, Maybelle nodded, set a plate before him, and the room fell silent.

The next morning, a soft knock sounded at the door. From inside her bedroom, Maybelle heard Anna pacing outside, peering through the windows. Then Anna called, "Maybelle? Are you there?" Maybelle emerged and sighed, "My man's upset—says I'm not doing my work, so I have to keep to myself for a while." Anna simply smiled. "I understand." The day after that, Anna came to the peanut stand. Maybelle confessed, "He thinks a white woman helping me will scare customers off." Anna suggested, "Let's pretend the business is mine and you're my assistant. No one will object to that." Maybelle chuckled. "Grandma started this stand—no one will believe it's yours. I'll manage on my own." She waved goodbye, and Anna walked back up the road alone.

Several days later, as Maybelle loaded jars of peanuts onto her wagon, the breeze picked up. "Grandma, are you trying to tell me something?" she whispered to the sky. But she reminded herself, "I can't stop—customers are waiting." With a sudden slip, a jar tumbled from the wagon and shattered, spilling vinegar across the porch. Maybelle wiped her hands on her apron. "If today's a good day for business, nothing's letting me get to it," she muttered. Finally, she strapped the remaining jars in place and trudged down the road to her usual spot. Two hours passed without a single customer. Just as she decided to pack up, a man on horseback rode up.

"Hand over your money," he demanded.

"I-I don't have any," Maybelle stammered. "I've been here two hours and haven't sold a thing."

The man sneered. "White folks don't like colored folks doing business here. Go pick cotton on a plantation, you've got the perfect hands for it. Don't let me see you here again, or I'll kill you."

Trembling, Maybelle scrambled back into her wagon and fled for home. When she burst through the door, Anna was waiting. "Maybelle, are you all right?"

she asked, her voice gentle. Through tears, Maybelle told of the robbery. Anna's brow darkened. "Did you have any money to give him?" Maybelle shook her head. "Good," Anna said. "But if I'd posed as the owner, he wouldn't have dared." Maybelle wiped her eyes. "It's all right. My man's opening a juke joint soon—we'll serve our own people. I won't need the roadside stand anymore." Anna's mind raced. A juke joint—that promised far more than peanuts ever could. That night, she shared the plan with her husband. Together, they decided to wait for bigger—and better—opportunities.

Opening Night

Anna and her husband finalized every detail of their scheme. Anna would continue to pose as Maybelle's friend and slip into the juke joint alone on opening night, discover where the cash was kept, then signal her husband waiting to rob the place —just as he'd done with the peanut stand.

Over the next few days, Maybelle collected her custom-made dress and Cotton's tailored suit from the seamstress. She rifled through the rag box for a pair of men's shoes, polishing them until the leather glowed. The catalog order arrived the same afternoon: a crisp shirt, golden cufflinks, and a bold tie for Cotton, plus delicate silk stockings and shiny new shoes for Maybelle herself. The following morning, Maybelle found herself seated at the hair salon, steam from the straightening comb wrapping her in warmth, while

Cotton emerged from the barber's chair with a neat, stylish cut.

That afternoon, they stepped into the big house—the elegant juke joint they'd built. Maybelle ran her fingers over the gleaming wooden bar; Cotton traced the brass footrail with satisfaction. Then Cotton cleared his throat. "Maybelle, do you mind if we rent out the upstairs rooms? Some guests might want a little privacy after getting to know each other." Maybelle smiled. "This was your idea, so do as you think best. Anna might drop by tonight—hope that's all right."

Cotton's smile faded. "I warned you about that white woman. She could ruin everything we've built."

Maybelle slipped her hand into his. "She's my only friend—she was there when I got robbed by the roadside. Not all white folks are the same. Trust me."

Cotton studied her, then nodded. "Okay. But I'll be watching."

Late afternoon, the cook arrived, filling the kitchen with bubbling pots and savory aromas. Servers took positions behind the bar and at the door. The blues singer entered last, her gown beaded with emeralds that flickered in the lantern light, followed by her musicians tuning their guitars.

As dusk settled, Maybelle and Cotton changed into their finest. Cotton's suit was crisp; Maybelle's dress hugged her curves, the stockings whispering against her legs.

When the doors opened, a wave of guests streamed in—women in silk frocks, men in pressed shirts, laughter, and the scent of moonshine filled the air. Cotton moved from station to station, collecting money, while Maybelle greeted each guest with a warm smile and a heartfelt thanks.

Shortly after ten, Anna arrived in a vivid red dress, her lips painted the very shade of Maybelle's. Anna stopped cold. "Where'd you get that lipstick? I thought makeup was for white women only."

With a light laugh, Maybelle replied, "It's a secret."

The blues singer faltered; the room stilled as every eye turned. Maybelle lifted her chin. "Friends, this is Anna—good folk who was with me when my grandmother died. I owe her everything. Welcome her!" Music swelled again, and the celebration resumed.

Maybelle guided Anna through the crowd: domino players with calloused fingers, ladies in feathered headbands gossiping over collard greens, corn bread, fried chicken, and Cotton himself—now more a businessman than a sharecropper—moving among the guests with quiet authority. Anna relaxed, amazed by the shimmering spectrum of brown faces lit by the lantern glow.

As the night deepened, Anna watched the dancers, the beat and laughter soaring around her. She tasted honey cakes and sipped corn liquor-spiked iced tea, and found herself drawn to Cotton's confident ease, his dark eyes reflecting the promise of something greater than sharecropping.

When the final notes faded, Anna asked Maybelle to drive her to the end of the dirt road so she could walk the rest—no one would dare harm a white woman. Maybelle waved as Anna climbed down, and a few steps away, her husband waited in the shadows.

"How did it go?" he whispered when she joined him.

Anna brushed a curl from her face, a slow smile drifting across her lips. "It went perfectly," she said. "But let's wait a few weeks—let the business grow. We don't want to strike too early and lose out on the extra cash. She laughed softly, the promise of the night's success lingering between them.

Forbidden Fruit

Over the next few weeks, Anna made regular visits to Darcy's grand mansion, climbing the narrow servant's staircase to the dusty rooms at the very top. Motes of light danced through the tall windows as she sanded and scrubbed the old pine floors and polished the carved mahogany dressers that had once belonged to the Browns, who owned the plantation. In payment, Maybelle slipped Anna an envelope of bills—crisp bills that smelled faintly of ink and hope. And yet each time Anna buffed the silver drawer pulls and smoothed the cool wood, a burning jealousy coiled in her chest. Maybelle presided over this vast house and a thriving peanut plantation, could afford silk stockings that hugged her calves and bright red lipstick to match, while Anna's life was tethered to Bubba— who struggled to keep a single hog alive—plus long days behind the counter at the mercantile just so they could scrape by. Masking her resentment with polite smiles, Anna dreamed of seizing everything Maybelle enjoyed, Cotton included. Night after night, she lay beside Bubba thinking of the juke joint, where Cotton wore a charcoal-gray suit and golden cuff links that caught in the flickering tea candle lights of the tiny tables filled with money-spending customers.

The week crawled by, then Saturday arrived with the heavy promise of moonlight and music. Bubba pressed against Anna's back in their cramped bedroom, his whisper rough as gravel: "Soon I'll gather the men—torch that joint, and take every cent." Anna silenced him with a soft "Not yet," and pressed her palms flat against his shoulders. "I need more time. I need to know where they keep their money." He chuckled, a harsh bark in the gloom. "Anna, if I didn't know you better, I'd think you just like sitting around with those darkies." She straightened his collar with cool authority. "This is business—our ticket upward. Let me go. I have work to do." With that, she lifted her skirts and stepped onto the sunbaked road that led to the juke joint.

Inside, warm air was thick with sweat, and spilled corn liquor rolled over her. A few women clustered at a scarred wooden table, their laughter mingling with the wail of a bent guitar. Anna slipped into a vacant seat. "Mind if I join you until Maybelle arrives?" she asked, smoothing the folds of her calico skirt. As they traded gossip about all that entered the door, Anna ventured, "How can Maybelle afford all this—owning a juke joint?" One matron, her eyes bright, shook her head. "This ain't Maybelle's joint—it's Cotton's. She just helps run it. He worked the fields day and night—sun-up to moonrise—until he bought this place. Maybelle spent her pennies on frills. Cotton put every dime into that bar, and now the man's got it all." As the woman spoke, Anna imagined herself in Maybelle's place: a devoted man who labored so she could drape herself in silk and lace. If she could charm Cotton away, the mansion, the peanut fields, even the juke joint would be hers. She only needed a plan.

When the band's fiddle moaned its final note, Cotton and Maybelle swept in together—he in his crisp gray suit, she in a buttercup-yellow dress—and began hugging patrons at the door. Anna rose, smoothing her skirt, and edged toward Cotton as he collected cover charges from a grizzled doorman. Brushing lightly against the side of his thigh, she murmured, "Could you fetch me a drink? The bar's so crowded—I hate feeling those sweaty backs pressed on me." Cotton's dark eyes flicked with surprise, then warmth. "For one of Maybelle's closest friends? Of course. What'll it be?" Anna's pulse thundered. This was harder than she'd thought. "Iced tea—with a shot of moonshine," she said, forcing a coy smile. Cotton grinned and drifted away.

Moments later, he returned, placing a tall glass beaded with condensation onto the table. "That'll be twenty-five cents." He held out his palm. Anna reached into her purse, dropped the quarter into his rough hand, and let her fingers linger, tracing the lines in his wrist. She lifted her eyes and lightly wet her lips. Cotton tucked the coin into his pocket, nodded, then took Maybelle's hand and led her onto the dance floor. As they swayed beneath the lantern glow, Anna nursed her drink and plotted her next move—how to draw Cotton's gaze away from Maybelle, how to turn ambition into betrayal, and finally claim everything she believed should be hers.

As Cotton led Maybelle onto the dance floor, his mind drifted to thoughts of the enchanting white woman who had flirted with him. Her presence lingered in his thoughts like a soft melody. Throughout his entire life, he had never imagined that a woman of such elegance would cast her gaze upon him with interest. He recalled his childhood, when he would see white women with their alabaster skin, which seemed to make their crimson lipstick and dazzlingly white teeth all the more vivid. He had always admired them from a distance, knowing full well that even a fleeting glance in their direction could lead to a fate as grim as being hanged by the neck until death claimed him. And now, here was a woman, akin to one who had once offered him a passage out of the oppressive cotton fields, showing him attention. His mind wrestled with the intoxicating notion of being with a white woman, a thought so consuming that he found himself lost in the fantasy of what it would be like to share even a single moment with one. Yet, the question loomed heavily in his mind: Was it worth risking everything he had worked for, just for a taste of the forbidden fruit?

FANTASY

It had been four weeks since the grand opening of the juke joint. Although Cotton's days of toiling in the rows of cotton were behind him, he still had plenty to keep him busy on Maybelle's farm. The juke joint down by the road brought in enough coin to make ends meet, but each autumn the fields needed turning, so that next year's crop could have fresh ground to spring from. Under the wide, sunlit sky, Cotton hitched the old mule to the plow. The warm breeze riffled his shirt sleeves, carrying the faint tang of earth and sweat as he guided the mule along furrow after furrow. Each time the mule tugged forward, Cotton's calloused hands gripped the wooden handles a little tighter—yet his mind was somewhere else entirely. Anna's face drifted in on each puff of dust: her pale skin glowing in his memory like moonlight on water, her eyes glittering with something forbidden.

Maybelle's laughter crackled from the back porch: she was off to town, she shouted, to fetch supplies. Cotton only nodded, though his heart thudded with thoughts of the white woman he dared not love. He had every right to his gratitude—Maybelle had freed him from a life of servitude, given him the chance to manage his own little empire of music and peanuts. He dreamed of marriage, of children, of waking each morning beside the woman he truly loved. But this dream never featured Maybelle. Instead, at dawn and dusk, it was Anna's face that clouded his every thought—an impossible dream he knew he must learn to shake, even as the week crawled toward Saturday, when she would reappear.

On the other side of town, inside her half-dark parlor, Anna paced. The lantern on the mantel flickered across her sharp features as she smoothed the hem of her skirt and plotted her next move. Cotton's flirting—so brief and polite—had set her heart racing with opportunity. She envisioned the juke joint under her control, its laughter and music rebranded for white patrons, the fertile fields and peanut business claimed by her and her husband, Bubba. Tonight, she decided she would plant the seed of false desire in Cotton's mind, lure him to believe she loved him. Then, in some out-of-the-way town, she'd cry out "rape," and let the power of white outrage finish him. His land, his livelihood, all would slip into her hands when the noose tightened around his neck.

When Bubba returned home, Anna spun her tale. At first, he bristled, ready to defend her honor with gunfire. Then she leaned close, her voice soft and persuasive: "Once he thinks I'm his, Bubba, he'll fall for the trap. I'll claim he kidnapped me, that he violated me. They'll hang him for sure. And everything he owns—juke joint, fields, peanuts—will be ours." Bubba frowned, uneasy at the cruelty of her scheme. She brushed aside his misgivings with a flourish: "Everyone will pity me, see me as the injured lady. You'll be the hero who saved me. A little therapy story about trauma, and soon they'll think I'm near broken." Her eyes glittered as she reached for his hand. "Then we turn Maybelle out, move right into the juke joint's attic, and run her house as our general store. Peanuts, groceries, dry goods—all profit." He smiled, "Okay, I'll do it!"

As the summer heat gave way to autumn's golden haze, Anna and Cotton's stolen glances blossomed into something dangerous. Anna's visits to Maybelle's whitewashed cottage became more frequent, her laughter echoing through the juke joint's smoky air while Maybelle, blind with sisterly affection, poured her another glass of moonshine. Behind Anna's honey-colored eyes lurked calculation, each smile masking her desire to claim everything Maybelle's grandmother had built. One humid evening, Anna watched Cotton through the juke joint's grimy window, his broad shoulders silhouetted against the kerosene lamps as he collected crumpled bills from the doorman. She waited until he slipped into the darkness before following, her patent leather shoes silent against the packed dirt. Cotton's path wound through tangled honeysuckle bushes toward the house, the canvas bag of money clutched in his fist. Anna's heart thundered as she darted forward, her fingers closing around his muscled elbow. "Cotton," she whispered, her voice like warm molasses. He turned, catching the sweat beading on his forehead. Her pale face glowed ethereally against the night as she stepped closer, the scent of jasmine perfume mingling with his earthy musk. "I've dreamed of touching you," she breathed, "Since that first day in Maybelle's parlor." Cotton's resolve crumbled like riverbank soil, though guilt shadowed his eyes. "What about Maybelle?" he asked, voice cracking. Anna's ruby lips curved upward as she promised escape, freedom, a life beyond America's cruel boundaries. When Cotton reached for her, she pressed her palm against his chest, feeling his heart race beneath his worn cotton shirt. "Not yet," she warned, painting vivid images of lynch mobs and ruination. As Cotton nodded, Anna's triumph blazed behind her careful mask. She retreated toward the juke joint's yellow windows, leaving Cotton standing alone, the money forgotten in his hand as he imagined a future with the devil who wore an angel's face.

The next morning, a pale light filtered through the thin curtains as Maybelle pressed a cool hand to her forehead. A wave of queasiness rolled over her—she told herself it was just the onset of her monthly cramps.

She forced a small smile, tied an apron around her waist, and set about preparing breakfast: soft, golden eggs fresh from the chicken coop and thick, steaming grits. Cotton sat at the worn pine table, arms folded, watching her with a distant expression.

"I hope you like the eggs," Maybelle said brightly, placing the plate before him. "I fetched them myself just this morning."

Cotton grunted. "Eggs again? Maybelle, why can't you make pancakes like white women do? All you black women ever serve is grits and eggs. I'm a businessman—I deserve pancakes, like proper white folk."

Maybelle felt her cheeks burn, but kept her voice gentle. "You sure woke up in a foul mood, sugar. I hope it eases as the day goes on." She rose, smoothed her dress, and announced, "I'm heading to the dressmaker to pick up my fitting." Cotton nodded without interest, and Maybelle slipped out into the bright morning.

At the seamstress's sunlit shop, bolts of silk and cotton lined the walls in jewel tones. As the dressmaker slipped the half-zippered gown around Maybelle's hips, she frowned. "Darling, this dress feels tighter than before. Are you expecting?"

Maybelle smiled ruefully, pressing her hand to her lower belly. "No, ma'am. It's just that time of the month—I always swell up a bit."

The seamstress laughed gently. "Well, next time I'll add an extra inch around the waist, just for those times." With a deft tug, she finished the zip and admired her work.

A week passed, and at home Cotton's chill grew colder still. He sneered at her meals, poked at her grits, and mocked the faint swell of her midsection. One evening, tears stinging her eyes, Maybelle slipped away to Anna's house—a little shotgun cottage painted sunflower yellow.

Anna greeted her with a warm hug. "Oh, honey, I know how it is with ambitious men," she said, guiding Maybelle to a rocking chair on the back porch. "They carry the weight of the world and let you feel every blow of their frustrations. Just smile, and be grateful you've a man as successful as Cotton. Plenty of women would kill for what you have."

Maybelle forced a grateful smile. "You're right, Anna. I'm so lucky to have you—and him."

But as nights lengthened and Maybelle's belly rounded, Cotton's glances at Anna grew too familiar. He began to join her for walks down to the juke joint, lingering by the lamplight as Anna's laughter rang out over the blues band. One dusky evening, as the moon seeped silver across their path, Anna took Cotton's hands in hers.

"Cotton," she whispered, "we can't go on like this. I want more than scraps of affection."

Cotton's eyes gleamed in the half-light. "I'm tired of sleeping next to a woman who can't make me pancakes. When do you want to leave?"

Anna pressed her forehead to his in the soft heat of the night. "Two weeks," she murmured. "That'll give me time to pack, settle with my job at the mercantile, and set everything straight."

Behind them, the distant strains of guitar and the voice of the blues singer drifted on warm air—an unknowing anthem for the life they planned to steal away.

Steal Away

That night, Anna leaned close to Bubba in the dim light of their room, her voice barely above a whisper. "I've figured it all out," she said, tracing invisible patterns on the bed sheet. "I'll convince Cotton to take me to New Orleans. With all those light-skinned folks there, nobody will question seeing us together." Her eyes gleamed as she continued, "Then I'll cry to the sheriff that he forced himself on me. Meanwhile, you'll report me missing the next day, and when they realize Cotton's gone too..." She squeezed Bubba's hand. "You'll suggest New Orleans, lead them right to me. I'll be there waiting, looking every bit the victim, and Cotton's land and money will fall right into our hands."

The following day, Cotton devised a plan of his own. Anna would disguise herself as a man, donning trousers, a button-down shirt, and an old hat that Cotton had picked out from the rag box. His wagon would be loaded with all the money earned from the juke joint, and they would set off at around 1 a.m. This timing would give them a head start to cross into Louisiana, where Cotton could ride openly without fear.

That Saturday, Anna arrived as usual, leaving her belongings discreetly at the edge of the woods near the juke joint. She strolled around the bustling venue, greeting familiar faces with a warm smile, and exchanged a quick, knowing glance with Cotton. After receiving his whispered instructions for their getaway, she took a seat at the worn wooden bar and ordered a corn liquor mixed with Coca-Cola. The atmosphere hummed with laughter and music, yet Maybelle sensed an undercurrent of unease. Stepping outside to feel the cool night air, she paused when she heard a voice. It was soft but clear, like a gentle breeze whispering through the trees: "Move the money to the peanut patch." "Grandma, is that you?"

Penelope's voice seemed to echo through the cosmos, repeating the instructions. Acting quickly, Maybelle dashed to the house and reached beneath the bed, where the juke joint's earnings were stashed. She pulled out a bulging bag of change and a roll of dollar bills, then hurried to the peanut patch. With determination, she fetched a shovel from the shed and buried the money beneath the earth. Following her grandmother's spectral guidance, she filled a sock with dirt and rocks, placed it in the money box, and returned it under the bed. Satisfied, Maybelle went back to the juke joint, blending seamlessly into the lively crowd.

About an hour later, Cotton slipped away to the house, retrieving the seemingly untouched money box from under the bed. He loaded it onto his wagon alongside his belongings and the clothes he had prepared for Anna. With a steady composure, he moved through the juke joint, collecting the night's earnings from the door, bar, and kitchen, while subtly signaling Anna to head for the wagon and preparing to depart. Moments later, Cotton joined her, leaping into the wagon's back with a blanket covering him. Under the cloak of night, with the moon as their guide, they began their journey toward New Orleans, their hearts racing with the thrill of newfound freedom.

As the night drew to a close, neither Cotton nor Anna could be found. Maybelle, her heart heavy with worry, moved through the throng of lingering customers, demanding if anyone had seen them. Most shrugged, lost in their own revelries, having no clue where either could have disappeared to. The doorman, a gruff man with a shadowed face, recalled, "After Cotton collected the money at the door, he slipped out the back and never returned." A cold suspicion slithered into Maybelle's thoughts: Could her closest friend have run off with her man? She went to her little cottage, hurried inside, her heart pounding in her chest, and knelt down to peer beneath the bed. The box, usually hidden there, was missing. In that moment, realization struck her like a lightning bolt—Cotton was gone, deliberately vanished. She understood that if he were caught, the consequences would be dire, a noose waiting to steal his fate.

As Cotton and Anna arrived in the vibrant city of New Orleans, Cotton handed Anna some money to indulge in shopping while he went into a nearby hotel to secure a room for the night. The streets buzzed with life, a kaleidoscope of colors, sounds, and smells swirling around Anna as she strolled along the bustling avenue. Her attention was soon captured by a woman with piercing eyes and a mysterious aura, who beckoned her over with a wave. "Come here, deary," the woman called out, her voice as smooth as honey. "It will only cost one dollar to have your fortune told."

Intrigued, Anna smiled and approached the woman, thinking to herself, "This should be fun." As she sat down, the woman, whose name was Mary, grinned knowingly. "You think so? Let's see what the cards have to say about you," she said, her fingers deftly shuffling a well-worn deck of tarot cards. With a practiced flourish, Mary laid out the Queen of Wands and the Ace of Swords. Her eyes widened with feigned surprise as she declared, "Ooh, I see you are a thief, a woman of deception."

Anna recoiled slightly, her brow furrowing in confusion. "Excuse me?" she retorted, her voice tinged with disbelief. Undeterred, Mary continued with a sly grin, "You have arrived here by deceiving a woman, making her believe you were her friend while you stole her man." Anna's heart skipped a beat as she stammered, "How do you know that?"

Mary chuckled softly; her laughter resembled the rustle of leaves in a gentle breeze. "I don't know anything, but the cards know it all," she replied cryptically. "So, you are here with a man belonging to a woman named Maybelle. You took him, knowing full well she was expecting a child, leaving that baby fatherless for your own selfish desires." Her voice took on a foreboding tone, "You will suffer for what you have done. Before the night is over, you will face the consequences."

Anna's eyes widened in alarm, yet defiance flared within her. "Now, that will be a dollar," Mary concluded, her hand outstretched expectantly. Anna rose to her feet, her voice resolute, "I am not paying you anything." The woman laughed again, her cackle echoing ominously. "If I were you, I would pay me. You're already in enough trouble," she warned, her words lingering in the morning breeze.

Anna reached into her purse, pulled out a dollar, and threw it at the woman before walking away. The woman laughed, "You'll pay for that too!"

To get her mind off of what she heard, Anna entered a dress shop, the bell above the door tinkling like delicate crystal. The shop smelled of lavender sachets and new fabric, bolts of silks and cotton stacked in rainbow rows against the walls. A beautiful woman of small stature stood behind the polished mahogany counter, her coffee-colored hair pulled up in a bun with a light blue satin ribbon wrapped around it, the ends dangling like twin waterfalls down her neck. Her skin was the color of fresh cream with just a hint of caramel, and her eyes were as sharp as a hawk's.

"Hello, I am Edna Baptiste," she said, her voice melodic with a thick New Orleans drawl. "What brings you in here today?"

Anna smiled, fingering the lace trim of a midnight-blue gown. "I'm just looking around, maybe find something nice to wear to dinner."

As Anna spoke, the woman's gaze intensified, studying Anna's face like she was memorizing every curve and hollow. "You look like someone I know. Can't quite put my finger on it, but you look like someone from around here. Are you from New Orleans?"

Anna shook her head. "No, I'm from Mississippi."

The woman laughed, a sound like wind chimes in a summer breeze. "Mississippi ain't too far from here. Maybe you have relatives here. Hell, I might be one. What's your last name?"

"Simpson," Anna replied, running her palm over a bolt of emerald silk.

"Is that your real name or your husband's name?" Edna pressed, leaning forward over the counter, her gold bracelets clinking together.

Anna looked up, suddenly noticing the woman's eyes—amber with flecks of gold, just like her own. But this was her first time in New Orleans. "My daddy's name was Mitchell," she said hesitantly.

The woman cut her off, her voice eager. "What about your momma's?"

"My mother's maiden name was Baptiste, like yours."

Edna's face lit up like a lantern, and she clapped her hands together, the sound sharp in the quiet shop. "I knew it! I knew it! What's your momma's first name?"

Confused, Anna said, "Rachel."

Edna rushed around the counter and grabbed Anna's hands in her own, her fingers warm and soft. "Girl, we been looking for you! Your momma was the biggest whore in Storyville until she started passing and ran off with a white gambler. You see, we are all the dependents of Jean Baptiste, so we look white. Most of us are concubines of white aristocrats—oh, but not your momma. She wanted to be a white man's wife. So, when a gambler came to town and met her, she ran off and married him without telling him about her past. Although we tried to find her, she left no trace until today. You are the child of Rachel Baptiste, my long-lost cousin."

Anna jumped back, her heart hammering against her ribs like a trapped bird. "There must be some sort of mistake."

Edna smiled, her teeth pearl-white against her rose-colored lips. "Honey, there ain't no mistake. You look just like us!"

Anna bolted from the shop, clutching her face as sobs racked her body. "There's no way I can be Black!" she cried. "I have to get out of here before anyone finds out!" Just then, Cotton caught up to her. "What's wrong, Anna?" he asked gently, though he couldn't hide his smile.

"My skin's so damp in this humidity, it looks like I'm crying—but I'm fine," she forced out. "Can we go up to the room now? We need to talk."

Cotton nodded. "Sure. Dinner in the room or out? We're in New Orleans—nobody will bat an eye. They'll just assume you're mixed, and they won't question us being together."

Anna frowned at the idea of being labeled "mixed" and walking beside a Black man so openly, yet among these French Creoles, it genuinely felt safe. As they entered the hotel lobby, she added, "I hope you booked separate rooms. I'm not sleeping with anyone without a commitment. I need time to know you." A passing maid offered a discreet smile.

"Of course," Cotton laughed. "This is your room. Mine's down the hall. Let's talk first." They ascended the stairs, and Anna's expression grew hard.

"Now that we're here, how soon can we force Maybelle off your land?"

Cotton paused, stunned by her bluntness. "Anna, we just arrived. She'll need time to process us leaving together. And she's pregnant—why rush her?"

"Her baby isn't my concern," Anna shot back. "I want her husband—and everything that comes with him: the house, the juke joint, the peanut business. She can keep the baby."

Cotton sank onto the bed, burying his face in his hands. "You can't have it. She owns it all: the land, the house, the peanut stand, it's all hers. Even the juke joint belongs—in trust—to a woman named Lisa Hartford from Yonkers. It was divided in the plantation mistress's will."

Anna's eyes flared. "So we own nothing?"

Cotton rose and pulled a small wooden box from beneath his coat. "Anna, this is all I have. It's enough to start our new life." When he opened the box, to his surprise, it was a sock full of dirt and rocks.

Anna threw her hands in the air. "I gave up my entire life for a penniless Black man? I'll be a laughingstock—and for what?"

Cotton's voice cracked with hurt. "Anna, I thought you loved me, not money you assumed I had. I lost the woman who saved me—who turned me from a sharecropper into a businessman."

Anna leveled a finger at him. "It's me or you. I choose myself. You'll be shamed in public; I'll be pitied." Without another word, she fled the room and went straight to the sheriff's office to report Cotton for kidnapping and rape.

As Anna entered the sheriff's office, tears cascaded down her cheeks, painting a picture of anguish and desperation. Her voice trembled as she recounted a harrowing tale of deceit and betrayal. She spoke of being lured into a wagon at gunpoint, where the illusion of friendship with a woman had masked the sinister intentions of a man who desired her. This man, driven by a dark obsession, had taken her to New Orleans, where he had seduced and forced himself upon her.

Just as her story unfolded, the door swung open with a forceful creak, and Bubba appeared alongside their town's sheriff. His voice was firm and insistent as he demanded the arrest of Cotton. "We want to take him back," Bubba declared, his words charged with the fervor of seeking justice. "The good people of our town want justice; we want to see him hang for tainting this decent white woman."

The sheriff, however, responded with a dismissive laugh. "A good white woman, you say? Word around town is that this is Rachel Baptiste's daughter. She is not white. Has she been passing off as white? You know there's a law against that," he said with a tone that dripped with disdain. "Now, unless you want to spend the next ten years in jail, I suggest you go home. We will investigate, and if necessary, he will receive a fair trial."

Anna's heart pounded in her chest as her ears caught the sharp edge of the sheriff's words. "Now, where is this Cotton fellow?" the sheriff inquired with a hint of impatience in his voice.

"He's at the hotel on Bourbon Street, next to the Voodoo Lounge," Anna replied, her voice quieter now, weighed down by the sheriff's dismissive attitude. With that, the sheriff nodded curtly, said goodbye, and strode out of the door, leaving Anna standing amidst the remnants of her shattered courage.

Moments later, three sharp knocks rattled the peeling paint on Cotton's hotel room door. The sheriff stood there, his weathered face shadowed by a wide-brimmed hat, silver badge catching the dim hallway light. "Hello there, you Cotton?" Cotton nodded silently, his throat too dry to speak. The sheriff's thin lips curled into what might have been a smile, revealing tobacco-stained teeth beneath his salt-and-pepper mustache. "Well now, seems you've been accused of some mighty serious crimes—rape and kidnapping—by that lady you strolled into our town with." His voice was honey-slow but edged with steel. "I ain't gonna clap irons on you just yet, but you need to stay put while we sort through these accusations." The lawman's calloused fingers tapped rhythmically against his holster. "If you take it upon yourself to leave town, I can't guarantee your safety. There's folks 'round here itchin' to string up a man like you." His eyes narrowed to slits. "And for what? A woman I saw with my own two eyes pocket your money and prance through dress shops, face lit up like Christmas morning. She's cut from the same cloth as her mama—a woman who trapped a good man in marriage, bore his children, all while hiding who she truly was. Deceit runs in her veins like river water." The sheriff adjusted his hat with a deliberate motion. "Stay put today. Come nightfall, we'll move you someplace safer, just in case they come sniffing around." With that, he turned on his heel and strode away, boots echoing down the corridor, leaving Cotton alone with his shattered thoughts and a heart as heavy as a stone in floodwater.

Meanwhile, Maybelle had to endure the gossip of the townspeople; they'd say, "Cotton done run off with that white woman. I knew aint no way a white woman would be hanging around all of these black folks unless she wanted something. I feel sorry for Maybelle, but that's what she gets for trusting those people." Maybelle's depression grew long and hard. She had lost her grandmother; she never knew her mother, and now this. Maybelle had to be strong; she had to get ready to have the baby alone with no help from a man or family. She would have to provide for the baby, so the best thing for her to do is act as if she had never met Cotton and continue selling the peanuts on the side of the road.

HOME AGAIN

Before Anna and Bubba climbed into the carriage bound for home, they begged the sheriff not to tell anyone about Anna's past. They intended to go back to their former lives—as respected white townspeople— and pretend nothing had happened. The sheriff agreed, though he warned them the town was still furious over Anna's abrupt departure. "Maybe you should start fresh somewhere else," he suggested. Bubba bristled. "This town is my life—my mother and the rest of my family are here. No way we're leaving. Once that nigger's hung, folks will pity Anna and forget in a month or two." Convinced, the sheriff tipped his hat and rode off toward town.

As Anna rode in the buggy back to the place where she lived, the late afternoon sun cast long shadows across the dusty road. Her mind wandered back to the way she treated all Black people, like that time she'd curled her lip at a mother trying to quiet her crying baby in the general store. She thought about the popularity of being prejudiced—how folks at church would nod approvingly when she'd make a cutting remark. She had been one to jump on the bandwagon like so many did with Christ. She pictured the multitude who watched the crucifixion on Calvary, their faces blank as stones while His blood dripped into the dirt. She remembered Maybelle at the counter, how she'd stared at her with cold eyes, and how she was appalled at her wearing makeup at the juke joint, the red lipstick that had made Anna's stomach twist with disgust. When Maybelle was trying to run her business, to rise up and take her rightful place in society, Anna had been there like the snake in the garden of Eden waiting to take it all away. She was not only a spectator; she was a partaker with hands as dirty as Pontius Pilate's. Could the Black people ever forgive her, like Christ forgave the crowd when he said "Father forgive them for they know not what they do"? Anna knew in her heart she did not want to be like the ones who crucified the Lord, and so she closed her eyes, feeling tears slide down her cheeks, and asked God to change her heart.

The next morning, the sheriff found his deputy sipping coffee at his desk. "What happened down in Louisiana?" he asked. Then he stopped, eyes wide. "You won't believe this: Anna is colored. Word got out in New Orleans—her grandmother was a mulatto in Storyville, her mother so fair she passed for white, married Bubba, and moved here. Anna says she never knew she was black."

The deputy sat up, stunned. "A nigger? I can't wait to see their faces when they learn she's been passing. She wasn't doing those colored people any favors by sticking around." The sheriff sighed. "This stays between us—no one else can know." The deputy grinned. "Your secret's safe with me."

That evening, the deputy returned home and found his wife in the kitchen. He kissed her neck. "What's for dinner, baby?" he purred. "Pork chops, corn, and taters," she answered. He turned her face to his. "I've got gossip, but you can't tell a soul." She nodded. "You know I never spill."

He whispered, "Remember Anna? She's not white—she was passing. When she ran off with Cotton, her family in New Orleans ratted her out." His wife gasped. "So they'll throw her in jail for passing?" he shook his head. "No—they'll hang Cotton for rape and forget Anna's secret in time." She laughed. "No one will ever forget she's black." He squeezed her hand. "Not a word." She pressed a finger to her lips and smiled.

The next day, the deputy's wife sold eggs at the mercantile. "Have you heard from Anna?" she asked the owner. "No," he said. "It's a shame—she left Maybelle pregnant, running off with Cotton. Maybelle's all alone now." The deputy's wife's eyes brightened. "Anna was passing for white—tricked Cotton into marriage." The clerk let an egg slip. "Anna's colored?" "Yep," she nodded. "Just like Maybelle. I hope they hang her." The storekeeper slammed the counter. "Where is she?" "She's returning from New Orleans," the woman answered. At that moment, Anna stepped inside.

"Hello," Anna said softly. "I'm sorry for everything. I was always a good worker—never late. Could I get my old job back?" The shopkeeper glared. "You forgot one thing—you're a liar." Anna blinked. "Liar?" he shouted, "You're black—a mulatto passing for white. How can my customers trust you with their money? If you'll lie, you'll steal. And everyone now knows what you did to Maybelle—lured Cotton away, got him nearly hanged, left an unborn child fatherless. Get out unless you want to buy something. I won't employ your kind."

Anna fled the store, heartsick, as several customers watched. She wondered how many people would learn her secret before nightfall.

Baltimore

The next day, the sheriff visited Cotton's hotel. "You're free, but you need to leave town. In case Anna's husband comes after you." He asked, "Got money?" "She stole it," he groaned. The sheriff laughed. "Rachael's daughter, no doubt. Don't worry—I know a man who runs a jazz club. There, you can earn money until you figure out where you want to go. I'll wire the other sheriff that you're in the clear. By the time he arrives, you'll be safe elsewhere." Cotton agreed gratefully.

That night, Cotton donned a suit and reported for work at the jazz club. The owner greeted him warmly. "Heard you ran a juke joint in Mississippi." Cotton nodded. "I've got you collecting money—just like back home. We don't offer rooms; the girls know where to go." Cotton smiled. "First time in New

Orleans?" the owner asked. Cotton nodded again. "It's the jazz capital—people come for the Cajun cooking and music."

In the weeks that followed, Cotton fell under New Orleans's spell: beignets dusted with powdered sugar, strong chicory café au lait, shrimp and fried salmon po'boys for nickels. He admired the cream-skinned women, especially one mulatto named Lula Mae. Every night she sauntered past, brushing her red nails across his chest. He hadn't been with a woman since Maybelle; he ached for her touch. Finally, he asked Lula Mae for a meeting. She smirked, "Ten dollars an hour." He paid without hesitation. "Tomorrow night," he said. She agreed.

The next morning, the sheriff burst through the hotel's peeling door, his weathered face slick with sweat. "Cotton—you gotta leave now. I just got word; your accusers may be arriving on the dusty afternoon train. The next one out of here leaves in ten minutes." Cotton's trembling hands stuffed wrinkled shirts into his worn leather suitcase. He pleaded with desperate eyes for a chance to say goodbye to Lula Mae, but the sheriff firmly shook his head, his silver badge catching the morning light. He handed Cotton a crumpled yellow ticket to Baltimore, Maryland. "Here you will meet a friend, Cecil Petunia, who said he was in desperate need of a preacher. He runs the Church of God and Sweet Jesus there." Cotton gasped, his dark eyes widening, "I don't know nothing about preaching,

I am strictly juke joint." The sheriff smiled, revealing tobacco-stained teeth. "Ain't nothing to preaching, just learn a few Bible verses on that rattling train ride and you are in business. You will love it—good money, and lots of beautiful women with Sunday hats and perfumed necks. Maybe you can meet yourself a wife and settle down. Lula is good for a good time, but she ain't someone you take home to momma." He pressed a small, leather-bound Bible into Cotton's palm. "Change your name on arrival, so no one can find you. Safe travels." With Lula Mae's jasmine scent still lingering in his memory, Cotton boarded the train, the floor vibrating beneath his feet, vowing to return once the dust had settled and he could resume his life in New Orleans.

An Introduction

Cotton stepped off the rattling train at Baltimore Station exactly at 11:33. Steam hissed from the iron wheels, and the sharp tang of coal smoke mingled with the distant clang of trolleys. A mild breeze carried the scent of Chesapeake bay salt and the promise of a new beginning. He surveyed the platform, cheeks warmed by the noonday sun.

A tall, dark-skinned man in a perfectly tailored black suit and crisp clerical collar approached him. His shoes shone like polished ebony, and his broad shoulders filled the doorway of the carriage behind him. With a deep, resonant voice, the stranger smiled and said, "Praise the Lord, Brother Cotton. Is that your surname?"

Cotton blinked, uncertain. The reverend's eyes twinkled as he asked, "Is that the name the massa gave you, or something you chose yourself?"

"I chose it," Cotton answered quietly.

The man laughed—a rich, rolling sound. "So you've named yourself after the plant that nearly broke your spirit: a living reminder of slave labor. Well, soon you'll have to change your name again." He extended his hand. "I am Reverend Strawberry. I took my name from the sweet fruit—dipped in chocolate, no less—a treat that shares the color of my skin. When people hear 'strawberry,' they think of summer's warmth. It brings a smile."

Together they strolled past vendors hawking newspapers and pretzels, past steam whistles and pigeon flocks bobbing on iron beams. Reverend Strawberry turned to him. "What would you like to call yourself now?"

Cotton chuckled. "I only became 'Cotton' a year ago—and now I must shed it already."

"Then think of something pleasant," the reverend said, nodding at a bright enamel sign overhead: BALTIMORE STATION. "A name that makes you smile."

Cotton let his eyes linger on the word "Baltimore." The capital "B" looked like a fat coin. The name whispered of opportunity, of leaving all past burdens behind. In that instant he knew. "What about B'Moe?"

Reverend Strawberry's face glowed. "Perfect. You can build a legend around it. Tell them your great-grandfather was enslaved alongside Reverend Petunia, escaped the chains to work with Frederick Douglass and Harriet Tubman, Maryland's own hero. After they founded a church here in Baltimore for the glory of our Lord. So proud was he of his freedom that he took the name Reverend B'Moe, and now you carry that mantle."

"How does it feel to be Reverend B'Moe?" the man asked.

Cotton straightened his back. "It feels real good."

"Excellent. Now, before we begin, is there anything we should know? Any children? Debts? Secrets that might come back to haunt the church?"

Cotton shook his head.

"Wonderful." The reverend beamed. "Let me show you your home."

They walked two blocks to a three-story brownstone trimmed in red brick and crowned with wrought-iron railings. Inside, the parlor smelled faintly of lavender polish; shafts of late afternoon sun slanted through tall windows, dust motes dancing like tiny angels. Reverend Strawberry led him upstairs to a spare room where a neatly made bed waited, its quilt patterned in deep blues and golds.

Cotton sank onto the edge of the mattress, his bones aching from the long ride. In the hush, his thoughts drifted to Lula—her skin the color of melting white chocolate, eyes bright as polished amber, hair coiled like midnight silk. He remembered their stroll along the riverbank in New Orleans, the lazy currents of the Mississippi rippling against the levee. She laughed when he teased her about her wide hips, said they were the secret of her power.

He pictured her again: temple archways of Storyville behind them, gas lamps flickering, while outside the grand mansions loomed like gilded tombs. He fantasized about marrying her—a reverent first lady at his side, bearing him sons to carry on with his ministry. Yet his heart tightened with guilt. He had lied about a past littered with betrayals: the little boy he'd never visited, the woman whose faith he'd broken, and the secret he'd buried even deeper—those men captivated him just as much as women.

He closed his eyes and felt the memory of Reverend Strawberry's soft lips, the way the man's question at the depot—"Is there anything we should know about you before you enter our sanctuary?"—had sent a tremor through him. He'd wanted to confess, to say, "I find you astonishingly attractive." But he bit back the words, smiled politely, and followed along.

Now, lying on this crisp linen quilt, Reverend B'Moe let himself drift into sleep. Tomorrow, he wondered, would he wed the woman of his dreams, the man of his heart, or remain alone—charming parishioners by day and slipping away for secret liaisons by night? He smiled to himself in the dark. What a splendid plan.

BANISHED

When Anna arrived home, Bubba sat at the kitchen table. "We made a mistake trying to rob that juke joint," he said. "Everyone, white and black, hates us now. We'll never be welcome here again. I sold most of our things. Use what's left to buy yourself a ticket out of town." He rose, saddled his horse, and rode off. Anna was alone, with limited funds and, friendless—except for Maybelle, the woman she'd wronged. Not only would she have to face and confess to her if she truly wanted her sins to be forgiven; there was also a community whose trust she had betrayed with every dismissive glance and cold shoulder. If she wanted to right her wrongs, she would have to stand before the weathered faces of people who had endured generations of contempt just like hers, apologize for her cruelties both spoken and unspoken, and transform herself from the marrow of her bones to the expressions that crossed her face. Anna would have to bow her head before their judgment; accept whatever bitter words they might hurl back at her. She would have to make amends to Maybelle—whose dignity she had tried to strip away at that counter—and to all the others she'd looked through as if they were glass, not flee to some distant town where nobody knew the ugliness that had lived in her heart.

Determined to make amends, Anna went to Maybelle's home.

When she walked up to Maybelle's weathered porch, the old pine boards groaned beneath her trembling feet. The late afternoon sun cast long shadows across the yard as she raised her hand to the peeling blue door and knocked three times. Maybelle opened the door, her dark eyes rimmed with red, tears glistening on her cheeks like morning dew. "What do you want?" she demanded, voice cracking. "Don't you think you've caused enough trouble around here?" Anna couldn't meet her gaze, instead focusing on the worn threshold between them. Her voice came out barely above a whisper, "Maybelle, I want to apologize for the wrongs I've committed against you. I want to make amends and help you through this difficult time. You can't manage the house and the business with the baby coming. Please, let me stay and help you."

As Maybelle listened to Anna's desperate pleas, her swollen belly tightened with each conflicting emotion, the child within her seeming to sense the tension hanging in the humid air between the two women. With a feeling of desperation, Maybelle turned, walked into her empty house and Anna followed her.

That afternoon, the sun slanted through dusty windows, illuminating Anna's tear-streaked face. Maybelle's fingers traced circles over her fifth-month bump while the familiar ache of betrayal burned in her chest. The farmhouse creaked around them, too large for one person but too empty without Cotton. Outside, the fields stretched golden and untended, demanding work her pregnant body could barely manage. Her mind raced through scenarios: labor pains striking at midnight, no buggy to take her to town, no hands but her own to deliver this child. The practical reality settled over her like the heavy quilt her grandmother had made—Anna's presence, despite the betrayal, might be the difference between life and death. With a deep sigh that seemed to come from the soles of her worn boots, Maybelle nodded slowly, giving Anna the chance to stay until the baby came.

When Maybelle agreed, Anna cleaned the house, tidied the kitchen, made the beds, and cooked a meal. That night, the townspeople crowded around Maybelle's house and demanded she turn Anna away. "Kick her out," they insisted. Maybelle refused. "Anna's paid dearly—lost her husband, her status, her white identity. She works for room and board, which none of you would do.

A man with skin weathered by years of fieldwork thrust a calloused finger toward Maybelle, his voice carrying across the dusty yard. "Maybelle, Nelly would be turning in her grave if she knew what kind of woman you turned out to be. You let that smooth-talking man into your grandmother's home, and he leaves you swollen with child while that woman—that betrayer—is laid up in her house!" Maybelle's eyes flashed like summer lightning. She drew herself up tall, her cotton dress stretched tight across her belly. "I ain't no fool," she shot back, her voice steady despite the tremble in her hands. "I loved that man with every beat of my heart. I had no idea the snake he'd turn out to be. My Grandma was from Africa—royal blood ran through her veins whether you believe it or not. Look around you! Most Colored women in these parts got babies and no husband to speak of. My Grandma would cradle this child in her arms because she understood the cruel ways of this world." Maybelle's chin lifted higher, proud as her grandmother's had been. "She'd see this situation through clear eyes—like the shrewd businesswoman she was. Anna is the only soul willing to move into my home and tend to things until I find my footing again. She works for nothing but a roof and meals, which not one of you would do, and one more thing! My Grandmother's name is not Nelly, its Penelope!" Her words hung in the humid air like Spanish moss. One by one, the crowd turned away, boots and worn shoes kicking up little clouds of red clay as they retreated down the path toward home.

God's Love

Once the crowd drifted away and Maybelle's breathing settled into the ragged rhythm of sleep, Anna sank to the rough floorboards. Her shoulders shook as sobs tore from her chest. "Father in Heaven," she murmured, fingers laced so tightly that her knuckles blanched, "I confess my sins— against You, against every soul I've wronged." Tears glistened in the flickering candlelight as she glanced toward the thin partition that separated her from her friend's shallow slumber. "Most of all, forgive me for betraying the one who trusted me when I had nothing but falsehood to offer." Her prayers wove through the cabin's rafters, floated over the moonlit cotton fields with their shimmering white bolls, swept past the nearby farms— past Utopia, Penelope, and Melanie, soaring over the sprawling Star plantation, and upward through the velvet darkness where stars hung like distant lanterns, until they reached the ears of the Almighty. "Oh Father God," she whispered, her voice raw and barely audible. "Dear Lord," Anna breathed, voice raw with regret, "pardon these hands stained by cruelty, this tongue sharpened by lies, this heart that coveted what was never mine."

As her confession spilled from her lips, Anna felt a sudden crack inside her chest—like fragile glass fracturing—and a cold emptiness replaced the dark ambition she'd harbored. At that moment, a gentle golden light enfolded her, warm as a summer breeze, soft as a mother's caress. From their vantage beyond the sky, Penelope, Utopia, and Melanie witnessed the miracle: the hard, icy core of Anna's spirit melted away, giving birth to a new pulse of compassion. A halo of soft radiance crowned her bowed head, and her tears, once bitter, turned to a sweet exhalation of relief. She lifted her face toward heaven, awed by the grace she felt fill her being.

Wiping her cheeks on the hem of her cotton nightgown, Anna crept into the narrow bed. The springs groaned beneath her weight as moonlight spilled through the tattered curtains, painting silver patches on the quilt. Fingers clasped, she thanked God for Maybelle's forgiving heart—so vast and unexpected, like rain in a parched season—and prayed that one day she might repay her friend's kindness.

Before dawn broke, Anna was already stirring in the kitchen. She cracked four brown eggs into a cast-iron skillet of sizzling bacon grease, the aroma filling the air. A steaming mound of white grits went into a blue bowl, a pat of butter melting into golden rivulets. Coffee percolated, dark and fragrant. Carefully, she arranged the meal on Penelope's old wooden tray, tucking a red-and-white cloth around its edges, and carried it gently into the bedroom. Maybelle, heavy with child, blinked awake beneath the patchwork quilt. "You didn't have to," she whispered, propping herself on a pillow.

"It's the least I can do," Anna replied, placing the tray across Maybelle's lap. Perched on the bedside, she traced a finger over Maybelle's rounded belly. "While you rest before the baby arrives, I need you to trust me with the peanut stand. We'll count every peanut, track every penny—I've got to prove myself."

Maybelle's hand settled over Anna's. "And what will I do all day?"

Anna squeezed her friend's fingers. "Whatever you like—rest here or come with me. For once, the choice is yours." Maybelle nodded, tears glimmering, but her smile was steady.

Later, Anna filled the woven corn-husk basket with jars of steaming, red-hot pickled peppered peanuts. She hoisted it onto the donkey's back and set off down the dusty clay road that snaked between towering cotton stalks. At the crossroads of three counties, she lay out her stand beneath an ancient live oak draped in moss. Wagon wheels creaked past, and riders sneered, one woman leaning out to jeer, "Does Maybelle know you're out here? You stole her man—what makes her think you won't steal her peanuts, too?"

Anna ignored the taunts until the afternoon sun cast long shadows across the road. A weather-beaten man stopped his mule cart in front of her. "Where's Maybelle?" he asked, voice gentle as creek water.

"She's resting—expecting soon," Anna said, offering a polite smile. "I'm helping her out."

He tipped his hat. "That's mighty kind. I'll take a jar of her grandma's spicy peanuts." He handed over a few coins, his calloused palm brushing Anna's. He studied the glass jar as the vinegar caught the light, then tucked it carefully away and waved farewell as his wagon rolled off, leaving a swirl of dust in its wake.

On Sunday morning, Anna woke Maybelle with another tray of breakfast. This time Anna wore a starched white dress, her hair pinned back with a bone comb, a small wooden cross hanging at her throat. "Where are you off to looking so fine?" Maybelle asked, rubbing sleep from her eyes.

"I'm going to church today," Anna replied, her face alight. "I'm going to ask the pastor to dip me in that cool water and wash these sins away. I want to be born again, clean as the day I was born."

Maybelle's fingers drifted over her belly. "I'm not much for church, you know that."

Anna's smile wavered, then returned firm. "I know we were raised different—Utopia's ways and mine—but I've strayed far enough. Today, I'm finding my path back to God. And when your baby arrives, that child is going with me to service every Sunday."

"Alright," Maybelle said with a soft sigh. "I'll have peanut stew waiting when you get back."

Later, Anna stepped into the white-washed building of the 2nd God and Christ Negro Church. The wooden floorboards creaked under her polished shoes. As the choir's hymn faltered, every head turned to stare at the pale woman whose complexion they'd always assumed meant she was white. The preacher's booming voice fell silent for a heart-stopping moment.

Finally, Anna rose slowly. Heart pounding, she cleared her throat. "First, I give honor to God, to the pastor, and to all of you gathered here. Second, I must apologize for deceiving you all these years."

A voice from the back shouted, "Why not go to the white church you've been attending?"

Anna's breath caught, but she pressed on. "Just a week ago, I learned the truth: I'm Negro, by blood and by birth. I was denied this knowledge—denied my place—until now. That's why I stand before you today. This pew, under Calvary's-stained glass, is where I truly belong. I know I must bear the consequences of my deception, but with the Lord's grace, I will show you I'm a changed woman. As scripture says, 'If any man be in Christ, he is a new creature.' I ask, with all humility, for the chance to prove myself and be welcomed among you."

The pastor—a tall man with burnished mahogany skin and silver-streaked hair—stepped forward. "Do you accept the Lord Jesus Christ as your personal Savior?"

Anna nodded, tears gleaming on her lashes.

"And will you commit to this church as an active member?"

Again, she nodded. The pastor opened his arms, and Anna stepped into his embrace. "We welcome you, Sister Anna."

One by one, the congregation rose—women in colorful hats, men in crisp shirts, children clutching hymnals—and came forward to embrace her. Their warm welcome and whispered blessings washed over Anna, sealing her new life in faith and forgiveness.

An Education

In the days that followed, Maybelle slipped into her new rhythm with surprising ease. Each morning, the sun crept through the narrow windows of their little clapboard house, illuminating dust motes that danced above the pine floors. Maybelle would sort handfuls of fresh peanuts at the worn kitchen table—cracking the shells by hand, and discarding debris. As Anna perched on a wooden crate beside the mule-driven wagon, the warm breeze tugging at her skirts as she called out to passersby, urging them to sample a handful of pickled peanuts still warm from the sun. At week's end, Maybelle counted out Anna's earnings, handing over a few bright colored coins as Anna slipped a folded note with ten percent of her earnings into Maybelle's nightstand drawer—her quiet gesture of thanks for room and board.

When Anna returned each evening, the house glowed with candlelight and the sweet aroma of simmering stew. The parlor, scrubbed spotless, held only a small round table draped with lace and Maybelle's grandmother's rocking chair, its wood polished to a deep honey sheen. All Anna had to do was wash her hands, settle into the chair, and let Maybelle bring dinner—tender meat, root vegetables, fresh biscuits—to her. Gone were the days of endless chores and a husband's demands; here, Anna found a haven.

After supper, Anna would pull a well-worn romance novel from the shelf—its spine cracked, its pages soft with use—and read aloud to Maybelle. Maybelle sat cross-legged by the kitchen hearth, where the wash tub stood brimming with soapy water warmed by the afternoon sun. The table was set for two: a chipped plate for Maybelle's supper, a glass of cool spring water. As Anna's voice wove tales of distant ballrooms and moonlit dances, Maybelle felt carried to far-off worlds she'd never seen.

One evening, Anna came in with her basket empty and her pockets jingling with coins. She dropped onto the rocker, her shoulders sagging from a long day's labor. "I'm so tired," she sighed. "Maybelle, could you read to me for a change?"

Maybelle's face flushed; she lowered her eyes in shame.

"Don't tell me you can't read," Anna pressed gently. "Can you write?"

"A little," Maybelle admitted in a whisper.

"Oh, Maybelle," Anna exclaimed, lifting Maybelle's chin. "After all you've done for me, let me give you the gift of learning. Reading can carry you to places you've never been—right alongside the characters I read to you." Her eyes shone with excitement. "I'll teach you how to write. While I'm away each day, you'll practice your letters. When I return, we'll sound them out together before bed. We'll start tomorrow—though tonight, both of us need rest."

Maybelle lay awake that night, her heart fluttering like a bird. At dawn, she tiptoed into the kitchen, the dew still clinging to the windowsill flowers. She set a steaming bowl of grits before Anna, whose eyes flickered open as if greeted by a sunrise. "You're giving me an education," Maybelle said, pouring milk into coffee and stirring with trembling hands. "I owe you more than words can say."

After breakfast, Maybelle retrieved a fresh notebook and a handful of sharpened pencils. She placed them on the table, the paper's crisp whiteness inviting possibility. Anna smiled, gathered her napkin, and wrote in careful loops:

A a – Apple

B b – Boy

C c – Cat

With each letter, Anna spoke the sound aloud while Maybelle traced it, her pencil scratching softly against the page. By the time the first three pages were filled, Maybelle's cheeks glowed with pride. Anna kissed her forehead. "Practice these letters and their sounds," she said. "Soon, we'll turn them into words."

Dressed in her worn work skirt and sturdy boots, Anna climbed onto the basket hitched to the mule. As the animal's hooves crunched down the red clay road, Maybelle stood in the doorway, notebook clutched to her chest, ready to begin her own journey into the world of words.

That night Anna returned home, washed away the day's dust, and settled at the table for supper. After dinner, rather than opening her romance novel, she spread out paper and pencil for Maybelle's lesson. They practiced letters, with Anna guiding Maybelle's hand as she formed each curve and line. Peanuts became counters—five in a row, then take two away. Days turned to weeks as they moved from simple addition to subtraction, from single numbers to pairs, then groups of three. Letters grew into small words, then phrases. By the harvest moon, Maybelle could sound out passages from Anna's books and calculate their peanut earnings without a single error.

One afternoon as they sat shelling peanuts, Maybelle rested her hand on her swollen belly and asked Anna, "What do you plan to do after the baby arrives? I know you don't plan to sell peanuts for the rest of your life. I think you would make a fine teacher." Anna's eyes lit up, though her smile remained hesitant. "You think so, Maybelle? I always dreamed of it, but I don't have a formal education. I never went past the 11th grade. Had to drop out to help Mama put food on the table, then I married Bubba, and that was the end of that." Her fingers traced the worn edge of the tablecloth. "College costs money I don't have." Maybelle reached across the table, her dark fingers contrasting against Anna's lighter skin. "Just go down to the nearest school and have faith that God will work it out." The next day, after the midday rush at the peanut stand, Anna penned a careful letter to the nearest Negro college, her handwriting precise and hopeful. When the reply came weeks later, an interview with the college. Maybelle was nearly bursting with excitement. While Anna worked, Maybelle lovingly pressed the cornflower blue dress she'd secretly commissioned from the dressmaker, the fabric crisp beneath the hot iron. She polished Anna's Sunday shoes until they gleamed like black mirrors. That Sunday, Anna approached the pastor, her voice steady despite her racing heart, and asked to teach Sunday school. By service's end, the entire congregation stood in prayer for her, their voices rising like a flock of birds toward the whitewashed ceiling. Anna clutched her worn Bible to her chest, feeling for the first time that her dream might actually take flight.

When Anna arrived at the school several weeks later, the brick building loomed against the cloudless blue sky, its windows gleaming like watchful eyes. Inside, the secretary—a thin woman with wire-rimmed spectacles perched on her nose—asked Anna for her High School diploma. Anna's throat tightened as she confessed, "I never got one. I never went past 11th grade." Her fingers twisted the fabric of the beautiful cotton dress gifted by her trusted companion, Maybelle. While she waited for rejection. Instead, the secretary's weathered face softened. "That's okay. Looking at your letter, you'll be fine with the curriculum. We'll test you to see where to place you." In the testing room, wooden chairs scraped against the polished floor as other women entered—their skin ranging from deep mahogany to caramel. Anna felt their eyes boring into her light complexion. One girl with tightly braided hair leaned toward her friend, her whisper carrying across the silent room: "Look at her—almost white. She could pass. Those mulattos always have the upper hand." Another girl with a beauty mark beside her full lips added, "Probably dumb though. Doesn't need brains with that shade—boys flock to her anyway." Anna's cheeks burned hot as a coal stove, a pain she had instilled in her earlier years. Then a tall girl in a pressed blue dress approached, her smile revealing a slight gap between her front teeth. "Hello, I'm Gracie. Don't mind them." Her voice was honey-smooth, comforting as a warm blanket. After the test, as afternoon shadows stretched across the wooden floor, Gracie touched Anna's elbow. "Let's have tea. When does your train leave?" Anna's tension melted like spring frost. "Six o'clock." Gracie's eyes crinkled at the corners. "Mine too! We have plenty of time to get acquainted. I just love meeting new people."

During lunch, Gracie shared stories of her family with pride in her voice. Her father, a professor at a Negro boys' college, had walked ten miles to school each day for his education. He'd ridden in empty train cars, facing terrible racism, all to help his community. Her grandmother's father had been a tailor who built his own dress shop from nothing, now serving Mississippi's finest families.

Anna sat quietly, unable to speak of her own past. The shameful truth—that she had once believed herself white and harbored the same prejudices as those who had tormented Gracie's father—stayed locked behind her lips. Instead, she nodded and fabricated a story: she was an orphan living with her sister Maybelle, born to a Mulatto mother and Black father, unable to attend school until after her sister's baby arrived.

Weeks later, when Anna's acceptance letter arrived, a new worry surfaced. "How will I pay for it?" Maybelle suggested writing to request a bill. "We'll need to work twice as hard on our inventory," she said, determination in her eyes. "Once the baby comes, you'll be gone for six months at a time."

Several weeks later, a letter from the college arrived while Anna was working at the peanut stand. Maybelle, too excited to wait, tore open the envelope and found the invoice inside. She retrieved her savings from beneath the mattress—money earned at Cotton's Juke Joint—and made her way into town. At the bank, the clerk eyed her swollen belly as he handed over the check.

"Looks like that baby's coming any day now," he said with a smile.

"It does indeed," Maybelle replied, one hand resting on her stomach.

At the post office, she carefully addressed an envelope to the college, sealed the check inside, and watched as it disappeared into the mail slot. That evening, she said nothing to Anna about having paid for her education— tuition, room, and board—with earnings from nights spent serving drinks to rowdy patrons at Cotton's Juke Joint.

That night, Maybelle's cries gave way to new life—a boy they named Brown. Anna's heart swelled at the first sight of him, tiny fists clenched against the world. The midwife placed him in Anna's waiting arms with practiced gentleness. "What do we owe you?" Anna asked, her voice soft with reverence. She set the child in the crook of her arm, went to the pickle jar on the shelf, and emptied coins onto the wooden table, counting them carefully. "It's all there," she said, cradling Brown against her chest. "Thank you for bringing our little one safely into this world." The midwife nodded, tended to the exhausted Maybelle, and slipped away with a parting smile. Finding Maybelle deep in slumber, Anna nestled the newborn in a basket and carried him to the kitchen, where she began preparing dinner, his tiny breaths keeping rhythm with her movements.

In the weeks to come, Anna received her room number, keys, and schedule from the school. When she read the letter, she looked at Maybelle and asked, "how?"

The following Sunday, Anna stood before the weathered wooden pews of the small church, her voice ringing clear above the rustling of hand-held fans. She announced that Maybelle had given birth to a healthy baby boy named Brown, his skin the color of burnished copper in the morning light. Anna's cotton dress, pressed specially for the occasion, rustled as she shared her plans to attend college for a teaching degree. Her eyes, earnest and determined, scanned the congregation as she humbly requested that they look after Maybelle during her absence.

In the weeks that followed, Anna's fingers grew calloused from working the peanut fields, the rich earthy smell clinging to her clothes as she harvested enough to sustain Maybelle's business. When Brown reached six weeks, his tiny fists opening and closing like sea anemones, Anna approached Maybelle about christening him. On that sacred Sunday, they dressed Brown in a pristine white gown with delicate embroidery along the hem, the fabric so fine it seemed to float around his tiny body. After the ceremony, when Pastor Johnson announced the river baptism, Anna leapt from her seat, her voice cracking with emotion as she praised the Lord. Maybelle cradled Brown against her chest, his downy head nestled beneath her chin, and whispered into his ear with a smile playing on her lips, "This is your new Godmother, don't laugh." As the congregation processed to the muddy riverbank, their hymns rising with the morning mist, a church sister with silver-streaked hair offered to hold Brown so Maybelle could be baptized. Maybelle's eyes sparkled with unexpected joy as she joined the line of parishioners waiting to be immersed in the cool, redemptive waters.

For four years, Anna immersed herself in her studies at the all-Negro women's college, with Gracie by her side through every lecture and late-night study session. Each holiday, she'd return home clutching textbooks and notes, eager to share everything with Maybelle. Together, they'd gather Brown at the kitchen table, passing knowledge forward like a precious heirloom. "Just imagine," Maybelle would whisper, eyes bright with possibility, "the first doctor in our family." Brown absorbed their lessons like rainfall on parched earth. When Anna's graduation brought an offer to teach at a colored school in Baltimore, she begged Maybelle and Brown to join her new life. But Maybelle just shook her head, her fingers trailing along the worn doorframe of Penelope's house. The day Anna left, Maybelle pressed a small cloth pouch of money into her palm and said, "Remember, no matter what happens in Baltimore, Mississippi will always be home.

"In Baltimore, Anna found a room in a modest boarding house and settled into her new teaching job on the negro part of town. Every week, she sent money south for Maybelle and her baby.

One evening, the store's streetlamp glow fell across a familiar figure: Reverend B'moe, striding purposefully toward his church. At the sight of him, Anna felt a flurry of surprise—and rage. She dashed into the street, shouting, "Cotton! I thought they hung you in Louisiana! How dare you leave Maybelle with a baby and no support!". Passersby froze. B'moe faltered, cheeks flushing. A matronly pedestrian tried to calm Anna, but she backed away and spat, This man of clergy cloth treated my friend abominably ill, vanishing, leaving her with child and no support. The child constantly asks about his father and no one has heard nothing from him until today. B'moe bowed his head and brushed past her into the sanctuary. No sooner had he crossed the threshold than the senior minister approached. "Bad news," he said. "You're being transferred to Hempstead, Long Island. They need a pastor there. When can you leave?"

B'moe looked surprised but smiled. "I've been dreaming of New York. I'll pack tonight." The reverend's lips curved into a knowing smile. "You'll need something special to fill those pews," he told Cotton. "Something to set you apart." When Cotton asked what he meant, the reverend reached into an old wooden cabinet and retrieved a small box. Inside lay a tambourine, its metal discs catching the light. Cotton lifted it with uncertainty. "This?" he asked, turning it in his hands. The reverend nodded firmly. "Learn to play it. Incorporate it into your sermons. Trust me—they'll come to hear a preacher who can make music with the word of God."

And so the two lives, once intertwined in scandal and sorrow, each set off into new chapters—Anna chasing redemption, teaching her people in the black world of Baltimore, and Cotton, now Reverend B'moe, on his way to yet another pulpit, far from the past they shared.

Baby Boy Brown Brown

Maybelle woke each dawn before the sun slipped over the pines, her heart full of a dream that stretched far beyond the ramshackle shack she and little Brown called home. She longed for him a life richer than her own had been. Five miles away, a humble schoolhouse—its wooden siding worn silver by rain and wind—welcomed Black children whose hunger for learning matched his. Every morning, Maybelle spooned smooth peanut butter across two slices of coarse country bread, sprinkled them with ruby-red strawberry bits, and tucked a tiny jar of mild, pickled pepper peanuts into a battered tin bucket along with his chalk and slate. Brown set off down the dusty lane, the tang of peanuts and strawberry sweetness trailing behind him like a promise. When the last bell tolled, she waited beneath the moss–draped oak to walk him to her grandmother's peanut stand, their slow return journey a precious ritual of homework recitals, new facts, and the shy bloom of wonder in Brown's eyes.

One evening, when Brown was about nine, the mercantile's lantern-eyed owner, Mr. Henry, rapped at Maybelle's door. She opened it to find him pivoting on the threshold, lantern in hand and concern on his broad face. "Maybelle, we need to talk about Brown," he said softly. "The story of how he came into this world—it's a painful one, and he's old enough to wonder who his father is. Folks around here whisper that Anna took your man and nearly everything else. Cotton's vanished, and no one knows where. How long can you keep the truth from your son?" Maybelle's chin fell; her knuckles lightened against the doorframe. "I—I know," she murmured. Mr. Henry stepped onto the porch, the boards creaking underfoot. "That boy needs a man's guidance—how to work, save, marry, and provide. I want to employ him after school, teach him the store trade for a few hours. Saturdays, I'll take him fishing—teach him how to catch supper with his own hands. He needs a father's lessons, Maybelle." She nodded, tears welling behind her calm eyes. "Thank you," she whispered. Mr. Henry gripped her shoulder. "And don't worry: I won't feed him my version of your business. You're his mother—one day you'll tell him the rest."

The next afternoon, Brown lingered by the schoolhouse steps while a cluster of classmates headed home together. Maybelle knelt beside him in the late-afternoon hush and said, "You're growing strong now. You can walk home with the others. After school, instead of coming to the peanut stand, you'll head to Mr. Henry's store and help him." Brown blinked, excitement and pride in his chest. "Then on Saturday, he'll take you fishing," she added, brushing the sweat from his forehead. Brown grinned and ran alongside the huddle of children.

Inside Mr. Henry's mercantile, rows of kerosene lamps cast a honeyed glow across dusty shelves of beans, flour sacks, and tin cans. "Hey, Brown," the owner greeted him, slinging an affectionate arm over the boy's shoulder. "Your ma says you can help around here. Sweep that front stoop, dust these counters, wipe the windows. Around 5:30, we'll have our 'man talk'—just you and me. After that, I'll walk you home." Brown tilted his head. "Man talk?" "Sure," Mr. Henry said gently. "It's when two fellows talk about life. I ain't had a son to teach the ways of a man, and your father's not here to do it. It'd do us both good." Brown smiled shyly. "Do you know my father?" Mr. Henry's smile softened. "Not well—only glimpsed him once or twice. But from what I saw, if he walked in right now, you'd know the likeness." Brown's eyes lit. "Was he tall?" Mr. Henry looked at his watch. "Brown, you're on my time now. If you want to learn about your father, you'll have to ask your ma. I'm here to be a father to you in his absence." Brown nodded, content.

And so, each afternoon Brown polished the wooden floorboards, lined dusty bottles on the shelves, learned to tally inventory and greet customers with a respectful nod. Every day at half past five they shared confidences: Mr. Henry's youthful misadventures, Brown's school lessons, dreams of the future. On Saturdays, they stood by the sunlit lake's edge, rods in hand, the water's surface rippling like molten glass. They talked of grades and girls, of what it meant to be honest and hardworking. Yet still Brown asked, more softly each week, "Mr. Henry, who is my father?" Once, overhearing Brown pose the question to a passing stranger, Mr. Henry's brows furrowed. He clenched his jaw, then knelt to meet Brown's gaze. "Your father's not here," he said, voice tight. "If he ever comes back, I'll point him out to you. I'm sorry, son." His shoulders sagged, and he pulled Brown into a gentle embrace, tasting the boy's silent hurt as keenly as if it were his own.

Summers brought Anna back to their little clearing by the shack, her pale cotton dress fluttering in the warm Mississippi breeze. Brown—his amber eyes wide, dimples deep—peppered her with questions: Who is my father? Where had he gone? Year by year, her answers grew thinner until one evening, as cicadas drummed their twilight chorus, she sought Maybelle on the porch swing. "Maybelle," she whispered, voice trembling like a leaf in the breeze, "I saw Cotton." Maybelle set aside her knitting, heart thundering. "In town?" "No—Baltimore," Anna said, gaze fixed on the worn floorboards. "He spotted me across a crowded street and ran like the devil himself was chasing him. I called out about the baby, but he vanished. He's preaching in a grand stone church there—stained glass and marble columns. I asked the secretary of his whereabouts, but she shut the door in my face." Anna's fingers twisted her skirt. "What do I tell Brown?" Maybelle reached for Anna's hand, her voice soft as a hymn. "Tell him his father is gone for now. If God wills it, He'll bring them together. Let the boy trust in that—and promise him he won't end up like his father. Promise him an education, a life of his own making."

Mr. Henry, too, made his vow to Brown: one day this store, all its ledgers and shelves, would be the boy's inheritance—a living to call his own, a roof over his head should he ever need to come home.

At last, the day arrived for Brown's journey north. Maybelle stood in the dawn light, her worn shawl wrapped tight around her shoulders as she handed him a large pickle jar. "I've been saving this for your college fund," she said, voice steady though tears glimmered in her eyes. Brown clasped the cool glass. "Thank you, Momma," he said, voice gentle. "But I've been working every day after school, too. I saved some of my own. I'll make it in this world, and if I ever need that jar, I'll call you." He pressed a kiss to her cheek, shouldered his small satchel, and stepped into the morning mist. As the train carried him toward Hempstead, New York, Maybelle watched until the last railcar vanished, certain that in his heart, Brown carried with him the promise of hope, love, and a future luminous enough to outshine every shadow of the past.

Big Momma

The long afternoons on Long Island stretched golden and hazy, as if painted in sunlight and the sweet tang of melting ice cream. A salty breeze drifted in from the bay, rustling the willow trees that lined their quiet street. One sultry afternoon, the family piled into the wood-paneled station wagon for a trip to Grandma Sasha's. Willie—vivacious, quick-witted Willie— chattered about a scandalous novel she'd discovered, her laughter dancing like bright streamers in the confining car. Camile's face tightened; before anyone could react, she slapped Willie so sharply that a hush fell over the gathering of cousins and friends. Willie's hands flew to her reddening cheek as tears welled in her eyes. Sissy swooped in, pulling the stunned child close, voice low but fierce: "How could you treat her like this? One day she'll stand before you, and you'll need her mercy—and she'll have none to give."

That blow marked the beginning of Camile's zealotry. She dove headlong into the doctrines of the church, Bible verses memorized like sacred armor. Willow—tender, dreamy Willow—followed her mother to every revival meeting, absorbed every prayer shawl and hymn. Willie, by contrast, felt the walls closing in. She craved whispered confidence under moonlight, soft kisses on warm skin, and the approving smile of someone who saw her brightness instead of her sin. When she was sixteen, a handsome boy with eyes like storm clouds taught her the tender language of longing. But Camile, perched on the front porch in her Sunday bonnet, sneered, "He'll only get you pregnant and vanish. No decent man wants a wild child like you." Afraid to disappoint her—or risk her wrath, Willie slipped away at the dawn, leaving him a note that tasted of tears and regret. And so it went with every hopeful suitor: Camile's warnings drove them off, and Willie's heart grew hollow and cold.

On the eve of Willow's wedding—another church affair bathed in white lilies—Camile leaned close to Willie and whispered, "Promise me you'll never marry. Men only break your heart." Willie, dressed in muted gray bridesmaid's lace, felt the words like chains snapping shut around her chest. Then came the day Willie packed for college. Willow watched from the doorway as her sister shouldered trunks stamped with distant university crests. On the mailbox, letters bloomed each morning to Willie from Big Momma— olive-green envelopes, pastel postcards—all tokens of maternal pride. Camile never sent so much as a postcard.

Meanwhile, at home, Camile's single-minded faith eroded her marriage. Cecil—once sturdy and cheerful—grew restless under sermons and scolding alike. One frigid night, Camile and Willow sat in a revival tent under flickering lanterns, droning hymns into the damp air. Cecil slipped away and found himself in a dim bar, its jukebox humming a blues lament. He ordered bourbon on the rocks and sank onto a scarred oak stool, where a woman with cascading chestnut hair and velvet-dark eyes offered him a gentle smile. "Can I buy you a drink?" he croaked. Amid the haze of cigarette smoke, he poured out the loneliness Camile had never soothed. Nights turned to Saturdays. Their rendezvous shifted from the bar's sticky floor to coffee-stained tables in quiet cafés, then to candlelit dinners scented with rosemary. Finally, one throbbing night, they succumbed to each other—something Camile's icy devotions had denied him for years.

By dawn, Cecil knew he could not endure neither Camile's rages nor the guilt in Willie's haunted eyes. When the bank's foreclosure notice arrived, he whispered a goodbye in the darkness, packed a single bag, and slipped out. Camile woke to an empty house and Willow's stunned tears. Soon, she was forced to squat in Madame Hartford's ancestral home, its windows shuttered against the world.

Then came the letter. Willie, writing from a cramped Los Angeles apartment, learned she'd won a fashion scholarship at Hampton University. Pride and envy crackled in her mother's eyes like wildfire.

"She's going to live her life," Camile muttered, voice brittle. "I was trapped in a marriage that fell apart over nothing." Willow, left behind, fumed. She was rejected by every college; in Yonkers, ostensibly to preserve the family's meager inheritance. In the dusty parlor of the Hartford house, Willow tended to Camile's silver hair and the old schnauzer's salt-and-pepper curls, her deep brown eyes glinting not with compassion but calculation. Whenever Willie returned home, Camile whispered slander to their neighbors—rumors of drug use, lesbian affairs, extravagance—all aimed at painting Willow as the dutiful daughter and Willie as a selfish opportunist.

High above, the spirit Utopia hovered, invisible but unblinking, as malice spiraled through the household. She watched as grief gnawed at Camile's bones: first her legs blackened, oozing with pain; then a grotesque tumor bloomed at her throat. Willow herself began to decay—her bright smile darkened into gum-ridden hollows, each tooth dropping like raindrops from an empty sky. These were no accidents but divine justice for the poison they'd poured into an innocent life.

When Sasha died penniless—leaving her trembling in the drafty mansion—Camile leaned on Willow like a crutch. Together, they convinced Willie to sell her loft in California and ship her cherished gowns east to care for her dying mother. Willie's heart split in two as she hung up her phone: "What about my car? My clothes?" she sobbed. Camile's frail voice drifted back, crackling through the line: "Don't worry, child. You will get more. You only have one mother."

Willie arrived beneath a gray sky to find Willow on the sagging porch, arms crossed. Days stretched into weeks as the repossession agent hauled away Willie's car. Willow scrutinized Camile's pills, her broth, her every tremor—offering neither kindness nor a single dollar. "You had your life," she hissed at Willie. "Now it's my turn." "Your turn with someone else's money!" Willie shrieked, but the echo died in the empty halls.

When Camile finally slipped away, Willow staged her coup. She changed the locks by dawn's first light, emptied the bank account, and read the will in a candle-lit drawing room. "To my dear Willow I leave everything," she announced, venom dripping from her words. "Willie gets nothing." With that, Willow, shoved Willie out the door, slammed it shut, and dialed the police on her cell phone. At the precinct, bruised and bewildered, Willie curled into herself as an officer drove her to the battered women's shelter, its fluorescent corridors cold as tears.

Far above, Camile's soul drifted upward through pearly clouds toward the radiant realm of Utopia. Light caressed her face, yet every bitter memory clung like shackles. When she reached the throne of cosmic justice, she whimpered, "But she was always in the streets. I only gave to the daughter who obeyed me." Utopia's gaze was an ocean of stars—unyielding and infinite. "You had two children," she intoned. "The one you crushed with neglect is the one who cared for you in your final days. Look." Beneath them, a translucent floor revealed Willie huddled in the shelter's doorway, her life unraveling in desperation. Camile's chest convulsed, but her pleas dissolved into silence as the floor vanished beneath her feet. She screamed once, then fell into the scorching abyss, her wails a requiem of regret.

Below, the shelter's narrow rooms hummed with the harsh glow of fluorescent lights. Volunteers in faded jeans guided Willie to a tiny apartment in the nearby projects, where poverty clung to damp plaster walls like mildew. It was there she met Marvin, a carpenter whose rough hands bore the stories of oak and pine. His laughter was warm as a hearth fire, and under a canopy of paper lanterns in a humble courtyard, they vowed their love. Their modest home filled with laughter and the sizzle of frying chicken, the sweet chill of potato salad folded with creamy mayonnaise, each meal an embrace of comfort.

But happiness proved fragile. Late one night, the police raided the abandoned warehouse where Marvin worked, and the clang of steel bars sealed his fate. And on an icy winter evening, fire swept through their block like a merciless storm, swallowing every child they'd held dear. Bereft and broken, Willie found herself at dusk on the brick lawn of Fortum University, clutching a brown-paper bag of malt liquor and a pack of Kool cigarettes. The ivy climbed the clock tower, its shadow stretched long across her hollow cheeks. Yet even then, behind the weight of betrayal and loss, a spark of her old ambition flickered—fragile but unextinguished—beneath a sky that still remembered stars.

UNFAITHFUL

Bea Collins, the owner of a boarding house nestled in the historic Kingsley section of Buffalo, had built her establishment into a discreet fortress of desire over the course of twenty meticulous years. Catering exclusively to Buffalo's most influential elites, Bea orchestrated encounters that skirted the edge of morality—a hidden world where even a bishop's clandestine desires could be indulged. One bright, if morally ambiguous, day, Bishop Petunia arrived at Bea's establishment seeking forbidden female companionship and was immediately drawn to a youthful teenager. With a calm yet cunning smile, the bishop approached his trusted confidante. "How much for her?" he inquired, the weight of his desire palpable in the hushed corridor.

Bea's eyes twinkled with a mixture of mischief and business acumen as she replied, "I've been waiting for you, preacher man. You see, she's a virgin, which means she commands top dollar—five grand." The bishop's face paled for a moment as he recalled the modest building fund, securely tucked away in a battered shoebox on the top shelf of his closet. With a shaky gasp, he finally consented, "You got yourself a deal."

That very night, Bishop Petunia returned, clutching the precious shoebox filled with funds reappropriated from the church's building collection. As he approached the heavy wooden door, Bea swiftly reached out to embrace the money. Abruptly, the bishop recoiled and demanded, "Where's the girl?" Bea's lips curled into a mischievous smile as she explained, "Oh, she's upstairs, being bathed in rose petals, milk, and honey. It's her first time—naturally, we don't want her to be marred by the scent of virgin blood." The bishop, half agonizing over his transgression yet seduced by the details, handed over the money, allowing Bea to lead him up the creaking wooden stairs.

However, as they reached the top, a sudden commotion erupted. The maid, with a frantic gleam in her eyes, barreled toward them, shrieking, "The child done left!" The pair exchanged stunned glances. In a swift motion, Pastor Petunia snatched the shoebox of money and hastened down the stairs. Not missing a beat, Bea grasped his arm and cooed, "Honey, you need your manly needs properly attended to—and I can provide that for you."

Infuriated and yearning, Pastor Petunia roared in protest, "I want a young girl, you are too old!" Bea's smile turned seductively condescending as she countered, "That young girl would only have brought you complications—a potential baby that could jeopardize your congregation and livelihood. Though I may not be the picture of youth, with me, you need never fear a trailing child. I offer know-how in delivering superior womanly pleasure, and I'm charging a mere one hundred and fifty dollars—that's less than half the price of that little hussy!" Caressing him gently, Bea sent a shiver through the bishop; his arousal became evident as he whispered, "Alright, it's only a buck fifty and no babies." Bea's smile widened as she led him toward a dimly lit room.

That night, as the clock's hands crept toward the first blush of dawn, Bishop Petunia and Bea entwined themselves in a passionate liaison that stretched into the early hours of the morning. When the time came for the bishop to depart, Bea, ever the gracious hostess, prepared him a warm cup of tea—knowing full well that morning tea was a cherished ritual among ministers. As the bishop sipped the soothing brew, Bea carefully gathered his scattered belongings, remarking on the delight of the evening. Once the bishop had dressed and readied himself to leave, he retrieved his treasured shoebox and meticulously counted out one hundred and fifty dollars. "I'll see you next week," he murmured, traversing the threshold as Bea gently escorted him to the doorway.

With a heart burdened by sin, Bishop Petunia departed the brothel—a man painfully aware of the transgression not only against God and his wife, but against himself. In the solitude of his thoughts, he fervently prayed that his indiscretions would not culminate in a divine retribution, like the scourge of syphilis. And so, week after week, he returned to Bea's establishment, each visit ushering in a familiar, desperate prayer of repentance—until, one fateful day, everything changed.

Mrs. Brown

Whoreneesha Maxwell who was lovingly called Neesha, was conceived during a one-night stand on a bitterly cold night in a dimly lit room in a rundown hotel near the Rockville Center projects. Her mother wasn't entirely sure who the father was, though the baby bore a resemblance to a married man with whom she had had an affair. Not wanting the hassle of taking a man to court only to find he wasn't the father, Beverly chose to keep quiet. In those days, few cared to identify a child's father. When Neesha was born, her mother secured a bit of cash, some food stamps, and an apartment in the Freeport Projects from social services—standard procedure.

At Neesha's birth, Beverly was content with her modest apartment, despite the occasional roach or rat. There was food every first of the month, someone to love, and someone who loved her in return. Life was relatively good for Neesha during those times. On frosty winter nights, she and her mother would cuddle close in front of an open oven for warmth, since the heating in the projects was unreliable. Sometimes, her mother would boil water on the stove and stand by it, watching the steam billow out of the pot. When money ran short, they resorted to food pantries, where each visit held the surprise of not knowing what they'd receive.

Things took a downturn when her mother landed a job as a bartender—her moral restraint evaporated. Night after night, she spent long hours away from home, her neglect growing with every absence. She would stagger back into their small apartment, accompanied by a new man every night, retreat to her bedroom with a slammed door, ignoring Neesha entirely. Sadly, her only solace was the weekly visits from the neighborhood women attending the Jehovah's Witness meetings. Each Saturday, they arrived, their presence heralded by the delicate scent of gardenias. Their cocoa-brown hands, softened by moisturizing lotions from the local drugstores, offered Neesha a rare measure of comfort and peace, contrasting sharply with the rest of her life.

Neesha's stark contrast stood in stark contrast to Beverly Maxwell, infamous for her promiscuity. Known far and wide, she frequented bars, always enveloped in her signature fragrance, "Wild Irish Rose." Under the stage name "Bev the wine-o," she worked at a strip club, mingling with all sorts of men, whom Neesha was forced to call "uncle".

Each morning before school, Neesha served breakfast to her mother and her mother's ever-changing boyfriends. The meal was a curious assortment: heated Pop-Tarts, pickled pig's feet straight from a large jar on the counter, and a glass of Diet Coke with a shot of Wild Irish Rose, garnished with a lemon slice. Struggling to keep the Pop-Tarts sufficiently warm, Neesha would hurriedly drop the tray on the dresser and dash off to school, carrying with her the lingering scent of cheap liquor and cigarettes.

Meanwhile, Sylvia Silversmith navigated the supermarket aisles, gathering donations for the local food pantry. As she passed through an aisle, an elderly woman called out, "Hello, dear, could you spare a few dollars so a frail old woman might get a bite to eat?" Sylvia, compassionate and kind, retrieved her purse from the shopping cart, pulled out a crisp twenty-dollar bill, and extended it toward the old woman. As the woman reached for the money, she deftly slipped her basket into Sylvia's cart, snatched the bill, and exclaimed, "Thank you!" Unfazed, Sylvia quickly pushed the cart to the register, had her groceries rung up and bagged, then sped out the door. When the old woman realized her basket had been lost and Sylvia was nowhere in sight, she shouted, "The Peanuts!"

This prompted her to rush through the supermarket in a frenzy, only to peer out the window and see Sylvia speeding away with what appeared to be the magical peanuts in her possession.

PROPHECY FULFILLED

"Pastor, we're going to have a baby!" Bea's triumphant announcement rang out, her voice trembling with a mix of awe and defiance. Pastor Petunia's eyes narrowed as he fixed his gaze upon the elderly woman, his face contorted by shock and indignation. In a voice that boomed with authority and disbelief, he bellowed, "Get out of town!" The harsh command ricocheted off the room's linoleum walls, its cadence mismatched with the reverence expected of a man of God.

The old woman recoiled, her deeply etched wrinkles deepening as she absorbed his words, a stark betrayal of the sacred dignity associated with his role. Undeterred, she drew him into a hesitant embrace, her arms trembling with both worry and tenderness as she whispered, "The devil must have stirred your tongue, causing you to curse against me and our unborn child. Surely, you don't truly mean those words?" With a brusque shove, he reclaimed his space, settling himself on the edge of the modest bed. In the dim light, he looked upward—where shadows danced on the ceiling—and spoke in a voice that was at once calm and resolute. "This is not the work of Satan; it is my own doing. I am a married man, entrusted with a church passed down through generations. I must uphold a standard for all who depend on me, so, damn it, I need you to get the hell out of town."

Bea's eyes shone with compassion as she replied softly, "Honey, I ain't going nowhere. This baby is nothing short of a miracle. I never imagined, even once, that I could have children, and now, at this stage in my life, I'm about to be a mother! You are a true man of God!" Her words flowed with a fierce pride as she added, "You need not proclaim your divinity— let this child bear my name and silence all doubts. Oh Bishop Petunia, thank you for my child!"

Nine months later, Bea's miracle child was born into a world replete with whispered hopes and secret blessings, and she crowned him with the name Clive Collins. Yet, barely three weeks after this joyous arrival, Bea found herself contending with an unwelcome visitor: First Lady Petunia.

In the quietly opulent parlor, where Bea cradled little Clive in her arms and soft lamplight mingled with the shadows of dusk, Ella Mae's eyes darted disdainfully over the luxurious furnishings. Her tone was icy as she asked, "What do you plan to do with your bastard?" Bea, undeterred by the cutting remark, offered a serene smile and said, "I plan to raise him. What business is it of yours?"

Ella Mae's shocked stare, laced with indignation and incredulity, revealed her mounting dismay that a woman of questionable character would dare address a God-fearing first lady so crudely. "How dare you speak to me in that manner!" she thundered. "You know that child is my husband's. Hand him over to me, for I alone understand how to raise him properly. You—a woman of ill repute—what could you possibly teach him? Give him to me!"

Bea's laugh, rich with unyielding defiance, cut through the charged silence. "Why don't you have your own child and leave mine alone?" she retorted. Furious, the first lady shot back, "He looks exactly like my husband and nothing like you! We can raise this baby as if he were our own!" Bea's smile deepened into a confident grin as she declared, "Everyone knows I am his mother!" Lowering her voice, Ella Mae pleaded, "We will adopt him, and in time, people will forget the scandal. Just give me the child, I beg you, so we may raise him in the ways of our Lord—far from sin and shame."

With indignation boiling over, Bea rose to her feet and ordered the first lady out of her home with a commanding tone. In a desperate bid, Ella Mae sank to her knees, clutching Bea's leg as she sobbed, "Please, give me the baby! He is my husband's son— we deserve a child!" Without hesitation, Bea yanked her leg free and, in a moment of raw intensity, delivered a fierce kick to the first lady's face. Screaming, she declared, "Get off me! That very hand you clutched in the hospital was mine, and I warned you one day you'd yield to our truth. The answer is no—now leave!"

Crushed by humiliation and fury, the first lady staggered to her car, tears mingling with her despair as she realized that the secret of the pastor's adulterous sin would soon ripple through the sanctuary. That night, before sleep could claim her, she ascended into the silent sanctuary. Her head held high despite her lowered spirits, she knelt at the altar beneath flickering candlelight, praying fervently that God would fortify her against the forthcoming torrent of gossip and disgrace. When her prayers subsided, she returned home, creeping into bed beside her snoring, unfaithful husband—her mind heavy with the burden of scandal and the bitter taste of betrayal.

Snatched

When Sylvia reached the pantry, her eyes landed on the familiar wicker basket that had been nestled in the back of her car. With a swift motion, she retrieved the packet of peanuts from the basket and tossed them into a sturdy paper bag. She then strode purposefully into the bustling charitable organization, where the air buzzed with warm chatter and the scent of fresh produce. "Hello, Sylvia!" the volunteers called out in delight, their voices ringing with genuine warmth. "You're just in time—there's a child here, eager to take some food home to her family." One of the volunteers, positioned at the back, added with a hopeful lilt, "You can hand the bag to her, and we'll add a few more items to another bag. Neesha, do you think you can carry it?" The question echoed through the room, filled with the spirit of community and care.

Upon reaching home, Neesha unfastened the bag, and the very first thing that caught her eye was a dazzling jar filled with Penelope's fiery red hot pickled peppered peanuts. The jar was adorned with a charming brown string tied neatly around its lid, glinting in the light. With a mix of anticipation and determination, she placed her hand firmly on top of the jar and twisted with every bit of her strength, yet the lid stubbornly refused to budge.

Just then, her mother emerged from the next room, drawn by the commotion, and gently inquired, "Wat'cha got there, Neesha?" In a soft, hopeful tone, Neesha replied, "The food pantry gave me these peanuts, but I can't seem to open them. Could you help me, Momma?"

Her mother leaned in, examined the beautifully decorated jar and the enticing peanuts inside, and remarked, "Yes, they do look delicious. But have you noticed the little lever on the side of the jar? Did you try using that?" With a graceful motion, she attempted to raise the lever, yet it too remained immovable. With a mixture of surprise and humor, she mused aloud, "Wow, maybe you ought to ask the maintenance department at your school tomorrow and see what they can do."

The following day, Neesha carried the prized jar of peanuts to school, where the team of maintenance men gathered around to try every means to pry the jar open. They experimented with a can opener, a wrench, and even a screwdriver, yet nothing could break the jar's steadfast seal. Finally, one of the maintenance men picked up the jar, its vintage charm evident, and said, "This jar of peanuts is an antique—no wonder it won't open. It's probably worth a million dollars! Neesha, take this jar home with you and hide it well. And if anyone tries to claim it, just say you've lost it and send them on their way. Always keep it close because it's certainly valuable."

Neesha nodded solemnly, carefully placed the jar back into her knapsack, and later, at home, stashed it deep in the recesses of an old cabinet behind the kitchen sink. No sooner had she tucked it away than a sharp knock echoed through the house. At the door stood an elderly woman with an air of urgency. "Hello, deary," the old woman greeted warmly, her voice carrying hints of both gentleness and purpose. Neesha's mother exchanged puzzled glances with her as the visitor continued, "My granddaughter mistakenly dropped some groceries at the food pantry, and in the tumble, my peanuts ended up in the bag. Have you seen them by any chance?"

Neesha's mother offered an apologetic smile, "I'm sorry, miss, but my daughter took them to school, and only God knows what those mischievous kids did with them—they're so greedy, they probably ate them!" A brief laugh escaped her, yet the old woman remained stern. "Do you think I could speak with the child alone to see if she still has them?"

Stepping quietly from behind her mother, Neesha greeted the visitor with a tentative "Hello." Meeting her gaze with a calm, soothing tone, the old woman said, "Hello, my child. I'm in search of my peanuts. They were mistakenly placed in the bag you received from the food pantry."

Neesha's eyes dropped in remorse as she whispered, "I'm sorry, we ate them." The old woman's face twisted with sudden anger, and she shot back, "You must be lying. How could you have opened that jar? No one but me can open it. You couldn't have eaten them—return those peanuts to me at once; they are not meant for you."

At that moment, Neesha's mother intervened firmly, "Listen, Miss, my child said she doesn't have the peanuts. Now, kindly leave my house before I call the cops." The old woman's eyes widened as she imagined the possibility of a police visit, and, retreating slowly while pointing an accusatory finger at Neesha, she warned, "You may have gotten away with holding onto the peanuts for now, but when I have you alone, you will hand them over to me, or face the consequences." With that ominous declaration, the old woman turned on her heel and trudged down the street, muttering curses to the very sky above.

LIKE MOTHER LIKE SON

Bea cherished Clive above all, pouring her heart into ensuring he had the finest clothes and the most prestigious schools at his disposal. Yet as Clive grew, a storm of rebellion stirred within him. No matter the lengths to which Bea went, he would sternly declare that his singular dream was to emulate the path of his infamous mother—a life as a pimp. One fateful day, Bea resolved to reveal to Clive the truth about his father, secretly hoping that the revelation might steer him toward a path of righteousness rather than incarceration.

Bea summoned Clive into her modest, cluttered office, where the air was thick with years of secrets and sorrow. With a tremor in her voice, she said, "I know how desperately you long to follow in my footsteps, but remember, I am only half of you. You have a father, and for the sake of us all, I believe it's high time you honored his legacy." Clive's eyes, dark and stormy with contempt, fixed on his mother. "Who is my so-called Daddy? Is it that preacher? That's the chatter making its rounds!" he spat bitterly. "Clive, your daddy is a preacher!" Bea's voice quivered as she leaned forward in her creaking chair, her eyes searching his for understanding. "Yes, Clive, your Daddy is a preacher. You must embrace that Bible wisdom before you find yourself behind bars like so many other black men. I was a mistress because madams found it easier, but a black pimp is treated like a murderer. They plant evidence on pimps when they get arrested. You, selling white women, are treading on dangerous ground— society despises the sight of a black man with a white woman, especially one who abuses them. Think about what happened to Malcolm; even as a God-fearing Muslim, he received a large amount of unfair time for pimping white women. You will have to change course, or prison will be the one to change it for you."

With those harsh words echoing in the cramped room, Clive stormed out of the office and left the debased confines of the whorehouse. His furious steps carried him onto the street, where fate intervened as he collided with Bishop Petunia. The Bishop, taken aback by Clive's striking resemblance to someone he had long known, gasped in shock. "I'm so sorry, son!" Clive bellowed, his anger and heartache intermingling. "Sorry? For bumping into me, or for being a deadbeat father?" Bishop Petunia steadied him with gentle urgency, his voice soft yet tentative. "I am no deadbeat. Since you were born, I've sent your momma twenty dollars a week. You were conceived in sin, and while I cannot claim a bastard, I did the best I could by you." Clive, recoiling as if the Bishop's words were a physical blow, shoved him away fiercely. "Get off me! twenty dollars—is that all I'm worth? At least I'm not some raggedy preacher clinging to my dead daddy's legacy!"

Around the time Clive first cried out into the world, scandal quietly gathered steam within the church walls. The church secretary, who had long served alongside the pulpit, found herself pregnant—a secret rumored to be the Bishop's own child. As soon as her condition was confirmed, she was whisked away to Asbury Park, New Jersey. There, she gave birth to a son whom she named Sigmund. With practiced ease, she spun a tale to her new friends and neighbors: his father had been a military hero, slain by experimental explosives, and it was the military that had supported her and the child in their hour of need. No soul suspected that it was Pastor Petunia who had discreetly sent money to help raise the boy.

As Sigmund grew strong and steady, he was soon seated on a piano stool—his small fingers dancing over the keys under the tutelage of a nearby church musician. With each lesson, he nurtured a quiet dream: that one day he might journey back to Buffalo, play for the congregation under his father's watchful care, and offer solace to the old Bishop in his later years.

Way Out

Neesha never experienced the soothing comfort of a mother's love; instead, she was the reluctant caretaker of an alcoholic, burdened with sorrow from a tender age. Her threadbare clothes and worn-out appearance made her an easy target for cruelty, and at school, the other children mockingly dubbed her the "Coody girl." The pungent odor of cheap liquor mixed with stale cigarettes—reminders of her turbulent, dysfunctional home—had become something she instinctively despised.

As she grew older, Neesha resolutely abstained from drinking or smoking. Every sip or puff stirred up painful memories of a neglected childhood, unlike most girls who reveled in the dreams of glamorous proms, bustling college life, or carefree outings with friends. Instead, she nurtured a humble yet steadfast dream:

to create a stable home adorned with the laughter of beautiful children and supported by the loving presence of a devoted husband who would cherish her. Each night, in the dim solitude of her modest room, she would tenderly clutch the jar of peanuts kept on her nightstand. With a heart full of hope, she whispered fervent prayers, yearning to be whisked away from the clutches of Beverly and her destructive boyfriends. As she squeezed the jar tight, she imagined a future of security—a family where a protective husband and even an adopted brother would ensure that loneliness was banished forever. In the quiet of her nighttime prayers, Utopia leaned in and murmured, "Do not worry, my little child; one day these humble peanuts will guide you to the husband, adopted brother, and children destined for you."

One fateful night, the fragile cocoon of her existence was shattered when one of Beverly's unruly boyfriends stealthily slipped int Neesha's room. With sinister intent, he crept into her bed and attempted to violate her. Startled awake by the unwelcome presence of what she considered her mother's boyfriend, Mrs. Brown bolted out of bed and raced into the cold, shadowy kitchen. As he pursued her through the darkness, his grip on her wrist tightened like a vise. In that desperate, heart-pounding moment, she seized the first object within reach—a heavy skillet—and struck him forcefully on the head. The resounding thud echoed through the room as he crumpled to the floor. At that very moment, Beverly emerged, witnessing the chaos:

her boyfriend bleeding profusely from his forehead. Consumed with rage, Beverly lashed out verbally, accusing Neesha of being infatuated with men, and deceitfully informed the police that she had attempted to claim her boyfriend after being turned down, leading to an assault. In the aftermath of her outburst, Beverly demanded that the authorities send Neesha to a group home for unruly teens—and they did.

After her release, a spark of hope lit within Neesha. Desperate for someone to take responsibility for her, she pleaded with Beverly to locate her father, believing that his involvement might at last mend her fractured life. In a venomous reply, Beverly screamed, "Your daddy don't want you! He has 42 kids and doesn't know any of them. You're just another statistical mistake. Jail is where you belong, among the rest of the lost souls!" Overwhelmed by bitterness, Beverly raised her hands and shouted, "I want to be like your daddy! I want to shirk any responsibility, living free of obligations just as he does! I'm sorry, but you've got to go!" With a heavy heart and trembling hands, Neesha gathered the little she possessed—including that treasured jar of peanuts—and tucked them away into her meager luggage. Without a backward glance, Beverly drove her back to the detention center, callously tossed her out of the car, and sped away, leaving Neesha stranded on the roadside as the car door slammed shut behind her.

Dropped off at The Juvenile Detention Center by the very mother who had once been her only caretaker,

Neesha felt the crushing weight of despair. As she walked through the imposing, cold doors of the center, she wondered bitterly, "How can anyone love me when my own mother abandoned me? How can I ever hope to find a decent man who will provide the family I dream of, when my past has been marred by neglect and injustice?" Yet, contrary to her bleak expectations, the world within Juvie proved remarkably different. Though legally bound to the state until she turned eighteen, she encountered compassionate counselors whose patient guidance illuminated a path toward a life of independence. They taught her not only how to secure a job but also how to navigate the complexities of the world on her own, in the absence of both mother and father. Slowly, the warmth of this newfound family, the fellow girls and the kind-hearted staff—began to mend the wounds inflicted by Beverly's cruelty, and she found herself daydreaming of a distant future free from that destructive shadow.

Within those confining walls, Neesha began forging bonds that transcended blood. The friendships she formed blossomed into a sisterhood, and the correctional officers, with their genuine care, assumed the roles of surrogate parents in her heart. It was here that she not only earned her high school diploma but also discovered the transformative magic of small pleasures, learning the graceful art of makeup and finding solace in singing lessons during spirited music classes in the recreation center. With time, she emerged as a natural leader, captaining the choir and leading her newfound sisters to compete in a national contest organized by the Department of Corrections for Juveniles. The officers regaled her with stories of hope, recounting how Ella Fitzgerald, once a ward of the state, had defied the odds and risen to become one of New York's most celebrated jazz legends. They whispered that all it would take was one magnificent performance at The Apollo Theater to set her firmly on a path toward stardom.

When she was finally released, however, lingering doubts about her self-worth taunted her, and instead of journeying to the famed streets of Harlem, she found herself working at a humble local supermarket, conveniently located across the street from Pastor B'more Church of God and Sweet Jesus. One ordinary day, compelled by an inner call, she crossed the threshold of the church and began to sing "Precious Lord." In an almost magical moment, the congregation rose in spontaneous applause, their clapping merging as a powerful affirmation of her hidden talent. That day marked the first time she felt truly seen and appreciated by a wider community for her musical gift—a moment that tethered her spirit to the church, where she soon became a steadfast, cherished member.

Minister of Music

As Sigmond grew older, his delicate nature unfolded in increasingly feminine ways. He reveled in the joy of dressing in flowing women's clothes, carefully choosing each accessory as though it were a treasure, and spending hours playing with intricately detailed dolls while humming soft tunes. In the warmth of his imaginative world, he also discovered a passion for cooking, delighting in mixing flavors and aromas that reminded him of secret gardens of spice and sweetness. One bright school day, when his teacher gently inquired about his lifelong ambition, he answered with a mix of solemnity and playful rebellion, "I want to die and be reincarnated as the third wife of Lord Krishna," Sigmond announced, his voice cutting through the dusty afternoon sunlight streaming through the classroom blinds. Before anyone could react, his lanky frame sprang from the metal chair, arms outstretched like a Bollywood dancer. His sneakers squeaked against the hard wood floors as he twirled, hips swaying, fingers snapping, his oversized white t-shirt twirled around his thin torso. "To the left, to the right, and dip baby dip!" he chanted, eyes closed in mock ecstasy. "Come on now! Dip baby dip!" His teacher, whose copper bangles, jangled as she shot up from her desk, her silk scarf slipping from her shoulders. "Blasphemy!" she screamed, her face flushed. The classroom froze—twenty-seven pairs of wide eyes darting between Sigmond's improvised dance and their teacher's trembling finger pointing toward the door. Within seconds, security appeared in the doorway and escorted the still-grinning Sigmond down the silent hallway to the principal's office.

Later that day, when his mother arrived to collect him amidst the lingering echoes of his antics, her face was etched with worry and resolve. In a soft yet firm tone, she explained that she could no longer raise him on her own. "A boy needs a father to learn how to be a man," she declared, revealing with a trace of both hope and resignation that his father lived in Buffalo—a prominent pastor—and that they would soon journey there to establish a bond. The prospect filled Sigmond with a bubbling excitement; at last, he would meet the missing half of his identity. In preparation for this monumental day, he meticulously pulled out his finest white jeans, a dazzling yellow vest, a crisp white t-shirt, vivid yellow argyle socks, and a cherished pair of white bucks—shoes he had saved for many long months in anticipation of this moment.

Their arrival in Buffalo marked an abrupt departure from the familiar seaside charm of Asbury Park, New Jersey. Gone were the shimmering, sun-drenched beaches; in their stead lay streets littered with discarded needles and broken beer bottles, relics of a harsher reality. The clear, inviting blue skies of his childhood were replaced by a muted canopy of ashen clouds that loomed over factories relentlessly pumping clouds of dirt and smoke into the air, day and night. Frustration welled up in Sigmond, and he cried out to his mother, "Must I stay here?" His mother, offering a soothing yet pragmatic embrace, replied, "Yes, son, this is for the best."

Upon reaching the imposing old church, they patiently waited in the quiet aftermath of a departing congregation. Once the space fell singularly empty, his mother discreetly approached one of the stern-faced deacons and requested a private meeting with Bishop Petunia. Moments later, the deacon reappeared and led them through dim corridors to a small, well-worn office that served as the Bishop's domain. The unexpected arrival of the pair startled the Bishop so vastly that he nearly toppled backwards in his creaky wooden chair. "Why are you here? Don't I send you and the boy enough money?" he bellowed, his voice resonating off the stone walls. During the outburst, a defiant Sigmond interjected, "This boy has a name!"

His voice rang with both indignation and a peculiar tenderness for his own identity. Standing tall, he pointed an accusing finger at the man before him and proclaimed, "Damn money—what about time? I am your son, and I deserve your time!" His words, charged with raw emotion, were quickly hushed by his mother, who gently coaxed him back into his seat. In a low, measured tone, she reminded him, "Sigmond, control yourself. This is your father; you must show decorum." Yet, as he crossed his arms and the mist of his tears fogged his glasses, he questioned in a trembling, almost melodious voice, "What kind of father is he?" The bishop, his eyes narrowing in incredulity, murmured under his breath, "Don't tell me this boy is a sissy?" In that charged silence, Sigmond's gaze met his fathers with unyielding defiance as he affirmed, "Yes, this boy is a sissy!" The tension thickened until his mother interjected firmly once more, "Control yourself, this is a church." Sigmond's wide eyes shone with a mix of hurt and rebellion when he snapped, "So what are you saying? Sissies don't belong in church. Well, the sissy is in church, and what?!" The Bishop, his voice now edged with irate disbelief, demanded, "What the hell do you want from me, woman? Why did you bring this sissy to me?" With uncertainty flickering across her face, Sigmond's mother replied abruptly, "bishop, I don't know what to do. I have raised him as best I could, but it seems my womanly ways have rubbed off on him. He needs his father to teach him how to be a man. I am here because he needs his father." The bishop's face fell into a grave mask of despair; he felt the weight of a legacy slipping away. Without an heir to carry on his name or preserve his legacy, he feared that not only his personal heritage, but the very future of his church hung in the balance.

As the silence stretched and heavy thoughts swirled in the air, Sigmond's mother broke it once more. "Sigmond can play the piano and sing like no other," she declared with a blend of pride and pleading hope. "These are gifts every church cherishes. Can you employ him, give him a proper salary to earn his keep, and in the process, guide him to be the man he is meant to be? We ask only that his origins be kept a secret." After a long, contemplative pause, Pastor Petunia acquiesced, appointing Sigmond as the minister of music—a role that promised both responsibility and a chance at transformation.

That very night, Bishop Petunia led Sigmond and his mother through winding, dim corridors to the church's basement, unveiling a modest living quarter with creaking floors and a single, warm light illuminating the space. "This is where you will stay," he pronounced, his voice echoing off the cold stone walls. Turning suddenly to the boy, he inquired with a tone blending curiosity and command, "What is your name, son?" Sigmond's eyes flashed with incredulity as he retorted, "What do you think my name is? It's Sigmond Petunia—I am your son." The bishop's lips curved into a tight, calculated smile as he replied, "If you plan to stay here, you will change your name immediately and legally. Otherwise, you will leave, and I will deny ever knowing you." That night, as the cool air settled over him and the weight of his future pressed upon his heart, Sigmond resolved that he would change his name to Sigmond Asbury—a tribute to the town and the people who had loved and accepted him.

HEMPSTEAD

Brown arrived at the Hempstead Greyhound bus station in Hempstead, Long Island, on a sweltering August afternoon. The sun blazed down relentlessly, casting shimmering waves of heat off the asphalt. He carried with him only a weathered suitcase, a brown paper bag lunch lovingly prepared by his mother, Maybelle, and a heart brimming with hopes and dreams of love and family. Inside the bag nestled a simple sandwich and a jar of fiery red-hot pickled pepper peanuts, a cherished recipe passed down from his great-grandmother Penelope, who had journeyed from Africa in chains. Hempstead, Long Island, was where Mr. Brown intended to sow his seeds of hope, nurturing them in the fertile soil of opportunity and waiting patiently for his crop of fortune to flourish.

He found refuge in a modest room at a boarding house on Terrace Avenue, its walls whispering tales of past tenants. On the worn, wooden dresser, he placed the jar of peanuts—a poignant reminder of his humble beginnings and the poverty he vowed to transcend. They served as a daily incentive to secure employment at a nearby factory and embark on his new life up north. Settling into his cozy room, Brown resolved to build a future by finding a wife and starting a family. During those first, lonely nights in New York, he mused, "God created woman to help man, and the good Lord knows I need help," a thought that resonated deeply within him.

On his first Sunday in this unfamiliar land, he dressed with care, savored a steaming cup of coffee from the corner store, and set out in search of a church where he might find his beautiful, blushing bride. As he embarked on this new adventure, he smiled at the thought, "He who finds a wife, finds a good thing; that's biblical, so it must be true." His journey led him down Main Street, driven by an urgent need to discover a place of worship.

It was there he stumbled upon "Reverend B'moe's Church of God and Sweet Jesus," a humble storefront with an amusing name. Despite its unassuming appearance, he stepped inside, curiosity piqued. As he entered the small sanctuary, the air was filled with the scent of polished wood and echoes of heartfelt hymns. To his astonishment, the first sight that caught his eye was that of Whoreneesha —a tall, striking woman with smooth, brown skin, slanted eyes, and silky black hair. She stood at the front, her voice soaring as she sang "Precious Lord," and in that moment, Brown's prayers were answered.

Pastor B'moe's church didn't have a musician, so Neesha was left to sing without accompaniment. She cleverly used every sound—whether it was the cry of a baby, the crunch of gum, or any other noise—as a rhythmic guide to keep her in tune. To her, every sound carried its own beat; one simply had to listen and weave the lyrics in between. As she performed before the small congregation filling the church pews, she constantly wondered which sound would serve as her next beat. In the back of the church, Brown sat quietly, musing over how he might catch the attention of someone so beautiful and talented—a sentiment that made him feel like a humble country boy.

Every week, Brown faithfully attended church, secretly hoping that the enchanting songstress might glance his way as she sang her sweet melodies, yet that moment of connection never came. Watching her perform, he imagined her notes floating gracefully past her bright smile, sending out delicate bursts of pink glitter bubbles from her glossy coral lipstick. To him, Neesha was nothing short of a superstar.

Although the world saw her as nothing more than a cashier scanning groceries, though customers always remembered her smile. She'd flip through fashion magazines on break, lingering over spreads where no model shared her deep complexion. At night, standing in front of her bathroom mirror, she'd trace the contours of her face and wonder what might have been. When she sang, though—that was different. Her voice filled her small apartment, bouncing off the walls of what the landlord called "affordable housing" and what everyone else called the ghetto. She'd close her eyes and imagine audiences, record deals, escape. Then the song would end, and she'd open her eyes to see only herself, suddenly small again. Because of these doubts, she kept her singing voice within the protective walls of her church family. Perhaps her talent could have taken her further if not for one disheartening night that shattered her dreams. One day, while she was working at the grocery store, a customer mentioned that The Apollo was hosting an amateur night and urged her to audition. Filled with hope, Neesha left work early to practice at home before boarding the train to Harlem that very night, determined to showcase her gift. However, to her dismay, the legendary Aretha Franklin was also performing on that same evening. When the audience heard the queen of soul, they turned on Neesha, booing her off the stage. Heartbroken, she fled the stage, hurried out the door, and disappeared into the subway, vowing never to set foot in Harlem again.

For Neesha, escape from her cramped life in Hempstead, New York, began and ended with the prospect of marriage to a wealthy man. The tree-lined streets of her small town felt like a cage, each red-brick row house a reminder of bills piling up and dreams deferred. In Neesha's world, a husband's paycheck meant more than companionship—it meant a down payment on a suburban home with a white picket fence, the very emblem of the American Dream she hung in her mind like a prize ribbon.

To prepare, she signed on as a Mary Kay consultant, enticed by the promise of shimmering lipsticks in rose and plum, satin-soft creams packaged in glossy pink jars, and, above all, the chance to call herself an entrepreneur rather than "just the girl at the supermarket checkout." Each time she opened her cosmetic case—its mirrored lid catching the fluorescent kitchen light—she imagined herself handing a client a satin-wrapped compact and hearing her gasp at the smooth canvas of foundation. She pictured the coveted pink Cadillac gleaming in her driveway, its polished curves vindicating her every effort.

But when weeks of late nights calling prospects and hosting candle-lit "makeup parties" yielded only a handful of lukewarm orders, Neesha reluctantly traded cosmetics for overtime shifts. Under the supermarket's harsh overhead lights, she scanned groceries—cartons of milk, bags of flour, crates of wilted lettuce—while the constant beep of the register reminded her how far she'd drifted from her pink Cadillac fantasy. The pay was steady, at least, and allowed her to buy the occasional free lipstick from her Mary Kay stash, the one real silver lining that kept her cheeks dusted with color for Sunday's choir rehearsal.

Music was Neesha's true passion: the only place she felt free of bills and cluttered aisles. She loved the fragrance of polished wood pews mingled with the sweet hiss of hymnals being opened, the way her voice—rich and clear—could rise above the audience and it almost seem to touch heavens door. She believed that if she could become the church's shining soloist, a pastor or bishop would surely notice her gift and welcome her as "First Lady," draped in silk suits and seated beside him in the pulpit, her presence as luminous as her voice.

Night after night, she stood before her bedroom mirror, candlelight flickering against the wallpaper's faded floral pattern, practicing high notes until the glass rattled and rolling her shoulders with the ease of a seasoned performer. She worked on her smile—wide and welcoming, a silent invitation to the congregation—and perfected every soft curve of her expression. In hushed prayers before sleep, she used the power of attraction: she summoned an image of a tall preacher with warm brown eyes bearing a bouquet of a dozen long-stemmed roses and flashing a diamond the size of a promise. "Neesha," he would say, his voice low, "will you marry me?" and he would drop to one knee at the front of the sanctuary, crisp hymnals at his side.

During her shifts at the register, she drifted into daydreams in between scanning beans and bread: she saw herself in a sprawling backyard, her children laughing under a pergola draped in wisteria, while she relaxed in a rocking chair watching "All My Children." She imagined herself on Sunday mornings, heart pounding, as the announcer called her forward: "Sister Neesha Maxwell! Our very own angel-voiced songbird!" Clad in a designer silk suit that caught every beam of light, she would ascend the steps, the congregation hushed in reverent awe. Just as the microphone found her hand, the fantasy would dissolve with a chirp of the scanner and a familiar voice booming out: "Sista, Sista Nee! How ya doin' today? I just love your singin'!"

Smiling, Neesha would look up at the church sister waving from aisle three and tuck her reverie back behind the register keys. Even in these small, stolen moments, she was a star to the people of Hempstead: fans flocked to leave roses by her register, followed her after choir practice to the parking lot, or stood shyly at the grocery entrance on Nassau Road, hoping for an autograph or a smile. Yet none of those admirers stirred her heart like Brown, who sat every Sunday in the front pew, his eyes never leaving her, as though he alone believed in the bright future she was determined to claim.

IMPATIENT

Three Sundays slipped by, and Brown grew increasingly restless as he waited for a chance to speak with Neesha—until one crisp Sunday morning changed everything. That morning, Pastor B'more stood before the assembled congregation and proclaimed that the Church of God and Sweet Jesus would be hosting its much-anticipated annual picnic. All the sanctuaries of their organization were set to converge at the sprawling Eisenhower Park in East Meadow, New York, in three weeks' time for a day filled with jubilant festivities. With his heart pounding and his resolve hardening, Brown decided then and there that he must muster the courage to ask Neesha out for a "Shuga Shake" at the quaint local five-and-dime shop.

The very next day, Brown reached for the telephone, calling his workplace to request any available overtime opportunities, all in the hope of earning enough extra money to purchase new clothes that would allow him to make a striking impression at the picnic. A few days later, he received word from his employer that overtime was available only on Sundays. Though he detested missing the moments when he could hear Neesha's mesmerizing singing, he recognized the necessity of the extra work if he was to look sharp and confident for the upcoming event.

On the other side of these intertwined dreams, Brown radiated excitement at the prospect of the picnic. The moment she overheard the joyful announcement; her high heels nearly flew off her feet from sheer exhilaration. Finally, the opportunity to catch the eye of a prospective husband was before her—preachers and community members from all corners of the country would be present. Resolute, she planned to practice her singing immediately after work and confidently requested the organizer to secure her a solo spot in the program. In her heart, she felt like Cinderella about to step into a magical ball—except this ball was called the picnic at Eisenhower Park, and every detail mattered. Determined to look her very best, she inquired at her job about the possibility of working overtime. However, her manager's sympathetic yet firm reply was, "I know you love going to church, but Sunday is the only day I have available." With the flicker of hope dimming slightly, Neesha accepted, "I'll take it". Knowing that this might be her singular chance to create a lasting impression.

Over the next three Sundays, both Neesha and Brown found themselves working overtime. In the intervening weeks, they roamed the bustling, colorful arrondissements of Jamaica Avenue in Queens, hopping from store to store in search of the perfect outfit that would capture the spirit of the picnic. While Neesha poured her heart into perfecting her high notes, dreaming of dazzling bishop Petunia from Buffalo. In her daydreams, she would capture his attention and win his heart, the grueling hours she spent standing in the supermarket would come to an end, replaced by the promise of a blissful future. Every night, she envisioned a wedding set against the luminous backdrop of a casino in Niagara Falls—a shimmering union that would finally put an end to her years of hardship.

HOPEFUL

Meanwhile, Brown envisioned the moment he would ask Neesha if she might accompany him for a leisurely stroll around the park, and eventually, invite her to share an evening at the movies. In his quiet musings, their aspirations seemed to flank opposite horizons, yet there appeared to be a divine orchestration at play – a force so mighty that what God unites cannot be unraveled, not even by the influential hand of a bishop from Buffalo.

After three long weeks, on the day of the annual picnic, Brown made his way to the Hempstead Bus Terminal. He boarded the N 70, and as the bus rumbled along Hempstead Turnpike, his eyes wandered over a row of bustling storefronts. Amid the familiar parade of local businesses, his heart pounded when he spotted the supermarket where his beloved plied her trade.

Throughout the journey, his imagination danced with visions of the joy that would envelop him when he and Neesha finally tied the knot.

Stepping off the bus, he was immediately embraced by the sights and sounds of the festive gathering. The air was redolent with the smoky aroma of barbecue wafting from nearby cookouts, while the murmur of excited conversation rippled among the crowd. As he strolled into the park, his gaze fell upon a striking red Lincoln Town Car parked in the distance. Inside the vehicle sat a coffee-colored man whose jet-black hair was slicked back with meticulous care. Crowning his head was a pristine white hat adorned with a large, resplendent feather. The man's ensemble was nothing short of remarkable: a crisp white linen suit, a vibrant red shirt, and a matching white tie. Brown glanced down at his freshly ironed Levi's jeans and brand-new white Converse—clothes he'd chosen with such care this morning, feeling proud of his casual sophistication. Now they seemed childish, trying too hard yet not trying enough. Part of him wanted to straighten his shoulders, own his different style; another part whispered he should have known better, should have dressed to impress. "How can I possibly compete with him?" Brown thought, then immediately despised himself for caring. As he moved deeper into the throng, hushed whispers began to weave through the crowd, proclaiming, "That's Bishop Petunia from Buffalo, and he is single." In that moment, Mr. Brown felt his heart sink; each beat echoed his fear that Bishop

Petunia might steal away the affections of his sweet lady.

Bishop Petunia made his entrance at the forefront of the assembly, taking a distinguished seat in the front row reserved for clergy from various sanctuaries. Shortly thereafter, Pastor B'more stepped forward and introduced Neesha, who emerged in a graceful ensemble—a flowing mauve skirt paired with elegant black sandals. With a warm smile and a clearing of her throat, she attempted to serenade the gathering, beginning with a heartfelt, "God is truly A…" but the expected music of her voice failed to materialize. Undeterred, she tried once more, "God is truly…" yet the silence that followed rippled through the crowd like a startled gust of wind.

In a state of sheer mortification, Neesha bolted from the stage, collapsing to the ground as tears streamed down her face, accompanied by anguished cries, "I can't believe my voice failed me!" It was then that a firm and compassionate hand rested on her shoulder. Looking up, she found herself gazing into the kind eyes of Bishop Petunia. "It's okay, my child," he comforted, gently grasping her hand, lifting her to her feet, and encircling her with warm arms. "Jesus loves you, and so do I," he murmured with genuine tenderness. Retracting his embrace slightly, he placed his hands in hers and softly implored, "I want you to come to Buffalo to see me. I know just the right voice coach who can help you get your chords right. There's no need to rush; simply consider it and come when you are ready." With that, he reached into his pocket and withdrew a handkerchief. "Jesus will wipe away all of your tears," he assured her as he tenderly dabbed away the water from her eyes, he then produced his business card with the other hand. "Call me, I'll be waiting," he added. Neesha offered a weak yet grateful nod.

As Bishop Petunia strode away, he passed by Brown, whose eyes brimmed with unshed tears and whose heart seemed to shatter into a thousand fragmented pieces. With a gentle smile, Bishop Petunia mingled among the attendees, shaking hands with everyone at the picnic, while in that instant, Brown's cherished dreams crumbled to dust, even as it appeared that Neesha's dreams were gradually coming true.

Each week, Neesha eagerly picked up the phone to call Bishop Petunia, and they would spend endless hours delving into conversations about The Word, the Lamb of God, the intricate parables of Christ, and every facet of Christianity's rich tapestry. The bishop carried himself with impeccable courtesy until one fateful day, while driving along a sun-dappled road, he was suddenly rear-ended by another vehicle. In the shock of the moment when he relayed the incident to Neesha, his tone cracked, and he blurted out a harsh insult, calling the other driver a "stupid bitch." Neesha was taken aback by his uncharacteristic language, yet as he explained his calamity, it unfolded like a tragic play: he had missed his insurance payment and now faced the dire choice of either repairing the woman's car or risking jail time. When Neesha inquired about the cost of the repairs, his voice turned grim as he revealed the price: three thousand dollars. That sum, representing her entire life's savings, was all she had in her account; nevertheless, her devotion to the Man of God—her future husband—compelled her to help. The bishop had promised to reimburse her once she reached Buffalo, so with quiet determination, she made her way to the check-cashing place and exchanged her cherished savings—three thousand dollars plus an extra dollar to cover the money order fee.

Before completing the transaction, she called the bishop to update him on her plans, only to be met with frantic urgency as he shouted, "No, I need you to Western Union the money; this is an emergency!" Calmly and steadily, Neesha explained that while she didn't have sufficient funds for a Western Union transfer at that moment, she would ask a friend to lend her the necessary amount, with a promise to repay them as soon as her check was received on Friday. The bishop reluctantly agreed to this plan, assuring her that he would settle the debt once she arrived in Buffalo. With resolute faith, Neesha then ventured over to the boarding house and sought help from Brown, who, with a heavy heart, pulled out his last twenty dollars. Handing it over to her, he represented what little he could offer, and she departed to carry out the bishop's demanding request.

This was not the first time the bishop had sought Neesha's financial aid; on other occasions, he had requested fifty or a hundred dollars over the phone. Yet never before had he demanded as much as three thousand dollars—a sum she swallowed like a bitter pill, viewing it as an investment in the future with her destined husband. Despite his habit of calling only when in dire need, Neesha decided to take a leap of faith and journey to Buffalo, trusting in God's guidance that this man was indeed the husband meant for her.

Finally, six months after that memorable picnic in Eisenhower Park, the decision was made. Neesha, gathering her cherished, antique peanuts, prepared herself for the seven-and-a-half-hour move from Hempstead to Buffalo—a place colloquially known as "The Land of the Superfreak."

Meanwhile, Mr. Brown was utterly devastated by the departure of the woman he loved, her leaving for a life in Buffalo with a prominent preacher. Yet, in the quiet recesses of his heart, he clung to the hope that if Neesha was meant to be his wife, God would someday guide her back. One day after church, summoning all his courage, he approached her and asked if he might walk her to the bus stop for her long journey. With a tender, bittersweet smile, she consented.

The night before her departure, Brown offered one final prayer, his voice a soft murmur in the dim light, and lovingly packed a lunch for her—a meal that featured freshly baked chocolate chip cookies made especially with her in mind.

The next day, as the moment of farewell had arrived, he met her with a heavy heart and presented her with a humble brown paper bag holding the lovingly prepared meal. As he walked her to the bus, he whispered, "I'mma miss you, sweet pea. Take care of yourself," before pressing a gentle kiss onto her cheek and waving goodbye—a poignant parting filled with hope, longing, and unspoken promises that time might mend his broken heart.

CLIVE

When Neesha stepped off the bus in Buffalo, the crisp autumn air mingled with the aroma of wet pavement and fallen leaves. Awaiting her on the platform was Bishop Petunia, a peculiar figure dressed in a vibrant suit and accompanied by a young girl he introduced as his assistant. In one sweeping motion, as Neesha hurried toward him with an anxious smile, she yanked her worn suitcase so forcefully that it tilted over, spilling its contents in a sudden, chaotic burst. Clothes, like colored leaves in a storm, fluttered across the bus depot's cold tile floor, while a jar of peanuts—its glass sparkling under the harsh light—clattered and bounced, miraculously remaining intact.

With a graceful gesture toward the scattered belongings, Bishop Petunia signaled, and his dutiful assistant knelt to help Neesha gather every piece of her life back into her suitcase. "Hello, my dear," Bishop Petunia said with a kindly, yet mysterious smile. "I am so glad you made it here safely. I will now take you to your living quarters, where you will be housed alongside a few of my servants." The word "servant" cautioned Neesha, filling her with a disconcerting mix of bewilderment and apprehension at the thought that her future partner might have planned for her to reside among subordinates. Yet, as she allowed herself a tentative half-smile, her mind whispered that she had ventured too far to now turn back, and so she politely nodded.

Arriving at an elegant vehicle waiting nearby, the bishop swung open the back door with theatrical flair, beckoning Neesha to slide into its plush interior. As she did so, his young assistant mirrored his actions on the opposite side, climbing in with quiet confidence. "Welcome, my name is Elizabeth," she introduced herself warmly, clasping Neesha's hand as if to offer both guidance and comfort. "We are so happy you came; I've heard you have a lovely singing voice." Though Neesha maintained her composure with a measured smile, she could not shake the uneasy uncertainty that swirled around the woman named Elizabeth and her cryptic welcome.

The car eventually took them to a grand white Victorian mansion—a majestic six-room home with intricately painted yellow doors and a perfectly manicured lawn. Freshly cut grass and clusters of daffodils dotted the sweeping front porch that gracefully curved to the back, evoking images of idyllic countryside charm. Inside, the mansion was a pristine vision of elegance. Gleaming hardwood floors were concealed under lavish oriental rugs, each a tapestry of intricate design that Bishop Petunia proudly claimed to have acquired from the Emperor of China himself. Exquisitely crafted furniture, hand-carved by Europe's finest artisans, harmonized with the vibrant stained-glass windows that bathed the rooms in a kaleidoscope of colors reminiscent of the mystique of the Russian Empire. It was, without a doubt, the most breathtaking residence Neesha had ever seen. And if this magnificent home was reserved for the Bishop's servants, one could only let the imagination wander to the grandeur awaiting its inhabitants.

Elizabeth turned to Neesha, her eyes glimmering with a mix of excitement and mischief. "Do you like it?" she inquired softly. Neesha offered a small, uncertain nod before Elizabeth continued. "Come on, let me show you to your room." Elizabeth led her through ornately decorated corridors to a modest chamber furnished with three twin-size poster beds, each accompanied by a matching dresser and a neat closet tucked beside each bed. Standing beside the bed closest to the door, Elizabeth explained, "This is your bed and your dresser. We eat breakfast at 6 sharp, lunch at 2, and dinner at 6. Every resident has assigned chores to be completed before lunch—yours is to clean each room on this floor."

Neesha's voice trembled as she repeated, "Clean?" to which Elizabeth responded with a gentle, yet knowing smile. "Yes, you will start off as a servant. With time, you may work your way up, perhaps becoming a cook or even a helper on the second floor. But for now, you are too young to be a supervisor. Clive will have you sing in the choir until you get the hang of things." Neesha's brow furrowed in confusion. "Who is Clive?" she asked softly.

"Clive," Elizabeth began, her tone taking on a darker edge, "is the man who picked you up at the bus station and drove us here. He is one of the largest, most notorious pimps in Buffalo. He usually seduces women and lures them up here to work on the second floor, but he brought you back for his elderly father, Bishop Petunia. He claimed he met you at a picnic— an event his father was too sick to attend—so he sent Clive instead. Clive, however, has his own ulterior motives. He intends for you to work with Reverend Asbury, the church's minister of music because of your beautiful voice. And because you are so attractive, Clive secretly hopes that the arrangement fails, giving you the opportunity to learn the art of turning tricks."

Elizabeth's sudden burst of excitement filled the small room as she continued, "Let me guess—you are completely penniless?" She explained further that Clive had a cruel habit of emptying the bank accounts of women, leaving them financially crippled and entirely dependent on him for even the simplest necessities.

Once isolated from friends and family and stripped of support, many found themselves forced onto the second floor, compelled to resort to the demeaning work of turning tricks. "Where are your parents? Do you have any relatives?" Elizabeth pressed. Mrs. Brown shook her head in silent despair. "Then it's the drugs," Elizabeth went on, her voice dropping to a conspiratorial whisper. "Most start off clean, but soon, as they mix with everyone else here who indulges, they too begin. And once that happens, there is no turning back. You become trapped in Buffalo for life."

The revelation struck Neesha with a devastating blow. Alone, with neither family nor friends, she felt duped into coming to Buffalo only to be led toward a life she never imagined—one haunted by the specter of forced prostitution.

That very evening, after a somber dinner in the grand dining hall, Neesha retired straight to bed. Throughout the night, she tossed and turned amid a tumult of worry and sorrow, her thoughts racing as she contemplated how to escape the suffocating nightmare that had become her reality. With her mother gone, no knowledge of her father, and the isolation of being an only child, she had already stripped her bank account bare. Through tear-filled prayers, she begged God to free her from the grip of Clive Collins and the impending ruin he heralded.

The following day, Elizabeth returned with clear, regimented instructions. "You will clean the rooms, lunch is at 12, and don't forget your voice lessons at Bishop Petunia's church at 2," she announced briskly, handing Neesha a small sheet of directions to the church. "Walk quickly. If you are late by even a few minutes, you will not eat until the morning."

At precisely one-thirty, a firm reminder stirred Neesha to leave for her voice lessons—promptness was not a luxury with the minister. Taking the note from the table with trembling determination, she stepped out through the mansion's back door, the cool breeze mixing with her rising anxiety.

The church, a magnificent structure reminiscent of a vast Catholic cathedral, loomed ahead—a stark contrast to the modest storefront in Hempstead. Boldly inscribed over the entrance were the words: "Welcome to the Church of God and Sweet Jesus, come As You Are." As Neesha entered, the gentle, soulful strains of music floated through the air, emanating from a grand baby piano positioned at the front. Behind the piano was a tall, slender man with thick glasses, his fingers dancing across the keys with deliberate passion. Noticing her approach, he rose with a welcoming smile and said, "Hi, you must be the one with the beautiful voice. My name is Reverend Asbury, and I am the minister of music. I assume you are here for voice lessons?"

Neesha could only nod in agreement. "Well, let's get started," he said, gesturing for her to come closer to the instrument. Throughout the lesson,

Reverend Asbury noted that Neesha listened intently, her responses a subtle nod rather than any outpouring of opinion. Her silent attentiveness struck a chord with him—here was an eager confidante for his own concealed sorrows. In quiet moments, he confided the burdens of his dual life: his impassioned love for the Lord entwined with the sufferings of a forbidden, hidden desire. Being gay, he lamented, was regarded as an abomination in his world, and his heart ached as he revealed that his dreams of living openly with the man of his heart were forever stifled by his mother's harsh words and an unforgiving society. His deepest wish was to escape to a bustling city and join others like him in the warm embrace of acceptance—if only someone could help him break free.

Moved by his vulnerability, Neesha vowed silently to keep his confidences, promising never to divulge his secret plans for escaping Buffalo and the oppressive clutches of the Church of God and Sweet Jesus.

Music

Reverend Asbury was a man of many dreams; a fabric interlaced with many lively strands of creativity. Often, his dreams painted him as a gentle lady, an opera singer with a voice that could shatter the stars, gracing the grand stages of Broadway in a Shakespearean theatrical show. Alone in the hushed, sacred stillness of the church, he would indulge in these dreams, practicing hitting those soaring high notes that hung in the air like crystal chimes. His soft, gentle hands would flutter gracefully, imitating the delicate gestures of a woman. With fingers poised around his waist, he would artfully mimic the sweep of a gown, pinching his fingers together as though gathering the fabric of an unseen dress. Then he would bend his knees, dipping gracefully into a curtsy that echoed with the elegance of an imagined past. Approaching the rows of empty pews, he'd smile and, with a voice lifted to its highest, say, "Thank you," to an audience that existed only in his heart.

Whenever he indulged in fantasies of becoming a female opera singer and performing in a Shakespearean production, a hint of sorrow would cross his face, as he was painfully aware that these dreams would never come true. Such freedom of expression could only flourish in a place where a gay man could live openly and without fear—a village of acceptance far from the rigid confines of his current world. In his heart, he understood he would never leave Buffalo; the courage to seek a life beyond the church's walls eluded him. The modest salary he earned was a slender thread, enough to cover a few small necessities and keep him fed, but not enough to fuel the pursuit of dreams. His mother had ingrained in him the belief that the world would shun him for his true self, that no one would employ a gay man, and that he would be met with hatred. Thus, he remained in the protective cocoon of the church, concealing his true identity behind the sanctuary's walls, despite the discomfort it brought. Isolated from those who could offer solace, he found himself tied to teaching singing lessons and leading the Sunday morning worship at Bishop Petunia's Church of God and Sweet Jesus.

That was until one fateful day, a day that shimmered with the promise of change. Neesha Maxwell, a woman originally from the bustling heart of Hempstead, Long

Island—a mere forty-five-minute train ride along the Long Island Railroad to the dazzling City of Manhattan —extended an unexpected proposition. It was after practice, in a moment tinged with possibility, that the course of his life began to shift.

Escape

Every day at precisely two o'clock, the determined Neesha would meet Reverend Asbury for their cherished singing lessons. Amid gentle harmonies and soft hymns, he would always hand her a neatly wrapped sandwich, a small but thoughtful provision for her journey back to Clive's extravagant dwelling, ensuring she wouldn't miss her evening meal. As the slow march of weeks brought them increasingly close together, their sessions evolved into a deep and unspoken camaraderie. One humid afternoon, beneath a sky that hinted at summer's lingering heat, Neesha, with a tremor in her voice, revealed the tangled web of deceit that had led her to Buffalo. She explained how she had been lured there by false promises, led to believe that Clive Collins was Bishop Petunia. In her faded hopes, she had imagined marriage as a rescue from poverty, yet soon realized the cruel truth: Clive Collins was not the ecclesiastical figure she envisioned, but rather Bishop Petunia's very own son—a man whose dark dealings in pimping shattered her naïve dreams. Desperate and frightened of a fate that could degrade her further, she devised a risky plan. She pleaded with Reverend Asbury, asking his consent to use the lone telephone in the pastor's office during their singing lessons—a lifeline that might connect her to the help she so desperately needed. With a conflicted but gentle heart, he agreed.

The following day, with hope and anxiety intermingling in her thoughts, Neesha called her only friend, Brown, only to discover that he was not home. She left a carefully worded message stating when she would ring him again. When she tried again the next day, Brown answered with an enthusiastic, "Praise the Lord!" Their conversation unfolded with a mixture of concern and informal warmth. "Brother Brown, is that you?" she inquired, to which a weary yet relieved Brown replied, "Yes, it's me. How are you doing up there? Have you been to Canada yet?" In a burst of desperation, she detailed her tragic predicament: "Oh, Brother Brown, I am in a complete mess. I was deceived into believing that man was Bishop Petunia, but his true name is Clive Collins. Not only is he the son of Bishop Petunia, but he's also a pimp. I'm trying so hard to come home, yet he's taken every bit of my money, and I have no time for work because I'm stuck shuttling between labor in his house and those endless singing lessons at his father's church. I'm trapped here in Buffalo, and I can't get out!"

Brown's voice, heavy with incredulity and sympathetic anger, responded, "Oh Lord, you're truly stuck in Buffalo? You gave up your place and everything, and yet you're still dreaming of coming home?" After a pause laden with hope and calculation, she said, "Yes, Brother Brown, I want to come home". Brown replied, "Let me call my dear Momma Maybelle. She always has a little money in her pickle jar. Call me back tomorrow, and I promise I'll see what can be done." Relieved yet anxious, she agreed before they ended their call.

Without delay, Brown reached out to his beloved mother in Mississippi. "Momma, is that you?" he asked on the line, and her familiar, crackling voice delivered, "Yes, it's me, Brown. How can I help you, dear?" Explaining his dire situation, Brown said, "Well, Momma, I have a small problem—I need five hundred dollars. Can you help me out?" With that warm, steadfast maternal resolve, she replied, "Well, Brown, I believe I have just about that hidden away in my pickle jar. I'll go to town, secure a money order, and send it right over." Her words carried the promise of a safety net, and Mr. Brown's gratitude was palpable as he thanked her.

The next day, determined and undeterred by her age, the little old woman set the phone aside and stepped into a large basket intricately woven from corn husks, its sturdy form balanced on two well-worn wooden wheels. At the front, a humble donkey waited, its gentle eyes reflecting a quiet resolve. Firmly grasping the reins, Maybelle called out in her distinctive drawl, "Getti up!" and with that, the determined donkey began pulling the basket along the winding road toward town.

Upon arriving at an empty check-cashing place, Maybelle maneuvered her way to the counter and carefully unscrewed her cherished pickle jar, letting its modest contents cascade onto the polished surface. "I need a five-hundred-dollar money order," she declared in a steady, no-nonsense tone. The cashier, methodically counting out five hundred and one dollars to ensure every cent was included, then inquired politely, "Would you like a stamped envelope?" "Yes," replied Maybelle without hesitation. Receiving the envelope, she methodically wrote her son's address on it. With measured steps, she strode to the nearby mailbox and sent the money order off, her actions like a small but significant beacon of hope destined to bring Neesha back home.

Later, after completing her errand, Maybelle called her son to confirm, "It's all done, Brown. You just need to wait until it gets to New York." Brown's voice brimmed with relief as he softly said, "Thanks, Momma."

The next day, Neesha reached out to Brown once more. With a determined tone, he assured her that he would soon travel to Buffalo to rescue her. Meanwhile,

Reverend Asbury, ever cautious, instructed her to leave all her belongings behind, "No one should find out about your upcoming departure," he said with a serious expression. Five days later, she took the peanuts from her suitcase, tossed them into a bag, and headed to her singing lessons with her confidante. What used to be a routine lesson now buzzed with the thrill of impending changes. Several days later, Neesha called Brown from a payphone outside the corner bodega, her fingers trembling as she pressed the coins into the slot. Brown told her he'd meet her at the Buffalo train station at precisely 2:15 PM on Sunday, when the express from Manhattan would arrive. That morning, Neesha stood before Reverend Asbury's baby grand piano, her Sunday dress clutched between tight-knuckled fingers, her voice steadier than her racing heart as she announced that today would be her final day at The Church of God and Sweet Jesus, because she was going home. The afternoon sun caught the gold cross on the wall behind him as his bushy eyebrows rose in surprise. In a moment of stunned solidarity, Reverend Asbury revealed a small suitcase he had hidden under the piano and declared, "I'm coming with you." Together, they raced to the Amtrak station, where Mr. Brown stood waiting like a steadfast sentinel of salvation.

Once aboard the train, Brown disclosed the painful reality: Neesha had lost not only her security but also her living quarters, leaving her stranded with nowhere to call her own. In a spontaneous yet pragmatic solution, he explained that they would have to marry—tying the knot to legitimize their living arrangement and to erase any semblance of sin. Although, Neesha did not find Brown particularly handsome, the promise of returning home outweighed her personal reservations, and she consented. Instead of heading directly home, their journey took an unexpected detour as they crossed the busy tracks and journeyed to the roaring majesty of Niagara Falls. There, in the luminous glow of the Peace Pipe Casino, they were wed in a ceremony as unconventional as it was heartfelt. Chief Light Foot, the charismatic owner, presided over the nuptials, while Reverend Asbury proudly assumed the role of maid of honor. In the end, although Neesha did not marry a bishop as she once fantasized, she found herself uniting in marriage at Niagara Falls in front of a casino—a wild, vibrant ending that made two out of three seem nearly perfect.

FAITH

As Mrs. Brown, formally known as Whoreneesha, Mr. Brown, and Reverend Asbury climbed aboard the old train bound for a fresh start in Long Island, the air was thick with hope and uncertainty. Outside, dusk had settled, painting the sky in bruised shades of purple and blue. Meanwhile, Clive Collins burst through the creaking doors of the grand mansion. His voice rang out in a furious crescendo: "Where is our minister of music and the little money songbird?! The church is in uproar—the congregation teeters on the brink of desertion, deprived of the entertainment that bonds them as its very soul!"

In the shadowy corridor, Elizabeth rose steadily and walked toward him, her eyes blazing with a mix of sorrow and determination. "They left," she said in a trembling tone, "and I don't know where they've gone.

How do you expect someone, lured up here under false pretenses, not to find a way out? And how can you confine a person in a basement devoid of love, expecting them not to flee in search of it?"

Clive's gaze fell to the worn floor as he murmured, "I do not know love—I only know money. And that is what we will lose if we don't devise another gimmick. Fortunately, my father is not the man he used to be, and the church has recruited a new minister from New Haven, Connecticut—a man born into an extensive lineage of devoted ministers. He is single, with the keen hope of meeting the woman destined to stand by his side." His tone grew sly. "I told him of Neesha and how beautifully she sings—a voice so angelic there's nothing quite like a pastor and his first lady harmonizing to fill the church. He agreed, dreaming of courting her to eventual marriage. Yet, let there be no mistake—I never asked her to trick anyone. I barely exchanged words with her, making it explicitly clear that her place was here, to serve the church's needs. Though she believed I was a preacher, as soon as she arrived, I distanced myself and paired her with the minister of music to ready her for the new minister's arrival."

Her mind took on bitter regret as he recounted, "They were the perfect gimmick for the church. Meanwhile, how did she end up cleaning the vast, echoing expanse of the second floor, all the while dreaming of a future illuminated by her singing. Who told her that cleaning the second floor was her destiny? Who introduced her to a life akin to that of a hooker?"

At these words, Elizabeth's eyes welled with tears that shone like broken glass in dim light. "Clive, it was I. I told her that if her singing career didn't take off, cleaning—and worse, a life like that of a hooker— would be her fate. That ultimatum is why she left. Had she waited, she might have met the man of her dreams. But lacking patience and failing to wait upon the Lord, she settled for a man she did not truly love."

In a surge of raw emotion, Clive rose and stormed over to Elizabeth, his anger manifesting in a swift, stinging slap that sent her reeling to the cool, hard floor. In a heart-wrenching cry, she exclaimed, "He is gay!" Clive's retort was bitter and resolute: "After my father is gone, he will be my only relative, and I need my family no matter what. You took him from me, and I shall never forgive you!"

Then, in a moment of profound, contradictory tenderness, Elizabeth gathered Clive in her arms. Amidst her tears, she pressed her cheek to his and whispered through the anguish, "Oh Clive, I pray that God brings your brother back to you. I have sinned deeply by uttering words to Neesha that instilled fear— fear that you would love her instead of me. I beg for forgiveness, yet I trust that if you hold onto your belief, God will guide your brother back into your life. And when your faith begins to waver, ask yourself: 'Where does my faith truly lie?'

Know that it rests in the mighty and boundless power of God."

Celebration

Over the years, the unassuming little storefront on Main Street in Hempstead, blossomed into a vibrant sanctuary under the nurturing guidance of Bishop Petunia. In the midst of his pastoral duties, Reverend B'more was introduced to a captivating woman from Baldwin, — a woman whose renown for baking the most delectable sweet potato pie on Long Island had already made her a local legend. Their paths first crossed at the annual picnic pie-eating contest, a spirited event where Reverend B'more emerged as the triumphant champion, his victory marked by contagious smiles and a sense of community pride.

Every Sunday thereafter, the woman who would become the future First Lady entered the church carrying with her the irresistible aroma of her signature sweet potato pie. Each slice, lovingly crafted and elegantly presented to Reverend B'more, gradually infused his every waking moment with the fond, comforting scent of home and tradition. Although Reverend B'more did not initially feel a passionate love for the small and sprightly woman—standing a modest four feet three inches tall—he soon recognized the undeniable necessity of having a partner, a true First Lady by his side. In a swift and heartfelt three months, he proposed marriage with one simple condition: the celebration must be conducted on a shoestring budget.

Six months before the wedding, Pastor B'more announced that the future First Lady wished to convene a special meeting with all the women of the church to cultivate closer bonds. Just fifteen minutes after the Sunday service, every woman in the congregation settled directly in front of the pulpit—a testament to their deep respect for the pastor's future union. Moments later, the future First Lady emerged onto the stage with quiet determination. With measured steps, she crossed in front of the podium, activated the microphone, and her clear, resonant voice echoed, "Amen, Amen." Then, imbued with a fervor that filled the room, she implored every woman to join her in a bold mission: to clear the path to the bridal gown of her dreams at the upcoming annual bridal sale in just two weeks. She stressed that it was essential to represent their beloved pastor in the most splendid manner, determined to procure a wedding dress that was not only stunning but also modest in cost. Concluding her impassioned announcement, she called out, "Are you with me?" and an enthusiastic, unified "Yes, we are!" resounded throughout the room.

Two weeks later, on a radiant Saturday morning at five AM, an eager assembly of women arrived at the Mavis Bridal shop, each driven by the desire to help secure the dream gown for their future First Lady. Their anticipation met the sight of a long, winding queue that curved around the corner to the end of the block. In that moment of mild despair, Mrs. Brown—a respected member of the Building Fund Committee and the head of the Woman's Club—stepped forward and bellowed with spirited conviction, "Sisters, do not be dismayed; the Lord is on our side! Father God, we ask that you clear away these dusty, thirsty heifers so that our beloved future First Lady may have her way to claim the gown of her dreams! Father God, we know You are mighty—now everyone say, Amen!" The resounding chorus of "Amen!" filled the air with hope and determination as the store doors swung open and the frenzy began.

Inside, the shop was a veritable wonderland of gowns in every imaginable hue. Amidst a dazzling display of champagne-colored, off-white, pure white, and even unexpected splashes of black, purple, and red, racks of dresses beckoned all who entered. Amid the commotion of excited pushes and grabs, the First Lady-to-be pointed with intent at the gowns that captured her discerning eye. In the heated moments of the search, Mrs. Brown, ever the staunch enforcer, tapped a woman on the head with her sizeable pocketbook, snatched a gown from her grasp, and declared in a tone laced with humor and authority, "Let it go, in Jesus' name!" The startled woman relinquished her prize and continued her search elsewhere.

As the day ended, the future First Lady clutched the gown that had ultimately won her heart. With a joyful cry that rang out over the din of the shop, she exclaimed, "Everyone, you may drop your dresses—the Lord has given me this one!" Carrying the gown with an air of triumphant grace, she approached the counter and placed a payment of three dollars and fifty cents, all the while shouting, "Thank you, Lord!" As the group dispersed, every attendee walked away with hearts full of gratitude, extolling the beautiful wedding gown that had been divinely bestowed upon the future First Lady B'moe.

BLISS

Their wedding was an enchanting affair held in the natural splendor of Central Park, where every detail spoke of humble opulence. The wedding cake, a culinary marvel created by the future First Lady herself, featured a rich sweet potato flavor enveloped in velvety cream cheese frosting, each bite a harmonious blend of tradition and artistry. The entire congregation of the church attended the celebration, which was lovingly organized by the dedicated mothers of the church. In the cool, bustling basement of the Hempstead church, the mothers prepared a sumptuous feast, which was then transported by the tireless brothers to Manhattan. There, they arranged the event in the park, meticulously setting up hot plates laden with savory dishes. The decorations, artfully executed by the woman's ministry, and the floral arrangements, tenderly designed by the children's choir, all came together to create a breathtaking setting—an elegant celebration completed with a mere twelve dollars.

On that momentous day, Reverend B'more cut a striking figure. His meticulously groomed cornrows cascaded like dark ribbons down the back of his sharply tailored black tuxedo, while his matching Casals—large, refined glasses—framed his eyes with a spark of gentle charisma. Equally impressive was his bride, the future First Lady, who epitomized the grace and poise that every First Lady aspires to embody. Her exuberance at the prospect of her new role was so palpable that she independently financed her bridal gown, a treasure she acquired during the once-a-year clearance event at Mavis Bridal.

The wedding unfolded on the edge of Central Park, closest to Harlem, near the bustling Malcolm X Boulevard. Beneath a clear blue sky, the gathering was seated on weathered folding chairs rescued from the church's basement, a humble reminder of the congregation's resourcefulness. Each guest had painstakingly crafted their own seat cover, a craft overseen with precision by the future First Lady, whose commanding presence and unwavering determination ensured that every detail was meticulously in place. At the stroke of one, all was carefully arranged in the park—a vibrant space that, despite its past as a resting spot for down-and-out winos and drug addicts, sparkled today with the promise of new beginnings, all converging to celebrate the awe-inspiring affair orchestrated by the Church of God and Sweet Jesus.

After the ceremony, a soul-stirring reception burst into life with a sumptuous Soul Food buffet. Guests clutched their mismatched paper plates as they returned to their seats, carefully balancing the offerings while silently praying that the cascade of aromatic, rich gravies and spicy collard greens would not betray them with a messy spill. Joy and anticipation mingled in the air as many admired the impeccable outcome of the festivities, while a few had come solely for the art of gossip. Amid the murmurs, Mrs. Brown's robust voice rang out: "Peace be still, the devil is always messing! This is a joyous occasion—it is the day that the Lord has made; let us rejoice and be glad in it. There will be no negative talk at our holy and magnificent Pastor's wedding. Let there be Peace! Peace be still!" and in that moment, the clamor subsided into a reverent silence, as everyone turned their thoughts toward the blessings of the Lord.

Yet, beneath the layer of celebration, the evolving story of the church began to mirror the growing complexities of its leader, Reverend B'more. As the congregation morphed into a grand, extravagant mega church, Reverend B'more, in a startling physical transformation, resembled a gentle, plodding baby elephant—a stark symbol of both his newfound status and creeping imbalance. In the months following the nuptials, as intimacy turned into routine, a disconcerting shift occurred; Reverend B'more found himself repelled by the presence of the very woman he was meant to love, the distinguished First Lady. The tender moments of a kiss grew scarce and mechanical, and when love was meant to bloom, he felt nothing but disdain. Oddly, the only delight he found in their union was in the delicate, tantalizing flavor of her sweet potato pies.

As time passed, financial troubles began to unravel the carefully constructed facade of harmony. The church's treasury dwindled alarmingly as the First Lady's extravagant spending—her frequent visits to opulent hair and nail salons—spiraled out of control. To salvage the situation, Reverend B'more pleaded with his congregation for additional funds to cover her lavish expenses, a gesture that only fueled her insatiable demands. Matters worsened when she took a daring step by selling records of Bishop Cecil Petune, one of the church's founding figures. The records, capturing his impassioned sermons and soulful melodies meant for his congregation, were not hers to part with, and her unauthorized act threatened to strip him of his venerable position.

In the end, a fraught reconciliation emerged between him and the First Lady, their union a fabric woven of tumult, bitter compromise, and the bittersweet escape found in those very sweet potato pies he had come to cherish so dearly.

FAMILY

It was within the warm, welcoming walls of the old storefront church that she first encountered her husband and dearest friend, Brown—a man who provided her with the family she had yearned for since childhood. Yet, despite the newfound love and security, the shadows of her past still lingered in her heart. Mrs. Brown had often spent long, reflective evenings wondering about the fate of her mother, questioning neighbors and friends alike, but the truth remained elusive—until one fateful day.

On that day, as the sun softly filtered through the stained-glass windows of Pastor B'more's church, a mysterious man arrived, his eyes carrying both hope and regret. When asked by one of the curious congregants what business he had with Mrs. Brown, he calmly replied, "I am her father." His words sent ripples through the quiet hum of the church, prompting the ushers to hastily inform the graceful First Lady. Her face suddenly lit with a mixture of surprise and a quiet, bittersweet joy. She instructed the ushers to escort the man to the little office tucked away in a corner of the church and assured him that she would join him shortly. Guided by gentle hands, the man was led into the office, where he sat in silence, absorbing the gravity of the moment.

When the First Lady stepped into the office, the air seemed to shimmer with anticipation. With open arms, she swept the man into a warm embrace. "Charles, what are you doing here?" she asked, her voice trembling with emotion. Charles returned her embrace with a crooked smile and explained, "I came to reconnect, to see if I could find my long-lost baby. You see, when I was married, I did what any so-called respectable married man might have done: I strayed to a local strip joint, where I became involved with a woman. When she revealed she was pregnant, I panicked, denied responsibility, and moved down south, clinging to the idea that it was cheaper to keep my wife, as Johnny Taylor sang." The First Lady's nod, though mixed with incredulity, invited him to continue. "Now, my wife has passed on, and I need to make things right. When I walked in today, there you were, standing with your preacher husband—still as fine as ever, , cupcake! You haven't changed one bit." Her gentle giggle filled the room before she playfully chided him, "Charles, stop; you're unbelievable!" Yet, even as she pushed him lightly away, his fervor persisted. "I know, baby, you experienced something like what my daughter went through. Back then, I was trapped in a marriage with no recourse, but now that my wife is gone, I have the chance to mend my past misdeeds. Why not arrange for me to meet my daughter? It's not too late for her— or for my grandchildren." With that earnest proposal, the First Lady promised to organize a meeting for the following Sunday, and Charles, with a final hopeful smile, departed.

Later that evening, under a slowly deepening twilight, the First Lady called Mrs. Brown with alluring news of a surprise awaiting her next Sunday. Mrs. Brown's heart swelled with joy and excitement as she presumed the nomination for the Burger King Gospel Fest in Mount Vernon was the cause for this mysterious delight. In her excitement, she confided in Brown, voicing her need for extra time to perfect the acceptance speech she'd imagine delivering. The very next day, with determined energy, Mrs. Brown penned a heartfelt speech and gathered an impromptu audience—neighbors, the diligent dog walker, the cheerful ice cream truck driver, and even the mailman, who was politely invited to sit down as she recited her words with passion, while the whole neighborhood waited expectantly for their checks to arrive in the mail. The preceding Saturday had been a flurry of activity as she lovingly prepared dinner and meticulously ironed her favorite dress. When Sunday finally arrived, she slipped into that cherished dress and took a moment to pop a Tylenol, ensuring that the tight patent leather shoes—known to pinch her left pinky toe—would not steal away her joy. With bubbling excitement, she joined Mr. Brown's sedan, each turn of the engine carrying her closer to a day she believed was brimming with celebration.

As the church service neared its conclusion, Reverend B'more rose from his pew and announced that the First Lady had a special proclamation to make. The congregation fell into a hushed anticipation as the First Lady strode gracefully to the front of the church, pausing to clear her voice amid the expectant silence. "I have an announcement for Sister Brown," she began, her tone both gentle and resolute. Mrs. Brown, nearly trembling with excitement, nodded for her to continue and rose to a standing position, bracing herself to deliver her prepared speech. With a mix of nervousness and hope, looked out over the sea of faces, uncertain of the reaction that would unfold. "Sister Brown, I have a surprise for you: your long-lost father is among us, and he wishes to forge a relationship with you." The revelation shattered the stillness as Mrs. Brown screamed, "What! Oh, hell no! Where were you when I was cast aside and sent to juvenile detention?" Turning sharply, she fixed her gaze on the man who claimed to be her father and demanded, "Where were you when I had nowhere to go and had to settle with Mr. Brown because he was my only option?" In that heart-wrenching moment, Mr. Brown's eyes welled with gentle tears as he looked upward, silently offering her strength. Yet, in a tender voice, she added, "But I am fortunate, for he is a good man." As she attempted to continue, Charles interjected.

"I know I haven't been the best father," he admitted, his tone holding both remorse and warmth, "but I still have a bit left over from my late wife's life insurance policy—I want to offer you some child support." The mention of money brought a brief, surprised smile to Mrs. Brown's face. "So, here's a hundred dollars," he declared. Shocked, Mrs. Brown bellowed, "Is that all you have from a life insurance policy?" Charles chuckled, "Come on, baby, you act as if you're my only child. I have forty-two children in all—I distributed at least forty-two hundred dollars among them. I may not have an abundance of riches, but what I lack in wealth I make up for in love. If you're willing to accept it, how about it? Come on now, give your old pops a hug." With arms outstretched, he said, "I've waited decades for this embrace." Mrs. Brown stepped forward hesitantly, then fell against her father's chest, feeling the unfamiliar contours of his shoulders beneath her trembling fingers. The congregation rose to their feet, hands coming together in thunderous approval.

BELLE

Maybelle learned she would move north with her young son under a pale dawn sky. She received the news with outward composure, though her chest felt heavy as wet sand. Inside her mind, sorrowful memories and bright hopes mingled in a dense fog. Ahead lay a tangle of decisions: first, she would part with the small plot of land that her grandmother left her—a stretch of red clay soil carpeted with wild grasses and haunted by the echoes of forced labor. Along with the earth, she would sell every tool, every relic that dwelled there. Next came the sale of her beloved Red Hot Pickled Peppered Peanut business, with it the weathered cornhusk wagon she had once guided down dusty lanes, and the old rocking chair that had cradled the late Mistress Darcy's frail frame.

That chair and its companion—the woven basket on wooden wheels—bore the deepest imprint of her family's past. Her mother, Melanie, had handwoven the basket from pale golden strands of dried corn husk, each fiber interlaced with the patience of generations. She'd brushed the woven form with shellac until it gleamed like honey under the sun. Two stout oak wheels, oiled smooth over the years, were affixed to the base so that Clover—Maybelle's stoic, grey donkey—could draw it effortlessly along the plantation's broad alleys of clay. In its early days, the basket had carried two people at once: enslaved women and men on errands or at the mercy of their masters' commands. In later years, Maybelle polished its surface until every knot and curve shimmered, her fingers tracing the delicate pattern with proud reverence. Travelers from Mississippi, art dealers, even city folk had tried and failed to capture its enduring strength and quiet elegance. This single artifact, this symbol of resilience—was all Maybelle had left of her grandmother's legacy. Yet she would sell it, for the new life awaited her on Long Island.

On the Monday of reckoning, a brisk morning breeze carried the tang of pine needles and fresh dew as Maybelle lifted the brass receiver of her worn telephone. She dialed Mr. Taylor, a dealer in Tennessee whose voice crackled through the line like distant thunder. When he heard she was ready to part with the basket, his tone brightened. "Fifty thousand dollars," he offered at once. Maybelle paused, her breathing steady. "Let me explore my options," she said coolly.

Before she could hang up, Mr. Taylor's voice boomed, thick with impatience: "No, Maybelle—one hundred and fifty thousand, and that's as high as it goes!" A faint, knowing smile curved her lips. "I'll call you back," she replied, and ended the call.

With decisive calm, she reached the three other dealers whose messages waited on her answering machine. For seven days she weighed each offer like a jeweler appraising gems. At week's end, she accepted the highest bid. In the same span of days, she placed her mother's land on the market. Developers—drawn to the property's border with a bustling brick-and-glass shopping center—quickly circled her parcel. When the contract was drawn up, Maybelle harnessed Clover once more, lifted the shining basket into place, and guided him along the sunbaked clay road toward the developer's sleek office. Inside, men in crisp suits shifted their ties and tapped pens on polished walnut desks. They explained that all but one hundred acres—preserved by for a distant heir—would transfer immediately. Maybelle listened quietly, sealed the agreement with a firm handshake, and promised to vacate in thirty days.

Two mornings later, the dealer reappeared to claim the basket and rocking chair then handed Maybelle a check that glowed with promise. The next sunrise found Maybelle mounting Clover once again, the check folded in her leather haversack, and setting off for the country bank. The building stood solid and familiar: white columns flanked a heavy oak door, and inside, the air smelled faintly of polished marble and ink. The bank manager emerged; spectacles perched on the tip of his nose, and asked how she would like her funds. "Hundred-dollar bills, please—if you can," Maybelle replied, her voice bright. Moments later he returned with neat stacks of crisp notes, each bundle wrapped in pale blue bands. She gathered them as though they were precious artifacts, tucking them carefully into her haversack.

That afternoon at home, sunlight danced through the kitchen window onto two thousand empty pickle jars she'd lined up along the table. Their glass sides caught every beam, throwing prismatic dots onto the wooden floor boards . Methodically, she unwrapped each band of bills, rolled them with exacting care, and slid the rolls into the jars until each vessel brimmed with cash. She then opened two sturdy suitcases and carefully placed each jar in the cases until they were completely full. Over the jars she draped her most cherished dresses—the faded calico that once saw spring festivals, the dark wool that kept her warm through bitter winters—and snapped each case shut. Then she made a simple noon meal of cornbread and pickled peppered peanuts, folded the soft blanket that once swaddled baby Brown, and tucked it into the haversack alongside the proceeds from the wicker wagon and rocking chair.

That night, under a moonless sky, Maybelle climbed onto Clover's back for the final time. His hooves clopped softly on the dirt road as she stole a last, lingering glance at her small white house—its shutters closed, its windows dark—cementing the scene in her memory's deepest well. At five o'clock, she reached the rickety bus station just as a pale sliver of dawn creased the horizon. Inside, the air reeked faintly of diesel and tar; benches creaked under the weight of early travelers. She loaded her suitcases into the belly of the bus, slung her haversack over one shoulder, and gave Clover a gentle pat before climbing aboard. Nestling into a window seat, she draped the worn blanket across her lap and closed her eyes for a hopeful nap.

Her rest was shattered hours later in Washington, D.C., when two masked men stormed the aisle, guns glinting under the half-light. Their voices were harsh commands: "Everyone, empty your pockets—or we'll fill you full of holes!" Passengers trembled, raising purses and wallets. Maybelle clutched her haversack tightly; one assailant sneered, "you can let that raggedy sack drop granny, we came for valuables ". She lowered the bag that traveled with Penelope from Africa slowly, closed her eyes, and whispered a prayer. When the thieves fled, sirens lulled in behind them and officers took statements. The bus resumed its journey north.

By afternoon she arrived at Hempstead Greyhound station, where her son stood waiting. The platform smelled of spent coffee and salt air rising from distant bays. Brown's arms opened wide: he introduced her to his new wife and their children, laughter and tears mingling in warm reunion. After he loaded her suitcases into his car, they drove along narrow, tree-lined lanes towards her new home on Long Island.

And so, Maybelle began her next chapter, her soul heavy with past sorrows yet buoyed by hope, a grandmother's haversack full of dreams and the enduring spirit of Penelope's red hot pickled peppered peanuts lingering deep within her soul.

To be continued